Broken Trust

by

C. B. Clark

Broken Trust

Cover Art by *Debbie Taylor*

The Wild Rose Press, Inc.
PO Box 708
Adams Basin, NY 14410-0708
Visit us at www.thewildrosepress.com

Publishing History
First Crimson Rose Edition, 2018
Print ISBN 978-1-5092-1952-0
Digital ISBN 978-1-5092-1953-7

Published in the United States of America

The thick carpet muted the tapping

of her high heels as she fled through the reception area and down the hall to the elevators. In spite of her cowardly retreat, she wanted to shout in triumph. She'd been terrified of angering the surly detective, but she'd dragged up her courage and told him what she thought. Blood buzzed through her veins, fueled by the adrenaline rush. Damn. It was good to have her old fire back.

She glanced down a short corridor on her left and stumbled to a stop. How had she missed the ropes of yellow police tape blocking the entry to one of the rooms? Her breath hitched in her throat. That must be where the grisly crime had occurred.

The shocking truth struck her like a blow—Jonas Waverley was dead. Murdered in cold blood. She staggered and grabbed onto the wall.

"Ms. Hartford, wait."

She glanced back.

Detective Brandon strode along the corridor toward her, his long legs eating up the distance, a determined expression on his face.

Her earlier spurt of courage vanished, and she whirled and dashed toward the bank of elevators. Chest heaving, heart pounding, she hit the button for the elevator, jabbing it again and again.

BROKEN TRUST

is C. B. Clark's fourth romantic suspense published by The Wild Rose Press, Inc. *MY BROTHER'S SINS* and *CHERISHED SECRETS* were published in 2016, and *BITTER LEGACY* in 2017.

Dedication

For Douglas…my biggest supporter.
I love you.

Chapter 1

"Who the hell are you?"

Natasha Hartford eyed the tall, muscular, scowling man. "I..er…um…I was just…" She winced at the thin squeak of her voice.

The man's frown deepened, and the large executive office was suddenly too small, the maroon walls too close.

She gulped and tried again. "I have an appointment with Mr. Waverley." She took in her accuser's short, dark hair, piercing hazel eyes and rugged good looks. He wasn't Jonas Waverley, that was for sure. The grainy photograph of Waverley in the *Port Hardesty Times* had shown an older man with graying hair, dark, bushy eyebrows, and a distinctive hawk-like nose. "Are you a security guard?"

His gaze settled on her hands, and his eyes narrowed.

A rush of heat flared up her neck, and she bit back a groan, wishing she could hide the two broken pieces of the delicate wood carving of a lioness and her cub. "This…this was an accident. I bumped against the table and…" The lump stuck in her throat threatened to choke her. "Of course, I'll pay for the statue." Although God knows how she'd do that. The carving likely cost more than she made in a year creating illustrations for greeting cards.

1

If possible, his mouth tightened even more.

"I'm really sorry." Tears stung her eyes as she forced out the words. She'd ruined the chance of a lifetime. After seeing the damage she'd done to his priceless work of art, Jonas Waverley wouldn't hire her to take out the garbage, let alone choose her to illustrate his company's best-selling children's book series.

She set the pieces of broken statue on the table. "Have Mr. Waverley send me a bill for the damage." Crossing the endless expanse of thick, cream-colored carpet to the door, she couldn't resist a last glance at the panorama visible through the wall of windows in the opulent office. Even with heavy, gray skies and the steady drizzle of rain, the million-dollar view of downtown Port Hardesty showcased the best of the seaside city. Snow-covered mountains draped in mist towered over the small bay where, in spite of the weather, sailing boats, their multi-colored sails billowing, flew across the waves.

"Who are you?"

She jerked and turned from the view. "I thought I told you. I'm Natasha Hartford. I have an appointment with Mr. Waverley." She grimaced. "Or, rather, I had an appointment."

"Had?" The ticking pulse in his strong, dark-stubbled jaw raced. His broad shoulders almost spanned the width of the doorway behind him, and even through the well-tailored lines of his suit, the play of hard muscles was evident.

"I doubt he'll want to meet me now. Not after that." She pointed toward the damaged carving on the gleaming, antique mahogany table.

"Let me get this straight." He stepped toward her.

"You're telling me you had an appointment, this morning, with Jonas Waverley?"

For a heartbeat, the unusual color of his eyes, more green than brown, distracted her. Long, dark eyelashes swept his rugged cheeks. In other circumstances she would have found him attractive. But not now, not when her dreams lay shattered like the broken statue. "Tell Mr. Waverley thank you, but there's no point in us meeting."

"Bullshit, lady." His eyes narrowed to slits of distrust.

She flinched at the steel in his deep voice. What was his problem? She'd said she'd pay for the statue. "I'm sorry. I didn't get your name, Mr...?"

"Chase Brandon." His large, bristling body sucked the air out of the room. "Detective Chase Brandon."

"You're...you're a policeman?" She stumbled back a step.

He nodded and removed a slim, black leather wallet from a pocket inside his dark-gray suit coat. Flipping the wallet open with practiced ease, he held it before her. A gold shield was on one side of the wallet and an official-looking photograph of him on the other.

Her mouth dried. "You're a cop? But this was an accident. I told you I'd pay for the statue."

"I'm not here about a piece of art." He waved his hand at the lavish office. "Perhaps you'd like to tell me what you're doing in here."

"I already told you. I have an appointment with Mr. Waverley. At ten o'clock."

"So you say."

"Why don't you check with his assistant? When she gets back, I'm sure she'll confirm my appointment." No one was in the reception area when Natasha arrived, but the door beyond the receptionist's desk had been ajar, and the temptation to snoop inside Waverley's office proved irresistible. He had a one-of-a-kind collection of ancient Middle Eastern art. No one was around. What would it hurt if she snuck a quick peek?

Touching the statue was another mistake, but the carving was so exquisite, the lines so detailed, she'd had to get a closer view. She'd been careful, but the soft thud of approaching footsteps on the plush carpet in the outer office had startled her, and her hand bumped the table. The fragile wood carving struck the sharp corner and broke in half.

She peeked through her lowered lashes at the intimidating man.

His eyes were an icy green, filled with suspicion. "We can't find Waverley's assistant."

"Well, then, ask Mr. Waverley. I'm sure he's aware of his appointments for the day." She shuddered under the twin laser beams of his eyes.

"What's your meeting with Waverley about?"

None of your business, she longed to respond, but he was a cop, and the hard expression on his face demanded answers. "This was supposed to be a job interview. I hoped he'd hire me to draw the pictures for a book series his company is sponsoring. I'm an illustrator of children's books"—she grimaced—"or at least I want to be." She babbled on, unable to stop the stream of useless information.

"Jonas Waverley's the number one publisher of children's books in the business. I've been applying for the past two years, and this is the first time I've managed to secure an appointment. I was thrilled when his assistant called and told me Mr. Waverley wanted to meet with me." She inhaled a much-needed breath. "I know if I can get him to look at my work, he'll hire me."

His face remained expressionless, his gaze probing.

The air in the spacious office was too warm in spite of the air conditioning system blasting frigid air down on her. She wiped her damp palms on her coat.

"If this appointment is so important, why are you leaving without meeting the man you've come to see?"

"Don't you get it? I blew it." She ran her fingers through her tangle of hair. "This has been one hell of a day. My car wouldn't start, and when I finally managed to get the damn thing going, traffic was backed up for miles on the bridge. Then it took forever to find a parking space."

She paused for breath, but it was like the tap had been left open and the words poured out. "Like I told you, the reception area was deserted, and I didn't see anyone. I figured the staff was at a meeting or something.

"I waited in the outer office for thirty minutes or so. Mr. Waverley's office door was open, and I didn't think he'd mind if I took a quick look." She pointed to the glass-fronted display cases set about the office. "I minored in Art History in college, and I'd heard his collection of Middle Eastern art is world class. I just wanted a peek."

Her gaze lit on the ruined statue, and a rush of heat seared her cheeks. "And then you walked into the room." She hung her head. "I screwed up. Big time. He won't hire me now."

"You're right. He won't. Waverley's dead."

****

Chase studied her face.

Shock, disbelief, sudden awareness, and sadness flashed across her expressive features. She paled and sagged, her body going limp.

He lunged and grabbed her arm to steady her, but the second his fingers curled around her coat sleeve, the brilliant blue of her eyes dulled, and she yanked her arm away as if she'd been scalded.

Jesus Christ! Did she think he'd hurt her? Or was something more going on here? "What do you know of Waverley's death?" He winced at his harshness. *Easy, boy.* No point scaring her silent.

Her face paled even more. "Me? I...I don't know anything. I didn't even know he was dead."

Was she lying? It was hard to tell. Her shock at hearing of Waverley's death appeared real. Either that or she was an excellent actress. She could be an actress with her creamy skin, silky blonde hair, and eyes resembling luminous blue pools. Tall and slim, she had curves in all the right places—the sort of curves that made a man forget his badge.

He'd caught her in Waverley's office searching through the man's possessions. Her explanation of an appointment was laughable. Waverley died two days ago. "How come you didn't hear about Waverley's death? It was on all the news sites."

She stumbled back as if shoved by an invisible hand. "I've been working on a project, and I haven't had time to watch TV or read the news." Her lower lip trembled, and tears shimmered in her blue eyes.

Yeah, right. Like he believed that story. Who in

6

this day and age stayed off-line for more than five minutes? "Who are you, exactly?" He advanced, using his bulk to intimidate, to force her to tell the truth.

She flinched, but held her ground. "I...I already told you. My name is Natasha Hartford." She dug in her purse.

He tensed and reached inside his coat and flipped open the holster of his service pistol.

She withdrew her driver's license, holding the laminated card for him to see.

Releasing a breath, he removed his hand from his holster and examined the license and the attached photo. The card looked legitimate, but anyone could buy a new identity and the accompanying I.D. "How well did you know Jonas Waverley?"

Fresh fear radiated across her face, and she toyed with a strand of hair, twisting and spinning the golden curl into a tangled knot.

A twinge of sympathy filtered through his badass-cop act, but Waverley was dead. Someone had killed him, and it was Chase's job to find the culprit. He narrowed his eyes and amped up his glower.

"I didn't know him." Her gaze darted around the room, and she crossed her arms in front of her as if she were cold.

She was afraid. No question. But why? Had she something to hide?

"I mean, not really. Of course, I knew who he was. I've researched him and his company on the Internet, but that's all. I haven't met him."

He kept silent. Suspects hated silence as much as nature abhorred a vacuum. Silence led them to slip up in their web of lies.

She brushed a lock of gleaming blonde hair from her forehead with a trembling hand. "What…what happened? Did he have a heart attack?"

He searched her face, delving behind the guile for the lie. Had she or someone she worked with murdered Waverley? Had she now returned to search for something she'd missed when she killed him? If she were involved in Waverley's murder, this whole doe-eyed, innocent routine she had going on could be an act—one designed to allay his suspicions.

He strode the last few steps toward her, stopping when mere inches separated them. Her perfume—something floral and delicate—surrounded him. "So you decided to wander around Waverley's private office? You didn't think he'd mind? Or did you already know he was dead because you murdered him?"

"I told you, the door was open and"—her eyes widened, and her face paled even more—"murdered?" She staggered back a step. "He was murdered?"

"That's what they call it when a man ends up lying in a pool of blood with three bullet holes in him." He'd intended to shock her into telling the truth, but when jewel-like tears glistened on her lashes, he gritted his teeth. *Damn.* He yanked a clump of tissues from a box on a nearby desk and stuffed them in her hand. He was a sucker for a woman's tears. Always had been.

She reminded him of a beaten dog he'd once rescued from a length of tangled chain. When he'd attempted to free the beleaguered beast, the animal had mewled and cowered and stared with the same fear that darkened Natasha Hartford's eyes. "Hey, take it easy." He kept his voice low and soothing. "I'm not going to hurt you. All I want are answers." Easing back a few

8

steps, he gave her the space she obviously needed.

"Someone shot Jonas Waverley?" She covered her mouth with the palm of her hand.

He nodded.

Stumbling to a maroon leather armchair, she collapsed into its depths. "He was killed here? In this room?" Her face turned a greenish hue as if she were going to be sick.

"No," he said quickly. "The homicide occurred down the hall in his assistant's office."

A hint of color returned to her ashen cheeks.

If she was acting, she was damn good. Maybe she was telling the truth. But why was she so afraid? Her over-the-top fear didn't jibe. Something was off. "Where were you on Wednesday morning between midnight and five?"

"Wednesday morning?" Her eyes widened. "I don't know, at home asleep, I guess. Why?"

"Can anyone attest to that?"

"No, I was alone." She sucked in a breath. "You don't think I"—her slender throat worked as she swallowed—"you don't think I had something to do with Mr. Waverley's death, do you?" Her hand pressed to her chest as if she were trying to slow her rapid breathing. "Oh my God, you do." What little color was left in her face drained, and she stared at him with wide, frightened eyes. "You think I killed him."

Her shock and fear were palpable, and he was suddenly filled with a desire to protect her, to tell her everything would be okay, but before he could speak and break a shitload of professional ethics, his cell phone vibrated in his pocket, saving him from making a mistake he'd regret.

He grabbed the phone. "Brandon," he barked, his gaze fixed on the woman.

"Hey, man, where are you? The chief's looking for you. He's pissed we don't have any leads. Thinks we're wasting time. Better get your ass back here ASAP."

Chase couldn't help but smile as the gruff voice of Mike Podborski throbbed in his ear. The two men had been partners for the past seven years, and Chase was used to the older man's cantankerous attitude. "I'm still at Waverley's office."

"What the hell? I thought you were just doing a quick walk-through before we released the crime scene."

"I did. And you won't believe what I found." He pinned Natasha with a hard look. "A suspect."

She cringed and shrank back in the chair.

He suppressed the twinge of guilt tightening his gut. His job was to investigate anyone suspicious. Finding her alone in the office of a recent murder victim reeked of culpability.

"Who is it?" Mike demanded.

Still watching her, Chase responded, "I'll tell you about her when I get back to the precinct."

"Her? Her?" Mike's voice thundered in his ear.

Chase clicked off his phone. Before he told Mike any more, he had to find out about Natasha Hartford. No point getting Mike's hopes up if this was another false lead.

Chapter 2

This was a freaking nightmare. Natasha was glad she was seated. All she'd done was show up late for her appointment, and before she had a chance to breathe, this hard-nosed detective appeared and harassed her with the third degree.

At one point, when he'd handed her the clump of tissues, his face had softened as if he believed her, but not now. Now his hazel eyes were shrouded with skepticism. His hard-eyed, cold gaze reminded her of Darien, and she didn't want to think of Darien, not here, not now.

She inhaled a deep breath. "Look, ah...Detective Brandon, I realize you have a job to do, but I can't help you. I'm sorry Jonas Waverley is dead, but I don't know anything about his murder."

One dark brow arched, his disbelief clear.

What on earth did he want her to say? He was obviously a man used to getting what he wanted, but he couldn't wring blood from a stone. She didn't know anything. How could she? Okay, so she was late for her meeting with Waverley, and she'd gone into his office uninvited and wrecked the expensive statue. Not good. Really not good. But she hadn't broken any laws, unless curiosity and impulsiveness were punishable offenses.

Her head throbbed. He had no right to keep

hounding her with questions. Inhaling a deep breath, she struggled to her feet. "We're done here." She fought back the quaver in her voice. "I've told you what I know." Tightening the strap of her purse on her shoulder and relieved her wobbly legs supported her, she strode toward the door and escape.

"You don't care Jonas Waverley was murdered?" His tone was condemning.

She halted her rush for freedom. "Of course, I care. The poor man's family must be devastated." She frowned at him. "Who could have committed such a heinous crime?"

"Exactly." He crossed his arms over his broad chest, his dark brows arched. "Who?"

She flushed at his implied accusation and dug deep for the anger buried beneath her fear. Planting her hands on her hips, she shot him a fierce look of her own. "What's your problem? From the minute you stomped in here, you've harassed and threatened me, implying I had something to do with Mr. Waverley's murder. I've had enough." She marched a few steps toward him. "If you have something you want to say, spit it out."

He opened his mouth to speak, but she cut him off, her fury too scalding to rein in. "As I've already explained, my name is Natasha Hartford. I had an appointment today at ten o'clock with Jonas Waverley. Believe me or not, but I'm telling you the truth." Her breath huffed in and out, but she wasn't ready to stop. Not anywhere near ready.

"I don't know anything about Jonas Waverley's murder. I never met him, never talked to him, and I certainly didn't kill him." She stiffened her spine. "You said his assistant's missing. Doesn't that strike you as odd? Why don't you find her and ask her your questions?" Lurching back, she struggled to calm her labored breathing.

The seconds ticked. If the silence were any louder, the room would implode.

She averted her gaze, refusing to look at the anger that must be on his face. The all-too-familiar debilitating fear swamped her, draining the last dregs of her momentary flash of courage. Legs quaking, she placed one foot in front of the other and strode past him and through the open door, feeling as if she were navigating a hundred feet rather than six.

The thick carpet muted the tapping of her high heels as she fled through the reception area and down the hall to the elevators. In spite of her cowardly retreat, she wanted to shout in triumph. She'd been terrified of angering the surly detective, but she'd dragged up her courage and told him what she thought. Blood buzzed through her veins, fueled by the adrenaline rush. *Damn.* It was good to have her old fire back.

She glanced down a short corridor on her left and stumbled to a stop. How had she missed the ropes of yellow police tape blocking the entry to one of the rooms? Her breath hitched in her throat. That must be where the grisly crime had occurred.

The shocking truth struck her like a blow—Jonas Waverley was dead. Murdered in cold blood. She staggered and grabbed onto the wall.

"Ms. Hartford, wait."

She glanced back.

Detective Brandon strode along the corridor toward her, his long legs eating up the distance, a determined expression on his face.

Her earlier spurt of courage vanished, and she whirled and dashed toward the bank of elevators. Chest heaving, heart pounding, she hit the button for the elevator, jabbing it again and again.

"Look, I'm sorry," he said, catching up. "I was hard on you, but I'm just doing my job. A man was murdered." He rubbed the back of his neck. "I have to examine every possible lead, question every person of interest."

She shuddered and stabbed the down button again. Person of interest? Her? She was a person of interest in a murder investigation?

"Can we go somewhere and talk?"

She shot him a look, making it clear what she thought of his suggestion.

He lifted one shoulder. "Maybe we could grab a coffee? I have a few more questions I'd like to ask."

The elevator pinged, and the doors opened with a hiss, revealing a middle-aged man and an elderly woman who stared at them with vague interest.

Natasha stumbled toward the elevator.

Detective Brandon grabbed her arm, holding her back. "Ms. Hartford, wait."

Warmth from his large tanned hand seeped through the thin material of her raincoat and raised goose bumps on her arm. "Let me go." Her voice was shrill with rising hysteria. She tugged, but he held on, his grip tightening.

"What's going on here?" the man in the elevator demanded. His dapper, military-style, red mustache bristled, and wisps of carrot-orange thinning hair stood at attention around his narrow face. Two patches of red bloomed on his cheeks. He stepped forward as if to intervene.

"Official business." Holding her arm with one hand, the detective yanked out his wallet and flashed his badge. "I'm a police officer."

Her would-be-rescuer shuffled his feet and hesitated, but Detective Brandon glared him down. The redheaded man paled and scurried back to the safety of the elevator.

The female passenger's lined face flushed red, and she gasped, clutching her oversized purse in front of her as if wielding a shield. She lunged for the control panel and slapped buttons.

The doors swished closed.

In the ensuing silence, Natasha remained frozen in place.

"Look, I'm sorry, but I couldn't let you leave. Not yet. We aren't done." Detective Brandon released her arm and eased back a step.

She rubbed her arm where his fingers had gripped. Even though his grasp had been gentle, her arm burned with an aching awareness. She fought to quell her rising panic. *He isn't Darien. You aren't a victim. Not anymore.*

Standing taller, meeting the detective's hard-eyed gaze with a fierce one of her own, she infused as much firmness as she could muster into her voice. "Detective Brandon, I haven't committed a crime. I've already told you what I know. You have no right to detain me." She sucked in a deep breath. "Now, unless you're arresting me, I'm walking out of here." Once again she stabbed the call button for the elevator. Her heart thudded in her chest like a cannon exploding.

"Ms. Hartford." His voice was gruff. "I apologize."

She risked a sideways glance in his direction.

A sheepish grin played across his lips, softening his rugged features. "Look, I need your help."

The elevator pinged, and the doors whooshed open. This time the compartment was empty.

"Please?"

She stepped toward the open elevator, but something in the pleading note in his voice stopped her. "You need my help?"

He threaded long fingers through his hair, setting the raven curls awry. "You're the first break in this case we've had in two days." He held up his hand when she opened her mouth to protest, silencing her. "Don't you want to help us find the person who murdered Jonas Waverley?"

"How could I be of any help? I told you, I didn't know him."

The warmth vanished, and his eyes hardened. "I could get a warrant and compel you to talk to me. Believe me, you don't want to go that route."

She shuddered. He was a police officer and a man—two strikes against him in her book. When had the police ever helped her?

"Well?" He arched his dark brows. "Which is it going to be—easy or difficult?"

She shook her head. "I don't have anything more to say. Let me know if I need to call my lawyer." Even as the bold words burst out of her mouth she was shocked. Knees rubbery, she staggered into the elevator and pressed the down button, desperate to escape before he vented his anger at her refusal to cooperate.

"This isn't over, Ms. Hartford." His voice was

chipped in ice. "Not by a long shot."

She flinched. Even the most hardened criminals must confess to any number of vile crimes when faced with the full force of Detective Chase Brandon's wrath.

The doors swooshed closed.

She sagged against the elevator's cold back wall, her legs weak, her breathing ragged. Had she really walked away from him? A faint glimmer of pride warmed her. Maybe she wasn't the pushover she thought she'd become. Maybe a little bit of the old Natasha remained.

****

Chase grimaced as he replayed his conversation with Natasha Hartford in his mind. He'd done a lousy job of questioning her. Hell, any rookie would have done a damn sight better. He hated to think what Mike would have said if he'd witnessed Chase's awkward attempts to drag answers from the skittish woman.

From the moment he'd found her in Waverley's office, his years of training and experience had disappeared, and he'd fumbled around like a raw recruit. Something about her caused his gut to clench each time he searched her wounded blue eyes.

He rubbed his hands over his face in an attempt to scrub sense into his addled brain. Just his luck the most attractive and intriguing woman he'd met in years was a suspect in a murder case. His murder case.

The unsettling thought continued to rattle through his brain later when, slouched in his chair behind his desk at the precinct, he filled his partner in on his encounter with Natasha Hartford.

Mike listened, chewing on the tip of a pencil stub. His faded blue eyes and weathered face hid the fact that behind the gray hair and sea of wrinkles, Mike Podborski possessed one of the sharpest minds in the Division. "So, we have ourselves a viable lead."

"I don't know what to make of her." Chase rubbed the day's growth of beard on his cheeks. "I believe her story of how she made her appointment with Waverley, but something about her rings false."

"You think she's telling the truth?" Mike's penetrating gaze fixed on Chase. "I mean, it's quite a coincidence you catch her in the victim's office searching through his stuff hours after the murder went down."

"She wasn't searching through anything. She was looking at Waverley's art collection." Chase shook his head. Why was he defending the woman? "He owns some interesting carvings," he finished lamely.

Mike narrowed his eyes, but for once, he didn't comment. "So, if you're so certain she's telling the truth, why are you investigating her?"

Chase shrugged. "I don't know." Time to come clean. He'd never been able to hide anything from his partner. "She's hiding something. If she were there for a simple job interview she wouldn't have been so nervous. You should have seen her. Fear fairly oozed off her, and I don't think it was because she'd broken a valuable carving."

He jumped up and paced, weaving between desks and avoiding collisions with the other detectives packed into the cramped office. His mind whirled as he struggled to sort out his thoughts. "My gut tells me Natasha Hartford's involved up to her pretty neck in this case." He raised his voice so Mike could hear him over the buzz of activity. "I just haven't figured out how."

"Your instincts are usually bang on."

The phone on Chase's desk rang, the loud clanging piercing the air. He stopped pacing and grabbed the receiver. "Yeah?" He listened for a minute. "Okay, send the file up, Bert. Thanks."

He faced Mike. "Seems we have a file in the computer database on Natasha Hartford. This may be our lucky day. Bert's gonna download the file and bring us a copy." A sour taste filled his mouth as his stomach rebelled at the hot dog stuffed with sauerkraut and fried onions he'd scarfed down after he'd left Waverley's office.

He should have been pleased. This murder investigation had gone wrong from the outset. The crime appeared cut and dried—murder committed in the act of an attempted theft. After all, Waverley's offices contained millions of dollars of rare art.

But that hadn't proved to be the case. Nothing was taken from Waverley's office or any of the other offices in the Waverley complex. The office where Waverley met his demise had been undisturbed as well, even though priceless, rare art hung on the walls.

As far as he could tell, only one item was missing. Video footage from that night showed Waverley holding a large manila envelope when he left his office and walked down the hall to his assistant's office. A team of trained investigators had searched the room, but hadn't located the envelope.

The assistant's office contained a large, glass-topped desk with a white leather partner's chair behind the desk, and two visitor's chairs. A minibar with a sink and a built-in fridge was set along one wall. Glass shelves behind the minibar were filled with a variety of expensive liquors.

Waverley had been sitting on the leather chair behind the desk. Two glass tumblers and a bottle of vintage single malt scotch whiskey were on the desk in front of him, as if he'd been expecting someone.

Somehow the murderer had gained entry into the locked building in the early hours of the morning, slipped past the night security guards, and surprised Waverley as he sat drinking scotch at his assistant's desk.

The intruder had shot Waverley three times, all three bullets hitting their mark. Waverley was dead before his head smacked the table. One of the glasses had been knocked over when he collapsed, and liquor spilled across the table, mixing with the blood from his mortal wounds. The office reeked like a distillery, but the sickening sweet, metallic smell of blood and death overpowered the expensive whiskey fumes.

The position of the body indicated Waverley hadn't seen his killer. He probably hadn't been aware of any danger until the first of the bullets ripped through his heart. And then it was game over.

Aside from the motive for the murder being a mystery, the forensics team hadn't found any trace evidence, no fingerprints, no weapon, not a single damn hair, as if the killer appeared out of nowhere and then vanished. Both glasses had been checked, but Waverley's fingerprints were the only ones present.

Somehow the killer had broken into a locked building with surveillance cameras posted in the halls and two security guards monitoring the building, and no one had seen a damn thing. After he'd shot Waverley, the murderer had taken the envelope and disappeared the same way he'd entered the building, leaving no trace.

Chase had watched the security tapes—nothing but hours and hours of empty corridors and closed office doors. The one break in the monotony had been the black-and-white images of the victim, as in the early hours of the morning Waverley had left his executive office carrying the envelope and strode down the hall to his assistant's office. After that, nothing, until the janitorial crew discovered the gruesome scene at five in the morning.

The persistent ache in his head amped up a notch. The murder smacked of a professional hit, but what could an art collector and a publisher of children's books have done to show up on the radar of organized crime?

Waverley must have known his killer. Why else would he have set out two glasses and a bottle of expensive scotch and sat there drinking as he waited for his visitor to arrive? And what the hell was in that envelope?

The case had been dead in the water almost from the get-go. In spite of their persistence and vigorous investigation, Chase and Mike hadn't been able to find a single clue as to the perp's identity. As Chase well knew, if a case wasn't solved within the first forty-eight hours, the golden hours, odds of solving the crime narrowed to near zilch.

Jonas Waverley, for all his wealth and influence, had been a well-liked man with surprisingly few enemies. The one person to benefit from the wealthy entrepreneur's death was the man's nephew, but he'd been in Hong Kong on business at the time of the murder and as such, had an airtight alibi. Their investigation was left with zip, a dead end with no leads in sight.

Until now.

Until he discovered Natasha Hartford in the middle of the murder victim's office looking as jumpy as a nun in a whorehouse. And the Port Hardesty Police Department had a file with her name on it in the department criminal record database.

Hot diggity damn.

Maybe this was the break in the case they so desperately needed. He sure as hell hoped so. About time they made some headway.

Funny how he'd been so wrong about her, though. He was pretty good at reading people, but her wide-eyed innocent act had fooled him. He'd actually believed her tale of wandering into Waverley's open office to look at the man's art collection while she waited for him to show for their appointment.

He'd felt guilty at the way he'd grilled her, but his inner alarm bells had been ringing, and he'd been pissed she was so damn skittish. Hell, she flinched when he so much as breathed. And so he'd gone on the offensive and charged after her. His threat of obtaining a warrant to force her to tell him what she knew was bogus. But if a file on her existed in the police database, the entire ballgame had changed.

"Hey, Detective Brandon, here's the file you wanted." Bert Shipton stood inside the door to the bullpen, a thick manila file folder in his meaty hands. Nearing retirement, Bert had worked as a file clerk deep in the dungeons of police headquarters since before

Noah built the ark.

He guarded the stacks of police case files as if they were gold. Ten years ago, when the back cases had been converted to computer files, he became an expert on searching law enforcement agencies' databases. If a criminal record existed, Bert tracked it down.

Chase shoved his dark thoughts aside and focused on the man in front of him. "Thanks, Bert." He held out his hand for the file.

Bert's beetled brows rose. "What's this about, Detective? I thought you and Detective Podborski were assigned to the Waverley murder."

"We are. Why?"

Bert's solid, gnome-like body swelled with importance, and he waved the file in the air. "Someone was messing around with my files. Whoever that was, he went to a lot of trouble to hide this." His croaky voice had a doomsday quality as if he were predicting the end of days.

"What the hell are you talking about?" Chase shoved his hands in his pockets.

Bert shuffled forward, and the sour stink of sweat, stale cigarettes, and fried bacon permeated the air.

Chase hid his grimace and breathed through his mouth. Did the man ever shower?

Bert's muddy brown eyes shone with excitement. "Like I told you, I had a hard time locating this file." He puffed out his chest. "No one else would have. I guaran-damn-tee you of that." He waved the file in Chase's face as if he'd found the Holy Grail. "Someone didn't want this found. They did a pretty good job of burying it, but they didn't count on me." He smirked. "When I couldn't find information on the suspect in the usual locations, I had to go on the mainline server and—"

"Thanks, Bert." Chase cut him off. Bert could go on for hours pontificating in mind-numbing detail on his search for obscure and arcane information. Chase didn't give a rat's ass where he'd found the file on Natasha Hartford. He wanted to read the damn thing. Now.

Sucking in a breath, he counted to ten, reining in his impatience. Bert was good at his job, and he didn't deserve to be yelled at. He gave Bert a playful slap on the back. "I've always said you're the best damn researcher in the business. The department's lucky to have you."

A flush of pleasure pinkened Bert's grizzled cheeks.

"Now let's see the file." Chase snatched the folder out of Bert's hand. The desire to tear it open and find what the hell Natasha Hartford was hiding seared through him like a wildfire. Whatever was in this computer file was integral to the case. As sure as God made little green apples, she was involved in Waverley's murder. She'd played him for a fool. But he was onto her now. The skin on the back of his neck prickled, and he slid a glance at Mike.

His partner's eyes narrowed, his bushy, gray eyebrows arching.

Chase flushed. "Something on your mind?"

"This woman," Mike said, "this Natasha Hartford. Something's different about her. What is it?"

Chase scrubbed his fingers through his hair. "Hell if I know."

Mike assessed him with a sharp-eyed look.

"Whatever's bugging you, you'd better figure it out. The chief will bust our butts if we don't catch a break in this case soon. He wants this murder solved yesterday. Waverley was an important man in this town, and the mayor's ridin' the chief's ass to find the killer."

Chase nodded. His partner was right. The media was all over the murder. They'd better find the perp soon, or he and Mike would be assigned to writing traffic tickets until they retired.

"Detective Brandon?"

Chase pinched the bridge of his nose. He'd forgotten Bert. Why was the man still here? Why wouldn't he leave so Chase could dive into Natasha's file? "What is it?" His voice was harsher than he intended.

Bert paled. "I...I just..." He shook his head, coughed, and shuffled his feet. "Let me know if the information in the file helps. Okay?"

"Sure thing, Bert." He held up the file. "Thanks again."

Bert beamed and scuttled out of the room.

With the file clenched in one hand, Chase snatched his coat from the back of his chair and headed for the door of the bullpen, avoiding Mike's narrow-eyed gaze. "I'm going home. I'll call you if I find out anything."

Chapter 3

Natasha stared at the blank paper in front of her. The steady ticking of the clock on the far wall echoed in the room, each tick a condemnation of her lack of progress. She'd been sitting at her desk since early morning and hadn't drawn a single line that was any good. Balls of crumpled paper were strewn across the floor where she'd pitched them. Grunting with disgust, she tossed her drawing pencil on the desk, jumped to her feet, and strode to the large picture window.

Sleek sailboats, their white sails flashing in the late afternoon sunshine, flew before a strong wind across the white-capped, emerald waters of Cranston Bay. Farther out, a cargo vessel, the decks loaded with stacked containers, chugged through the whitecaps, tall smokestacks trailing a plume of black smoke, heading toward port. Distant snow-capped mountains, their rugged slopes carpeted with dense evergreen forests, glistened. The view of mountains and ocean was the main reason she'd bought the tiny house. The stunning scene usually inspired her.

Not today.

Today, nothing worked. No matter what she did or where she looked, she couldn't dredge up any ideas for the latest greeting card designs. Pressure was mounting. If she didn't fulfill the contract, she didn't get paid. If she didn't get paid, the bank wouldn't be happy at not getting this month's mortgage payment, and she'd lose the house.

She'd been thrilled when Jonas Waverley's assistant called three weeks ago and informed her the man himself wanted to meet with her. She'd done her happy dance and celebrated with an expensive bottle of white wine at the prospect of meeting the man with the power to propel unknown artists like her into super stardom.

Once Waverley examined her drawings, he couldn't help but be impressed; impressed enough to sign her to do the artwork for *Turtle Town*, the best-selling children's book series on the market today.

The future looked bright. At least it had until the man she needed to fulfill her dream was found dead, murdered, no less. She shuddered.

An image of Detective Chase Brandon rose before her, imprinted on her brain. His tall stature and muscular build made him a formidable man. Add in his perpetual frown and suspicious hazel eyes, and he was the epitome of everything she feared. But then he'd offered her tissues to wipe her tears, revealing an unexpected, gentler side, and she didn't know what to think.

She'd researched Detective Brandon on the Internet. From all reports, the man was a hero. He'd been decorated at least five times for bravery in the line of duty. He was good at his job. Could have fooled me—unless rudeness and intimidation were now part of a police detective's arsenal of interrogation techniques.

She rubbed her eyes. Why was she wasting time thinking of him? She had work to do. With fresh determination, she pivoted from the window and marched back to her desk.

The doorbell pealed.

She blew out an exasperated breath. The bell rang again, and she cursed. If someone wanted her to buy something or support his or her religion, she'd give him an earful. Stomping out of the room and down the stairs, she flung open the front door. Her breath froze in her throat. "What…what are you doing here?"

"I wanted to see you, Natasha. Is that a crime?"

"It is when I have a restraining order prohibiting you from coming closer than a hundred yards." She glared at the man standing on her front steps.

As always, Darien McCabe was dressed as if he were attending a cocktail party. He wore an expensive, tailored dark suit, red-and-white striped silk tie, and matching handkerchief tucked into his jacket pocket. His blond hair was cut short and styled to hide the fact his hair was thinning. This flaw in the otherwise perfectly groomed man gave her comfort. Nice to know, in spite of evidence to the contrary, he was human.

He carried an expensive-looking metal briefcase in one hand. His thin lips curved upward in a parody of a smile, but the cold light in his pale blue eyes revealed his true character. He chuckled, the false sound grating. "I know you, Natasha. You won't call the police."

She steeled herself not to flinch.

"I did you a favor, and I've come to collect."

"What favor?" She stared past him at the shiny black sedan idling at the curb.

Two thick-necked men wearing matching mirrored sunglasses sat in the front seat watching her. Darien never left his office without at least two muscle-bound gorillas.

"The last time you did something for me, I ended up in the hospital." She grabbed the doorknob to shut the door, but his foot shot out, blocking her from closing it. "I'm not doing this, Darien. Not anymore. Leave, or I'm calling the police."

His foot, in the polished, handmade-leather shoe jammed in the door, didn't budge. The cold smile didn't leave his thin lips. "Come on, Natasha, is this any way to show your gratitude for what I did for you?"

The thundering in her chest was so loud she feared her heart would burst free. *Call the cops*! She closed her ears to the urgent demand ringing through her mind. He was right. She wouldn't call the police. Calling for help was a waste of time. Sure, the cops would come, she'd show them the restraining order, and they'd talk to Darien, but somehow he'd schmooze his way out of any liability. The police officers would walk away with tickets to first-class sporting events, and she'd wind up with a new set of bruises.

Wrapping her arms across her chest, she inhaled a shaky breath. "Okay, I'll bite. What is this big favor you did?"

His smile resembled a shark's feral grin. "How did your appointment with Jonas Waverley go?"

She longed to wipe her damp palms on her pants, but she didn't want him to know how his very presence destroyed her. "My...my appointment? How do you know I had an appointment with him?" She caught her breath. "Are you having me followed?"

He chuckled. "You're so dramatic, Natasha." His smile vanished, replaced by an icy stare. "I keep a close eye on all my possessions. You know that."

"How...how do you know of my appointment with Jonas Waverley?"

He smirked, his bleached white teeth gleaming. "I set it up."

"You what?" Her knees wobbled, and she sagged against the doorframe.

"I called Waverley and arranged the meeting." He shrugged. "He owed me a few favors. I knew how much meeting him meant to you, and I simply asked him to see you." His gaze narrowed. "Why are you surprised, darling? Surely you didn't think you secured the appointment on your own merits." He simpered, using her shock to shove open the door and step inside. "Your little drawings are pretty, but a man in Jonas Waverley's position has the pick of the best. And you're"—he shrugged his narrow shoulders—"well, you're not."

His words drilled through her, each gloating syllable chipping a layer from her earlier bravado. How could she have been so blind? She should have known. Snagging an appointment with Jonas Waverley had been too good to be true. Waverley wasn't impressed by her work, or her dogged persistence. The meeting had nothing to do with her. Darien had arranged everything.

The fight drained out of her. "What do you want, Darien?"

"I want to talk to you." His lips curled in a parody of a smile. "Surely that isn't too much to ask. After all, a man has a right to expect his wife to accommodate him when he wishes to see her."

Apprehension sprouted to life and seared through her, but she fought to hide her growing fear. He liked her afraid. Got off on her terror. "We aren't married anymore, Darien." She struggled to hide the quaver in her voice. "We haven't been for two years."

"So you say, my dear,"—his eyes narrowed—"but in my book, when one marries, the bond is for life. Only death severs the sacred union of a man and his wife."

She shivered at his thinly veiled threat and rubbed the goose bumps prickling the skin on her arms. They'd been having this same conversation since she'd screwed up her courage and left him and their disaster of a marriage. Two years, and he still refused to accept they were divorced.

He called her all hours of the day and night, appeared on her doorstep demanding entrance, and had his men following her. He was a cruel man capable of horrendous acts. With each passing month, her fear increased, building to a breaking point until she'd taken out the restraining order against him three months ago.

He hadn't liked that. Not one bit. But he'd stopped calling, and she hadn't seen him since.

Until now.

Mustering her courage, digging deep for her remaining embers of strength, she jammed her hands on her hips. "Look, Darien, I'm busy."

His face flushed, but when he spoke, his voice was calm. "This won't take long."

She glanced back into the house, wishing she hadn't left her cell phone upstairs in her office.

"Come on, Natasha. I'll be good. I promise."

She gazed into his pale-blue eyes and a slew of memories flooded her. Once upon a time she'd loved him enough to marry him. But then—

As if sensing her weakening, Darien added, "I've been so alone. Every day is a trial." He wiped at pretend tears in his eyes. "Let's talk for a few minutes, and then I'll leave." He grinned a boyish grin. "No harm, no foul."

He was toying with her. He didn't mean a word he said, but still she wavered, caught between her fear and the sure knowledge she hadn't left behind the cowed and broken woman she'd been. She grimaced in disgust when, as if from a distance, she heard herself say, "Okay."

His smile widened. "I knew you wouldn't refuse me."

A fresh veil of unease settled over her. She'd committed the one mistake her therapist had warned her against. Darien smiled his charming smile, and she reverted to her old, malleable self, and let him back into her life. She was still the pathetic, weak victim she'd always been.

She wiped her damp palms on her pants and followed him into her small living room. Her knees shook, and she was careful to put as much distance between them as the room allowed.

He sprawled on the sofa as if he were master of the manor and set his briefcase on the floor.

The tiny room with the river-stone gas fireplace and moss-green walls covered with framed drawings of her own work created a cozy retreat. His presence sullied the private space. She'd let the devil inside, now what?

The silence dragged on, tension mounting until the weight of it was a living, breathing entity.

Her heart pounded. She couldn't catch her breath.

He crossed his legs and sat back, looking relaxed. Too relaxed. "I'll have a drink. Scotch, straight up." He smiled. "You know how I like it."

She clenched her fists, her nails digging into her palms. Her face burned at his assumption she'd scurry off and do as he ordered. A part of her wanted to do just that. Obeying him had been ingrained through years of living with his threats and intimidation.

Times had changed. She'd changed. She wasn't his servant. Not any more. Besides, liquor and Darien were a bad mix. Alcohol made his hair-trigger temper more volatile. "I'll make some coffee."

His brow furrowed, but he didn't say anything, and she hurried from the room.

Her hands shook as she fumbled through the motions of making coffee. She'd made a mistake—a big one. Letting him into her home was something she vowed she'd never do. She leaned against the counter. Two years of therapy weren't enough to erase five long years of domination and abuse.

As the steaming water dripped into the pot and the familiar aroma of French roast coffee filled the air, she blew out a ragged breath. Images of the horror of the years she and Darien McCabe had lived together as man and wife swept over her, and she grabbed onto the counter, her nails digging into the granite. The pain stopped her from succumbing to the nightmarish memories and reminded her she wasn't the same broken woman she'd been two years ago.

She'd be damned if she'd let him abuse her again. Relaxing her rigid grip, she shoved away from the counter. She set a mug, a small pot of cream and another of sugar, and the just-filled coffeepot, on a wooden tray.

Turning to carry the tray into the living room, she paused and snatched a wooden-handled carving knife from the knife block on the counter. She slipped the knife into the pocket of her sweater and strode into the other room.

Chapter 4

"Ah, there you are, my dear." Darien smiled, but his eyes remained cold. "I'd begun to think you'd scuttled out the back door."

Her steps slowed and she stumbled, almost dropping the heavy tray. How many times had she fled to escape his anger and violence? But she wasn't the same person. That weak-willed woman was buried along with the corpse of her broken marriage. She inhaled a deep, steadying breath. "I'm not afraid of you, Darien." She winced at the ice in his eyes, but held strong to her lie. "Not anymore."

His mouth tightened in a thin line.

She repressed a shudder and fought to hold his gaze, but the air in the room was suddenly too close. She couldn't breathe. Her hands shook as she set the tray on the coffee table.

A satisfied smirk flickered across his fine-boned, handsome face. "You aren't joining me?" He pointed at the single cup on the tray.

She shook her head and rubbed the cold shivers rippling along her arms.

He stared, waiting for her to serve him like she always had.

She bit her bottom lip. Hard. A part of her, a very tiny part, wanted to tell him to pour his own damn coffee, but past experience had taught her the consequences of opposition. The best thing, the smart choice, was to do what he wanted and pray he departed soon.

Her hands trembled as she poured coffee into his cup, slopping a few drops on the maple table.

He tutted. "Still the clumsy woman I married, I see. You always were falling and hurting yourself." His voice was filled with affectionate scorn, as if he were talking to a wayward child.

Heat flared up her neck and over her cheeks, and she darted to the kitchen to get a cloth to wipe the spilled coffee. A sudden desire to keep running overcame her. She grasped the knob on the back door and twisted.

The carving knife weighing down her sweater pocket bumped against her hip, and she stopped. No. She wouldn't run from him. Not this time.

Releasing her hold on the doorknob, she grabbed a cloth from the counter, and returned to the living room, taking a measure of pride in the fact her hands didn't shake when she bent and wiped the table.

But that was the extent of her victory.

Head bowed, she stood before him, damp dishcloth hanging from her hand, and waited for his next instructions as he'd taught her. Her inner voice screamed in outrage, telling her he wasn't her husband anymore. He didn't have power over her. She was in control. *Tell him to get the hell out.* She heard the inner command, understood the words, but her innate fear overrode the outraged clamor.

"Sit down, Natasha." His words weren't a request.

Once again, her body obeyed, even as she rebelled in her mind, and she stumbled over to a chair and sank onto the soft cushion.

He made a loud tsking sound with his tongue. "You're such a little mouse, always so nervous and skittish." The menace in his voice was unmistakable. "When will you understand I only want what's best for you, my dear?" He sipped his coffee, set the cup on the table, sat back, and crossed one elegantly clad leg over the other. "So...about that favor."

He paused, but she remained silent, refusing to play his game.

He huffed out a breath. "I've been waiting for you to thank me, but when you didn't call"—he shrugged— "I decided you wanted to thank me in person." He brushed off a fleck of lint from his tailored slacks.

"I didn't ask you to set up an appointment with Jonas Waverley."

"And yet, I did." He steepled his fingers. "I must tell you, my dear, arranging that meeting wasn't easy. Waverley didn't take kindly to being reminded of his debts." He smirked, baring a row of blinding white teeth. "But of course, in the end, he agreed." He smoothed his hand along the crease in his slacks and chuckled. "As if he had a choice."

The throbbing in her head inched up a notch. "So that's why you're here." Her voice was leaden with resignation. "You want me to thank you."

"I did you a favor, my dear. Now I want you to do something for me." He spread his hands as if his expectation was the most normal thing in the world.

"I didn't see Waverley," she blurted. "He died before I had a chance to meet with him."

"Ah, yes. I heard. Someone shot him, I believe." He took another sip from his cup. "Rather an unfortunate event, I should think, both for the poor man"—he paused, his cool gaze piercing her—"and for you, of course."

"Me?"

"Don't tell me you haven't considered how Waverley's demise destroyed any chance you have of getting your little drawings into that ridiculous children's book that means so much to you."

Heat rushed to her cheeks.

He shook his head. "We're much alike, my dear. We're both willing to do anything to get what we want."

Her fury rose to the surface, and the words she should have said when she first saw him at her door spewed forth. "You're wrong, Darien. We're nothing alike, nothing at all." She glared. "I want you to leave. Now, before I call the police."

He sat back and sipped coffee. "About that favor."

"I don't owe you a thing. I didn't ask you to set up the appointment with Waverley."

He pursed his lips in a moue. "Come now, my dear. Don't make this difficult."

She shuddered at the calculating look in his eyes, but she'd started this; she had to finish. She made a point of inspecting her watch. "You have two seconds to tell me what you want before I call the police."

"I'll leave when I'm good and ready, Natasha, and not before."

"I told you, I didn't meet with Waverley. He was already dead."

"Unfortunate timing."

Springing to her feet, she pointed toward the hall. "I'm not doing this. Not anymore. Go. Get out of here.

Now."

He sat unmoving, a smug smile playing across his thin lips.

"I mean it, Darien."

"I'm sure you do." In a flash, he leaped to his feet and grabbed her arm, twisting it behind her back.

She screamed and scrabbled for the knife in her pocket with her free hand, but the pain was too much, his grip too tight.

"Do you think I like doing this?" He yanked harder, jerking her arm higher. "Do you?"

Tears of pain filled her eyes.

"Well?" He tightened his grip, his fingers digging like claws into her flesh.

She shook her head.

"What was that?" He yanked harder. "I can't hear you."

She gulped for air, fighting against the overpowering agony. "N...no."

His grip loosened, but his fingernails scored into her skin. "This is your fault. Our little meeting didn't have to come to this, but you make everything so difficult. You always have. I merely wish to ask my wife a simple favor."

A sudden weariness stole over her. Why fight him? What was the point? He always won. She opened her mouth to tell him she'd do anything he wanted as long as he didn't hurt her, but before she could get the words out, he dropped her arm and slammed his palms against her chest and shoved.

She yelped, arms flailing as she flew back. Her hip struck the edge of the coffee table with a loud crack, and she crashed to the floor. Shooting pain disabled her.

A whimper escaped her mouth, and she drew her knees to her chest in a protective ball.

He chuckled, though mirth was absent in the chilling laugh. "This is your fault, Natasha. You pushed me too far. You know how upset I get when you're contrary." His furious gaze seared her like a fresh blow.

He prodded her leg with the toe of one gleaming shoe. "Well, what's your answer, my dear? Will you do as I ask, or do we have to go through this tiring ritual again?"

She curled into a tighter ball, protecting her stomach, covering her head with her arms.

"Well?" He nudged her thigh.

"Okay. I'll do what you want. Just stop hurting me. Please." Her stomach twisted at the whine in her voice. She hated this. Hated the way he seeped into her soul like a vile poison and destroyed her self-respect. Hated how she cowered before him, willing to do anything to stop the pain. Hated him. Hated herself more.

He crouched beside her, and his long, thin fingers with their glossy, manicured nails connected with her cheek, caressing her skin.

She shuddered.

"Look at me, Natasha."

She closed her eyes, refusing to obey, determined not to give in to his command, fighting to regain the tattered remnants of her dignity.

His fingers tightened, squeezing her cheek, pinching the skin. He twisted her face toward him with a jerk. "I said, look at me."

She opened her eyes.

His gimlet gaze bore into hers. "I want you to keep something for me." He pointed to the metal briefcase on the floor beside the couch. "I want you to hide my briefcase somewhere safe where no one will find it." The burnished, silver-like metal sides shone in the light streaming through the window.

"Why? What's in there?"

"Nothing that concerns you."

"Why do you want me to keep it here?"

"It's only for a few days. I'll come by and retrieve the case by the weekend."

She rubbed the back of her head. "I don't know. I don't feel comfortable—"

He shoved her shoulder, and she fell back, her head banging against the hardwood floor.

Her teeth clamped on her bottom lip, and she tasted blood.

"I don't give a damn if you're comfortable or not. You'll keep my attaché case and guard it with your life." His eyes narrowed to pinpricks of menace. "If anything happens to it…" He let the rest of his threat trail off. "Well, you know the consequences."

She shuddered.

He sat back on his heels. "I understand you've met Detective Brandon of our illustrious Port Hardesty Police Force."

She blinked at the sudden switch.

"Don't look so shocked, my dear. I know everything you do. Everything. You'd do well to remember that." He rose to his feet, strolled across the room, and stood with his hands behind his back, staring out the window.

She inhaled a shaky breath, but his presence sucked the air out of the room, replacing the oxygen with something foul.

He faced her, his gaze intense. "Stay away from Detective Brandon. Don't talk to him, don't call him, and don't answer any of his questions. Don't say a word about me."

"What are you talking about? I have to talk to the police if they question me. Detective Brandon thinks I'm a suspect in Waverley's murder because he found me in Waverley's office."

He studied his nails. "Just make sure you keep your pretty mouth shut."

She sat up, wincing as a jolt of pain seared through her hip. "Why do you care? Waverley's death has nothing to do with you." Her breath caught in her throat, and she gasped. "Or does it? Is that what this is about? Is that why you're afraid of the police? You killed Jonas Waverley?"

He chuckled, though his laugh sounded forced. "Don't be ridiculous. No poorly educated, blue-collar, donut-eating cop scares me."

"I'm right, aren't I?" Her heart raced. "You murdered Waverley. Either that, or you know who did." Her fear vanished, replaced by a blaze of fury, and she climbed to her feet. "Get out, Darien. Now."

His hand snaked out and he caught her hair and yanked. He wrapped his other arm around her neck and jerked her against his body.

A cloying cloud of expensive cologne wafted over her. She gagged at the all-too-familiar scent.

"You'll do as you've always done, my dear wife." His coffee-scented breath fanned her face. "You'll follow my orders. If not—" His arm tightened on her throat, cutting off her air, his threat more than clear.

Struggling to breathe, she clawed at his arm,

fighting to break his vise-like hold. Breaking free, she staggered away, sucking air into her burning lungs. She tried not to look; didn't want to witness his gloating triumph. But she couldn't help herself.

He smirked. "I trust we understand each other."

She wiped her hand over her mouth with the back of her arm, too exhausted to fight any longer. "What do you want me to do?"

His lips curled in a smug smile. "I've already explained. Hide my briefcase somewhere in this little house of yours, and don't talk to Detective Brandon or any other law enforcement officer."

"Why is this so important? If you didn't murder Waverley, you have nothing to worry about."

"Believe me, my dear, the police are the least of my worries."

"I don't understand."

"You don't have to understand." His eyes were narrow and piercing, his mouth a hard, thin line. "Just do as you're told."

Her free arm brushed the knife in her pocket. How could she have forgotten? She dug in her sweater pocket, grasped the knife's hilt, and brandished the four-inch blade before her. "You've said what you came to say. Now get the hell out of here."

He stared at the knife and then at her. His lips curled.

She shuddered at the malevolence in his icy gaze and tensed for his next move.

"You really should be careful, my dear." He gestured at the knife. "Playing with knives is dangerous. You could get hurt."

She clenched the knife tight, but her hand trembled

so much she feared she'd drop the weapon. "Get out."

Ignoring the knife, he stepped closer, his body boxing her in. "You don't want to piss me off." His breath was warm on her cheek, his cologne stifling. "You'd better not say a word to anyone of my little visit here today."

Anger thundered through her. She leaped away and shoved the blade of the knife toward him, uncaring if she slashed him.

"Don't be stupid, Natasha." His voice was filled with malice.

She swallowed an icy lump. But instead of cringing in terror, she waved the knife before her. "Get out, Darien."

With a final glare, he wheeled around and strolled out of the room. He opened the front door and paused, turning back to face her. "Better be careful, Natasha. You don't know what you're messing with." He left, letting the door swing closed behind him.

She flew across the room and slid the dead bolt in place. With her back jammed against the door, she gave in to wracking sobs. The knife clattered to the floor. Her body shook, and she swallowed the rancid taste of fear.

Chapter 5

Chase sipped the cold coffee and grimaced at the bitter taste. He lurched to his feet and grabbed a bottle of water from the refrigerator. Screwing off the cap, he raised the bottle to his lips and gulped. The icy wetness soothed his parched throat. He leaned against the counter and eyed the open file on the table.

He was a trained police detective. He'd witnessed all manner of crimes—arson, rape, embezzlement, robbery, assault, even murder. Nothing one person did to another surprised him. Not after twelve years on the force.

But no matter how hardened he was to the misery he encountered on a daily basis, some cases stayed with him. Those were the ones that kept him up at night, the cases driving him to open the bottle of whiskey he kept in the top cupboard. But no amount of alcohol would drown the current images blazing through his mind in vivid, gut-wrenching detail.

He rubbed his hands over his face, the rasp of stubble loud in the silent apartment. When he'd first opened Natasha Hartford's file he'd expected to discover reports on any number of petty crimes resulting in her being in the police database.

He'd been prepared to find she was involved in criminal activities; a person who'd be an excellent suspect in Jonas Waverley's murder. Hell, she could

45

have been engaged in prostitution. Not the hard-bitten whores who worked the streets. No. She was too fresh, but maybe a high-class call girl or escort.

He gulped more water. Man, had he been wrong. He returned to the table and once again read through the stack of papers he'd pulled from the file Bert had given him. The first page was a copy of the restraining order she'd taken out on her ex-husband three months ago. That wasn't unusual. Many women had to go to those lengths to protect themselves from their ex-husbands or boyfriends. Some men didn't get the hint a relationship was over.

He scanned the next pages. Bile burned deep in his gut. Natasha Hartford's marriage hadn't been a happy one. Not by any stretch of the imagination. He'd seen similar scenarios dozens of times. Page after page of evidence outlining the physical abuse she'd suffered at the hands of her husband. Countless hospital records detailing broken bones, contusions and open wounds.

At one point, the bastard had beaten her so bad she had to be hospitalized for two weeks while her battered body healed. The abuse appeared to have started soon after their marriage began and continued for years.

Why had she stayed with the jerk? Why had she put up with him using her as a punching bag? He'd read that battered women were so under the power of their abusive partners they were too frightened to leave. Sometimes the man threatened that he'd find her or their children and kill them if she dared leave. Often the women had been raised in families where their fathers were abusive to their mothers. They were so damaged they saw the abuse as their due, as if being beaten was the natural order of life.

Spousal abuse wasn't so simplistic, but for whatever reason, women often stayed in abusive relationships for years before they escaped. Some never got away. Some stayed until the monsters they'd married followed through on their threats and killed them.

He should know.

His mother hadn't made it out. Not alive anyway. Her marriage had been a death sentence. His gut tightened as he fought the onslaught of painful memories. With a shaking hand, he raised the plastic bottle to his lips and gulped down the rest of the water.

He should have recognized the signs—Natasha Hartford's innate fear of him, the way she flinched when he touched her and cringed when he drew near.

His mouth was desert dry, his thirst unquenched in spite of the water he'd already drunk. Swiping his mouth with the back of his hand, he swung to the fridge, opened the door, and grabbed another bottle off the shelf. Twisting off the cap, he chugged half the water in one swallow.

The telltale markers were in the file—the too-frequent hospital visits, reports of police cruisers called to the house for domestic disturbances, and the recent restraining order. Natasha Hartford was an abused woman, all right. But she'd escaped her abuser. That took courage. A hell of a lot of courage.

And what about her bastard husband? She'd called the police for help, but she hadn't filed charges. He'd assaulted her repeatedly, and each time he'd swaggered away free and clear because his battered wife was too terrified to stand up to him.

The police could only do so much. After

responding to her call, the officers on scene would have followed standard protocol. They'd have ensured Natasha Hartford's immediate safety, encouraged her to file charges against her husband, and when she refused, they'd have referred her to Social Services. Their hands were tied. With her refusing to press charges, they had to leave her with her abuser, knowing full well the same scenario would play out time and time again.

He clenched his hands into tight fists, aching to smash her weasel of an ex-husband in the face. Only the worst sort of scum wanted to exert that kind of control over another human being.

He flipped back to the first page and reread the name of her husband.

Darien McCabe.

A prickle of awareness edged along his spine. The name was familiar. He rubbed his hand over his chin, his fingers rasping over the day's growth of whiskers as he fought to remember. Grabbing the phone, he called the precinct. When Mike answered, he explained what he'd discovered in Natasha Hartford's file.

Mike's raspy voice softened with sympathy. "Sounds like her ex-husband's a real asshole." He huffed out a loud breath. "Damn. I guess that's why she's in our files. And that lets her off as a suspect in our murder investigation. Come on, man. We need something…anything. The chief's ragging my ass. He wasn't any too happy when I told him we didn't have any solid leads."

"There may be something."

"Give it to me, man." Mike's words were garbled as he spoke around the stub of the chewed pencil perennially stuffed in his mouth. "I'm desperate."

"I have a hunch."

"Love your hunches."

"Natasha Hartford's ex-husband is Darien McCabe. Ring any bells?"

"Let me think." A rustle of papers and the click of computer keys echoed from the other end of the line.

Chase took another slug of water.

Mike's gruff voice came back on the line. "Looks like your spidey senses are bang on. You won't believe what I found."

Chase's heart raced at the excitement in the older man's voice. "Well? Don't keep me in suspense. Who is he?"

"McCabe's an interesting character. His record's spotless, but he's under a hell of a lot of suspicion. Has been for years. The Feds investigated him last year for fraud and money laundering, but they couldn't find anything concrete to pin on him. He has loads of cash and a team of high-priced, sleazy lawyers he hides behind like the snake he is."

"I remember," Chase said. "Doesn't the FBI have him linked to half the crime families in the country?"

"That's our boy." Again the crunching sound of wood and pencil lead filled the connection. "Are you thinking McCabe's involved in Waverley's murder? It's quite a coincidence you found McCabe's ex-wife snooping around Waverley's office." More crunching. "You know what they say about coincidences?"

"There's no such animal," Chase muttered. "Not in our business."

"Bang on, buddy."

"I'm not sure." Chase set the water bottle on the table. "They've been divorced for two years. She has a restraining order against him. Doesn't sound like they parted on good terms. Why would she help him?"

"From what you told me, he abused her," said Mike. "You know what these guys are like, once they get their claws into a woman, they don't let go. The poor women are so terrified they'll do anything the guy asks so they don't get slapped around."

Chase thought of Natasha and the fear dulling her blue eyes. "Yeah, I know what you mean. But, I talked to her, Mike. I don't think she knows anything. Whatever happened with her jerk of an ex is in her past. I can't see her having anything to do with him. If Darien McCabe's involved in Waverley's murder, she doesn't know."

"Hey, man." Mike's gruff voice softened. "Don't go there. Natasha Hartford isn't your mother. Maybe Hartford's not a victim. If she's helping her ex, she's guilty as shit."

"You haven't met her, Mike. You haven't seen the fear in her eyes. I have."

Mike surprised him by chuckling. "Big blue eyes, right? Isn't that what you said? And I'll bet she has a figure to die for." He laughed louder. "That's your hormones talking, buddy. You always were a sucker for a pretty face."

Chase opened his mouth to snap, but stopped. Mike spoke the truth. Natasha Hartford's presence in Waverley's office two days after the publisher was murdered was a red flag. Her explanation for being in the office was reasonable, but when you factored in her sleazy ex-husband, the situation took on a definite sour flavor.

If his cop instincts bristled around Natasha, they

soared into the stratosphere at the thought of Darien McCabe. He'd bet his cop's full, indexed pension the creep was involved in Waverley's murder. "All right. I'll head over to her house and try to get to the bottom of this."

"Are you sure that's a good idea?"

"We need to figure out if she's telling the truth. We can't afford to waste time chasing down false leads. I'll make sure we can rule her out as a suspect. No time like the present. Strike while the kettle's hot and all that shit."

"Chase, Darien McCabe's one bad dude. He isn't going to take kindly to you rushing over to his ex-wife's house and asking questions. If he's watching her, you could run into trouble. Why don't you wait until I'm finished here, and I'll come with you?"

"No way." Chase shook his head though Mike couldn't see him. "I'm doing this now. I can look after myself." Something inside compelled him to act. He had to find out if she'd lied. He ignored the tiny voice snickering in his ear. *Is that why you're so determined to see her tonight? Because of the case?* He picked up the almost-empty bottle of water and guzzled, silencing the voice. "And Mike? You don't have to worry. If she's holding back any useful information, you can be damn sure I'll find out what she knows."

Mike's chuckle was loud as Chase slammed down the phone. He vaulted to his feet. The chair toppled and clattered to the floor. Ignoring the overturned chair, he crushed the empty water bottle and tossed it on the table, grabbed his coat, and charged out of the apartment.

He'd talk to her, all right, and find out what she

knew. He didn't give a damn how her blonde hair gleamed like spun gold, or how a man could get lost in her luminous blue eyes. Before this night was over, he'd either charge her as an accessory to murder or clear her of any complicity in the crime.

****

He jabbed the doorbell for the third time.

Musical chimes echoed inside the small, one-story, Cape Cod-style house. The door opened and warm yellow light spilled onto the tiny porch.

His breath caught in his throat.

She was even prettier than he remembered. She wore a long-sleeved, full-length, blue velvet robe with a matching sash knotted around her narrow waist. Her feet were bare and slender; her toenails polished a soft pearly pink. He caught a tantalizing glimpse of shapely calves through the slit in the robe.

He tore his gaze from the fullness of her breasts outlined by the soft blue fabric and focused on her face.

A mistake.

Her blonde hair was a riot of curls, her face flushed, her eyes sapphire blue.

He gaped, transfixed by the rosy softness of her full lips, imagining what they tasted like. He couldn't stop staring, devouring her. He clamped down on his bottom lip, fearful a groan of longing would escape. If he stirred so much as a muscle, he'd take her in his arms and kiss her.

"Detective Brandon?" Her voice quaked. "What are you doing here?"

Her unbridled fear drew him out of his lustful thoughts. *Get a grip, man. This is business. Cop business. Better get that through your thick head.*

"Sorry to bother you." He winced at the hoarseness of his voice. "I have a few more questions I'd like to ask."

She paled and stumbled back a step.

The light from the hall glared in his eyes, placing her face in shadow, but her eyes shone with panic. Why was she so frightened? Was she guilty? Is that what this was about? Was she in cahoots with her ex-husband? If so, now would be the moment she'd demand a lawyer. Suspects with something to hide hid behind their lawyers. Would she?

"I have nothing more to say, Detective. I told you everything I know." Fear radiated off her in waves. Her gaze skittered past him, and she peered up and down the dark street.

The hairs on the back of his neck prickled, and he followed her gaze. The narrow residential street was dark and silent. Light from a single street lamp pooled on the sidewalk. A car was parked down the road against the curb in the shadows of an oak tree. Was someone inside the car watching? McCabe's men? He squinted against the glare of the porch light, but couldn't be certain.

She stepped back in the house and shifted to close the door.

He shoved the palm of his hand against the door, stopping her. "I really do have to speak to you, Ms. Hartford. It's important."

Her mouth tightened, and a tiny furrow appeared between her blonde brows. "I've told you, Detective. I have nothing more to say." She stared at the parked car down the street, and a visible shudder ran through her. "I can't do this now."

A dog barked from somewhere down the block.

The faint sounds of a television game show filtered through the open windows of the house next door.

He shoved the door open wider. "What is it? Why are you so frightened?"

"What are you talking about? I'm not afraid." Her stricken face proved her lie. "It's late and I'm exhausted." She shivered and wrapped her arms across her chest. "I...I want you to go." A car rolled past on the road, and she tensed. She watched the car until the vehicle turned the corner at the end of the block.

He scowled. She was as jumpy as a feral cat. He shook off his concern. He was here to find answers, not analyze her. "Ms. Hartford, I can return with a warrant and force you to talk to me if that's the way you want to play this." He fixed her with a steely glare. "Your choice." His threat hung in the air between them. He was bluffing. No judge in his right mind would sign a warrant based on Chase's cop instincts, but he counted on Natasha not knowing that. He tapped his foot and waited.

The high-pitched yapping of a dog pierced their standoff.

She blew out a long breath. "Great."

He followed the direction of her gaze.

A woman holding a straining leash attached to a small, fluffy, white dog marched down the street toward them. "Make doo-doo for mommy, Taffy." The woman's high-pitched baby talk carried over the dog's incessant barking. "Come on, Taffy, make doo-doo."

Taffy tugged on the leash, sniffing every bush and tree, ignoring its owner's pleas.

The woman's steps slowed as she approached Natasha's front yard. She paused on the sidewalk.

Chase nodded. "Evening, ma'am."

She studied him with narrow, suspicious eyes.

The dog apparently felt the same because he lunged on his leash toward Chase, snapping, sharp teeth bared.

Chase glared, giving the little dog his best cop's stare down.

Taffy stopped barking and whimpered, cowering behind the woman's legs.

Taffy's owner stumbled back, dragging the dog with her.

The white puff of hair yelped in protest.

The woman shushed the dog and called out, "Everything okay, Natasha?"

Natasha stepped onto the front porch. "Fine, Betty. Thanks."

The dog snarled again and strained on the leash.

"Hush, Taffy," Betty scolded.

Taffy squirmed to break free of the restraint, twisting until the collar slipped over his little neck, and he bounded away.

"Taffy!"

Taffy raced across Natasha's lawn, his stubby tail wagging, and squatted on a bed of flowers beside the front porch steps.

"Taffy, no." Betty's horrified voice squeaked as, cheeks flaming, she hurried over to where the little dog crouched. She bent and scooped a small mound of fresh dog poop into a plastic bag and hoisted the squirming dog in her arms.

With a last suspicious glance at Chase she scurried across the street, poop bag swinging in her hand, and disappeared through the front door of a white Colonial house. Seconds later, the curtains covering the large front window twitched as someone peered out.

Natasha exhaled a loud breath. "You'd better come in." She gestured for him to follow as she retreated into the house.

Thank you, Taffy. Not the friendliest welcome he'd ever received from a woman, but whatever worked.

Chase bit back a smug smile as he stepped into the house's warmth, closed the door, and followed the enticing sway of Natasha's hips down a short hall to a small tidy living room.

The room smelled of lavender. A gas fireplace, the orange and blue flames flickering, lent cozy warmth to the room. Several framed drawings of whimsical creatures painted in bright primary colors hung on the pale-green walls.

A large bay window filled one wall, but the view of the street was blocked by closed multi-colored drapes. A floral-patterned recliner and matching sofa faced the fireplace. A brass table lamp was on the wooden end table beside the recliner, and a coffee table was set in front of the couch. The hardwood floors gleamed in the soft light from the lamp.

He shrugged off his leather jacket and laid the coat across the back of the couch. His pulse raced as he met the full force of her luminous eyes, framed by impossibly long lashes. Inner alarm bells clamored, and he tugged at the too-tight collar of his shirt. *Get a grip. This isn't a date. She's a suspect in a murder investigation. You're a cop. Act like one.*

"Would you like some tea?" She pointed to a ceramic teapot on the maple end table. A china cup and saucer sat beside the teapot, a thin spiral of steam wafting from the hot tea.

He shook his head. "This isn't a social call." When she'd first opened the door, he'd stammered and stuttered like a fool, but what man wouldn't when confronted with such a sight? He had himself under control now.

He hoped.

A sturdy aluminum briefcase sat on the floor beside the couch, looking out of place in her feminine living room. He strolled over to the couch, studied the burnished metal case, and bent down and tapped the side. The briefcase was solid. He lifted it, surprised at its weight. The initials DCM were inscribed in block letters on a discreet silver plaque on the top of the briefcase by the leather handle. DCM? DCM!

He rose to his feet. "What are you doing with your ex-husband's briefcase?"

Chapter 6

Natasha's breath caught in her throat. Why hadn't she hidden Darien's briefcase like he'd told her to? Her mind whirled, and she struggled to think of a response. Darien had warned her what would happen if she talked to the police. She rubbed her hand over her bruised hip and winced.

The detective was bluffing, trying to unsettle her. He couldn't be certain the briefcase was Darien's. She pasted what she hoped was an innocent look on her face. "What are you talking about? That's not—"

He arched his dark brows, cutting off her lie.

"It's not…I mean, I'm…" She tugged the collar of her robe tighter and crossed her arms over her breasts. Under his probing gaze she was vulnerable and exposed.

And guilty.

All afternoon, she'd thought about what Darien had said. Even considered going to the police. The briefcase contained something important, something he didn't want to be found at his home or office. Otherwise, why was he so determined she hide it?

He'd told her he had people watching her. She believed him. The prickling awareness of being spied on was strong, though she hadn't seen anyone suspicious in the neighborhood. But his minions were out there. They'd know if she approached the police.

And they'd know a detective was here right now questioning her.

She eyed the police detective standing in the middle of her living room, his hard eyes watching her, and shuddered. He was a complication she didn't need. "Why are you here?"

The spark of pleasure that had shot through her when she'd opened the door and found him on her doorstep had shaken her. His rugged cheeks were flushed from the cold, and his dark hair had been tousled by the wind. Under the porch light his amber eyes had gleamed with an intensity that took her breath away and heated her blood, liquefying her bones.

Her first thought had been to turn him away. The last thing she wanted was Darien to think she'd talked to the police. But her nosy neighbor from across the street had appeared, and she sensed the burn of a dozen sets of eyes. The scenario didn't look good...a man on her doorstep at this time of night, and her in her bathrobe. Far worse if they figured out he was a police detective here to question her about a murder.

He paced closer, crowding her. "I told you. We aren't finished. I have more questions."

She shrank back, desperate for room to breathe. "I...I don't understand." Surely he didn't still think she had something to do with Waverley's murder. Another thought struck her, and her legs weakened. She grabbed the back of the couch for support. Did he know of Darien's visit? Of course he did. The briefcase was right in front of him.

"What are you hiding?" His dark, penetrating gaze raked her.

Heat flared in her cheeks, and she resisted the urge

to cinch her robe tighter and clutch the collar. "Hiding? Don't be ridiculous. I'm not hiding anything." She looked away so he wouldn't detect her lie. "It's late, Detective. Let's get this over with so I can go to bed. What do you want?" She sucked in a breath as the full impact of what she'd said struck her.

His eyes darkened, the pupils dilating until the hazel irises were hidden by coal black. The air sparked between them. He spun on his heel, strode to the couch, and sat down, stretching out his long, jean-clad legs, and crossing his feet.

Her heart lurched as he sat in the same spot on the couch as Darien had. The two men couldn't be more physically different. Darien was handsome in a refined, debonair way, but Detective Brandon, with his bulging muscles and dark ruggedness, was one hundred percent pure virile male.

Darien's dark-blond hair, cut short on the sides and longer on top, was carefully styled with a variety of expensive hair care products. The detective's tousled dark mane brushed his collar and looked as if he'd run his fingers through the glossy curls.

"I checked up on you."

His deep voice startled her out of her reverie. "On me?"

He nodded. "We have a file on you in the police database down at Headquarters." His gaze bore into her. "But I'm sure you know."

Her knees buckled, and she grabbed onto the arm of the nearest chair. "You...you're talking about the restraining order against my ex-husband?"

"Among other things."

Blood drained from her head. Too weak to stand,

she sagged onto the chair.

His eyes narrowed and his expression was unreadable, but when he spoke, his voice was gentle. "I know your ex-husband abused you."

Heat flared across her cheeks, and she jammed her knees together, her damp palms resting on her thighs. "I…I don't know what you're talking about."

Silence settled over the room, thick and cloying.

"Come on, Natasha. Is this the way you want to play this?"

She forced herself to meet his gaze. "I'm not playing anything, Detective."

"Why did you feel it necessary to take out a restraining order against your husband?"

"Ex-husband." The word tasted foul in her mouth. "Ex-husband."

"I fail to see what this has to do with your investigation."

"You tell me."

"I was under the impression you were here in regards to Jonas Waverley's murder." A chill rippled along her spine, and she rubbed her arms. The last thing she wanted to talk about was Darien and his abuse. Not after today, especially after today.

Another heavy silence ensued as he drummed his long fingers on his thigh. "You were married to Darien McCabe for five years."

Her breath hitched in her throat, and she nodded.

"Nice guy." Sarcasm riddled his voice.

"We divorced two years ago." Her heart pounded so loud she couldn't think.

The expression on his chiseled face didn't alter. "You're still in contact with him. I mean, in spite of the restraining order."

"No, I'm not." Her voice cracked. "Of course not."

"So you haven't seen him since the divorce?" He nodded at the briefcase on the floor.

Her skin prickled, and she surged to her feet, unable to sit still under his probing gaze. "What's this about, Detective?" She pointed her finger at him. "You read the file. You know why I required the restraining order. You know what he did to me." She paced to the window. "Do you really think I want anything to do with him?"

Thrusting the edge of the curtain aside, she peered out the window. The street was as deserted as a graveyard. The car that had been parked down the block was gone. She blew out a breath. Maybe it'd be okay. Maybe Darien didn't know a cop was here asking questions about him.

"You're afraid of something, Natasha. That's for damn sure."

She jolted at the sound of his voice and spun around. He stood inches from her. She opened her mouth to refute his claim, but he cut her off.

"Don't bother spouting any more lies." His amber eyes flashed fire. "I smell your fear." He threaded his fingers through his hair. "Whatever hold that bastard has over you, you're terrified." His eyes softened to a misty green, and he touched her arm.

She sucked in a quick breath and shrank back.

His eyes shuttered, and he withdrew his hand. He backed away, grabbed his coat off the couch, and shrugged it on. "If you decide you want to tell the truth, call me. Any time." He withdrew a small card from his pocket and tossed the card on the coffee table. "By the way"—he nodded at the briefcase—"don't leave town. Not any time soon." With an abrupt nod, he strode out of the room.

Her body frozen, her feet glued to the floor, she listened to his heavy tread march down the hall and then the opening and closing of the front door. A car engine rumbled to life on the street outside, and then there was silence.

Freed from her immobility, she stumbled across the room and collapsed on the couch. Her shoulders shook as the tears flowed, dampening the soft fabric beneath her cheeks.

****

Natasha blinked in the beam of dazzling sunshine streaming through her bedroom window and rubbed her puffy eyes. Images of the confrontation with Detective Brandon the previous night rose before her, and she groaned and yanked the sheets over her head.

She recalled his piercing gaze and shivered.

He knew.

The words blazed across her mind. He knew about Darien and the years of abuse. He also suspected the briefcase in her living room belonged to Darien. He probably assumed Darien was connected to Jonas Waverley's murder. And she was somehow involved.

Her cell phone rang on the bedside table. The loud ring shattered the morning quiet, and she tugged the sheets tighter and sank lower in bed, trying to block out the sound. Her head pounded, and her eyes were sandpaper.

The incessant ringing stopped, and she blew out a breath and rubbed at the tight knot in the back of her neck.

After Detective Brandon departed, she'd sobbed until she couldn't cry anymore. Sometime in the night, she'd dragged herself off the couch, dead-bolted the door again, and staggered up the stairs to her bedroom and collapsed on the bed. She'd tossed and turned, reliving the horror of her fight with Darien and the confrontation with Detective Brandon. Wishing she'd said this, done that, anything but what she'd done.

The clatter of the phone ringing split the air.

She shoved the covers back and sat up against the pillows and snatched the small phone. "What?"

Silence greeted her gruff question.

Her irritation mounted. "Who is this?"

Harsh breathing filled the line.

She was poised to punch the off button when he spoke. "Good morning, Natasha."

Her blood chilled, and she dropped the phone on the bed and stared at the phone as if it were a poisonous snake.

"Natasha?" Darien's tinny voice echoed from the phone. "Natasha?"

She bit her bottom lip until she tasted blood. Her hand shook so much she dropped the phone twice before she managed to raise it to her ear. "Wha…what do you want?"

His chuckle sent chills rippling along her spine. "Can't I phone my wife and wish her a good morning?"

She bit her lip harder, fighting back the rush of vitriol threatening to spew out.

"I understand you saw Detective Brandon last night."

"How did you—?" She stopped. The car. The black four-door sedan parked down the street. He'd been watching her. Or his minions had. Either way, he knew Detective Brandon had been there.

He chuckled. "I told you I was watching you." His voice hardened. "I trust you kept your mouth shut."

"I…I didn't say anything about you, if that's what you mean."

"Good, very good, my dear. And is my attaché case stowed away as I asked?"

A vision of the metal briefcase sitting on the floor beside the couch where he'd left the case flashed before her. It was on the tip of her tongue to tell him she'd rather face the fiery gates of Hell than follow through on anything he asked of her, but she sealed her lips and said nothing.

A whisper of static crackled over the phone line. "I trust your silence means you've done as I asked. Make sure the case remains hidden." A click and dead air as he severed the connection.

She fell back against the pillows. Whatever was inside the burnished metal case was important. Shoving back the blankets, she swung her legs out of bed and hurried downstairs to the living room. She lifted the briefcase, surprised at its weight, and carried it to the couch.

Setting the briefcase on her lap, she ran her fingers over the smooth, polished metal. Three letters were inscribed into a small metal plaque between the two locks on the top. Peering closer, she made out the initials DCM. Darien Charles McCabe. So that's how Detective Brandon knew the case belonged to Darien.

The briefcase was locked with two roller-style combination locks. She fiddled with the dials, trying a combination of numbers…Darien's birthdate, their wedding date, the date of their divorce, a series of random numbers. After a few minutes, she gave up.

Lifting the heavy case, she flattened her ear to the metal side and shook. Something heavy thumped against the inside of the briefcase. She shook the case again. Clunk. And again. Not papers. Something solid.

She tried prying open the case with a screwdriver and then a knife she grabbed from the knife block in the kitchen, but the seam was too tight, and she didn't want to risk scratching the burnished metal. If Darien noticed any marks, she'd be in real trouble.

Sitting back, she wiped dampness off her forehead with her arm. What should she do with the damn briefcase? Turn it over to the police? Detective Brandon would love to get his hands on the briefcase. But if Darien found out, he'd be furious. And she'd pay the price. She shuddered. Better to hide the case as he'd asked. He'd promised to retrieve it in a few days. What harm would it do to hide it?

Picking up the weighty briefcase, she lugged it across the room into the kitchen. She knelt on the tile floor and opened the cupboard below the sink. Pipes from the sink and the dishwasher hose filled the dark, cramped space.

She cleared away containers of dish soap, cleansers, and an assortment of pot scrubbers. Reaching into the back of the cupboard, she pried off a thin strip of wood paneling attached to the back wall, revealing a rectangular hole cut into the wall.

When she'd had the dishwasher installed after she'd moved in, the plumber had explained that in order for the ancient water pipes to tolerate the pressure of a dishwasher, he had to cut into the existing wall and run the hose through to the pipes behind. He'd covered the gaping hole with a piece of wood veneer that matched the wood of the cupboard. If she hadn't known about the hole behind the panel, she wouldn't have suspected the hidden space existed.

She hefted the briefcase and jammed it into the hole. With a bit of twisting and turning, the metal case fit. Retrieving the strip of wood veneer, she set the wood in place and repositioned the cleaning supplies. Sitting back, she wiped her hands on her nightgown.

No one would think to look for the briefcase under the sink. And if they did, they wouldn't notice the hidden hole behind the false-wood front. Not that anyone would come looking for the briefcase. Darien was paranoid. But at least now the case wasn't sitting out in full view.

She washed her hands under the tap and peered at the clock. Nine thirty and already the day had gone to hell. The wakeup call from Darien had started her off on the wrong foot. A run would clear her head and calm her nerves. The physical exertion would help her forget the mess she was mired in up to her neck.

She hurried upstairs to her bedroom, wiggled into a pair of running pants, and tugged a T-shirt over her head. Scraping her long hair back into a ponytail, she slipped on her running shoes and headed for the door.

Relief and the sweet taste of freedom swamped her the second she stepped outside. The smell of the previous night's rain lingered. A gentle breeze redolent of moist earth and the lilacs blooming in profusion on the bushes lining the end of her short driveway filled the air. The sun shone warm on her shoulders. The first robins of the season tweeted from high in the branches of the old elm tree in the middle of her front yard.

Betty Houston waved from her front lawn across the street where she was pruning her prized rose bushes.

Taffy, tethered to a long leash, bounded between Betty's feet, yapping and tugging at his restraint.

Other than Betty and Taffy, the street was deserted. No unfamiliar black cars were parked on the street; no giant, hard-muscled, sunglasses-wearing men watched from behind the bushes.

Inhaling a deep, cleansing breath, she plugged in her earbuds and headed down the street to the beat of her favorite, old-time rock-and-roll tune. Her pace was stiff and slow at first, but as her muscles warmed and the bruise on her hip loosened, she loped with long, easy strides along the sidewalk.

After three blocks, she crossed the road and followed a dirt path through a thick stand of trees to a narrow gravel lane leading to a road along the river. This was the best part of her run. Usually other runners, cyclists, and young mothers pushing strollers populated the busy trail, but today she had the path to herself.

Her heart lifted as she loped through the verdant forest. The trees were alive with birds and skittering squirrels, the air fresh, and the sun bright. Her breath whooshed in and out of her lungs in a steady, relaxing rhythm. The muscles in her legs burned with each stride. Sweat beaded her brow and soaked the nape of her neck and T-shirt as she ran to the beat of the Rolling Stones.

Crossing the lane, she jogged along the grassy shoulder in the dappled shade of the towering fir trees lining the road. Her foot struck a rut, and she yelped as she stumbled and fell. Her knees hit the soft ground with a thud, and her breath whooshed out.

Shaken, she struggled to her feet and brushed bits of gravel, grass, and dirt from her knees. She tested her ankle. Other than a slight twinge, her ankle was fine. Shaking off her spill, she continued her run, but her next steps faltered, and she slowed, and drew to a stop. A set of ankle-deep tire tracks gouged the grass and dirt of the soft shoulder and disappeared over the bank.

She stood at the edge of the steep hill and peered through the thick tangle of bushes to the ravine below. Something shiny glinted in the sunshine. Her heart lodged in her throat, and she edged closer.

A vehicle lay at the bottom of the steep ravine. The car rested on its side and was jammed against a stand of thick cottonwood trees. The wheels were still spinning. Dust hung in a cloud over the ravine.

She ripped the earbuds out of her ears. "Hello?" Her voice was a thin reed of sound as she called to the gully below. Taking a deep breath, she tried again. "Hello?"

An ominous silence, unbroken by the call of birds or the sigh of wind in the leaves of the trees, greeted her call. She fished in her fanny pack, yanked out her cell phone, and punched in 911. The phone rang forever before the call was answered.

"911. What is your emergency?"

"An accident!" Her voice was shrill. "There's been an accident. Out on Hawkins Road, down by Pederson's Corner. A car's at the bottom of a ravine. Someone could be injured. Send an ambulance." Without waiting for a response, she stuffed the phone back in her pack and zipped the pack closed.

Slipping and sliding in the mud and loose gravel,

she fought her way to the bottom of the ravine. She skidded and grabbed a bush to slow her descent, wincing when the sharp thorns of a wild rose bush dug into her palm. She slid on her bottom the rest of the way.

The sickly sweet tang of gasoline stung her nostrils, and her eyes watered. A loud crack split the air and echoed through the narrow ravine.

She froze. Was the car's gas tank going to explode?

Another crack.

Run! The warning screamed through her. She spun to flee but slipped in the muck and fell, landing on her bottom. Scrambling to her feet, she halted her fear-fueled flight. *Calm down. Cars only burst into flames in the movies. The people in the car could be injured. They need help.*

Heart in her throat, she slogged over to the black, four-door sedan. The back end of the car was crushed from the force of the impact, and the vehicle rested on its side. The tires had stopped spinning, but her stomach clenched at the stench of burning rubber, hot grease, and oil.

Sloshing through a narrow, shallow stream, her feet sinking in mud, she fought her way to the front of the wrecked vehicle. She jammed a fist in her mouth, stifling a scream.

A man sprawled on the hood of the car amidst a shower of tiny glass cubes from the shattered windshield. Splotches of white powder from the air bag covered his face and neck. Blood dripped from a deep gash in his forehead, forming a pool on the hood. His neck was twisted at an unnatural angle.

Hands shaking, she edged closer and placed her fingers on the side of his neck, feeling for a pulse. His skin was warm, but his dark brown eyes were filmed and milky as he stared sightlessly at the sky.

CPR!

She knew how to do the life-saving procedure. She'd taken a first aid course when she'd worked at the recreation center as an administrative assistant right after she'd fled from Darien. But you weren't supposed to move someone if he had a spinal injury.

She gulped at the man's twisted neck and bloody face. Her stomach rose and fell like an ocean swell. He looked familiar. Was he one of her neighbors? Someone she'd worked with?

Sirens wailed in the distance, growing louder by the second.

A wave of relief washed through her. Help was almost here. She jerked at a clatter of rocks and spun toward the unexpected sound.

A man dressed in black denim jeans and a dark leather bomber-style jacket stood on the far side of the clearing, outlined like a ghostly apparition in the glare of sunlight.

"I'm so glad you're here. Help me, please. This man's..." She shook her head and swallowed back bile. "But there may be someone else in the car."

The man didn't move. His eyes were cold, his expression hard. His dirty-blond hair was scraped back from an angular face into a tight bun. A wisp of dark-blond beard covered his pointy chin.

A sudden chill assailed her, and she stumbled back a step.

He groped in the pocket of his leather jacket and

withdrew a small black object.

Her breath froze in her throat. *A gun*! *He has a gun*! The words screamed through her in a frantic litany. Time stood still as she stared, transfixed.

He raised his arm and pointed the gun.

She dropped to the ground, throwing herself face first onto the mud and gravel.

A loud, booming crack reverberated through the gully, bouncing off the rocks and trees.

She whimpered and burrowed deeper into the muck.

Another deafening boom resounded, and a rock a foot in front of her exploded into a dozen sharp splinters.

Something hot struck her cheek, stinging and burning. She raised a trembling hand, and her fingers came away covered with blood. Scrabbling deeper in the mud, she slithered across the rocky ground on her belly to the side of the wrecked car. Her heart pounded, her breath chugging in and out in ragged pants. Why was he shooting at her? She wedged closer to the car, wishing she could part steel with her bare hands and squeeze inside the vehicle.

Every cell of her being vibrated, bracing for the next bullet.

A branch cracked off to her left.

She squeezed her eyes shut. "Please, please, please." The whispered prayer slipped from her lips.

Over the wail of approaching sirens, a flurry of footsteps sounded as if someone were slipping and sliding over loose rock, moving fast over the rough ground. The footfalls grew more distant as the man with the gun clambered away.

The screech of sirens spiked in an ear-splitting crescendo and abruptly ceased. Car doors slammed. Voices, loud and commanding, issued orders.

She shoved away from the fender and sat up. Drawing her knees to her chest, she laid her head on her arms as a warm bath of relief washed over her. Her hiccupping breaths eased to pants, and her heart rate slowed its frantic pace.

She stood on shaky legs. Her gaze landed on the dead man sprawled on the hood. She gagged as she met his sightless stare. Stumbling away from the car, she leaned over and spewed vomit into the muck. Again and again her guts spasmed until only bile remained.

"Are you okay, ma'am?" Someone grabbed her arm, steadying her.

She jerked away.

"Ma'am?"

She wiped her mouth with the back of her arm and met the narrow-eyed scrutiny of a silver-haired, middle-aged man wearing a blue police uniform.

He studied her for a minute, his gaze settling on her injured cheek. His brow furrowed, and he pressed the communication unit attached to the shoulder of his uniform and spoke into the microphone. "Peterson, get those damn medics down here." He slid a glance at the wrecked car and spoke again into the microphone. "I have at least one dead and another injured." He studied her with a penetrating look. "Was anyone else in the car, ma'am?"

His lips moved and he spoke, but his words didn't make sense. A deep weariness stole over her, and it was all she could do to remain standing.

"Ma'am?"

She opened her mouth, but her throat wouldn't work, as if her vocal cords were paralyzed.

He clamped his hands on her upper arms. "Ma'am, were you involved in the accident?"

She shook her head.

"You called this in?"

She nodded. Tears spilled from her eyes, dripping onto her T-shirt, mixing with the mud and blood.

His eyes softened, and he released his hold on her arms. "Look, I have to leave you for a minute. I have to make sure no one else is injured."

She shook her head with such force tendrils of hair that had escaped her ponytail whipped across her face. She grabbed his hand.

"You'll be okay. The medics are on their way. Stay here." He pried her fingers free and turned toward the damaged car.

"No." Her voice was an anguished wail. She seized his hand again, refusing to let him go. She had to tell him about the man with the gun. "No…don't leave me. Please."

He cast an anxious look over his shoulder at his fellow officers and then back at her. "I'll send someone to help you. I promise."

She shook her head, but words wouldn't form. Her gaze darted around the surrounding thick tangle of brush and trees. The blond-haired man could be hiding, watching, waiting for a clear shot. She shuddered.

"Sergeant, I've got another one."

With a last reassuring glance, the gray-haired cop freed his hand and hurried across the clearing, sloshing around the car to the far side.

She stood frozen as if in a trance. Her heart beat a

trip-hammer in her chest.

More skittering of gravel and mud, and she whipped around, her mouth open in a silent scream.

Two paramedics skidded down the bank in a spray of loose rock. Each man carried a heavy navy-blue nylon bag strapped across his shoulder. They packed a collapsible stretcher between them and slogged over to the car.

Her breath whooshed out. She studied the ravine, searching for the blond man with the gun. The surrounding bush was thick. He could be hiding anywhere.

Red and blue lights reflected off the leaves of the trees from the road above, and voices squawked urgent commands from police car radios. More sirens neared, their wails like a pack of starving beasts on the hunt.

She rubbed her arms in a vain attempt to massage warmth to counter the bone-jarring chill rattling through her.

"Come with me, ma'am. I'll help you up to the road."

A young police officer, clad in a mud-spattered uniform too big for his lanky frame, held out his hand. A bulky belt laden with a gun, nightstick, and handcuffs hung on his narrow hips. "The medics will see to you after they're finished down here." He nodded at the accident scene. "Come on. Let's get you away from here."

She shrugged off his hand. "Was…was anyone else in the car?"

"One other victim." His Adam's apple bobbed in his thin throat.

She studied his youthful, pale face with the light

fuzz of facial hair lining his upper lip. "He didn't make it either, did he?"

He shook his head.

Mind whirling as she took in this new information, she stumbled along behind him as he urged her toward the bottom of the hill leading to the road above.

"Easy, ma'am." He tightened his grip on her biceps and helped her climb over the loose rocks and up the steep slope. They trudged to the top, and he led her over to an ambulance.

The rear door was open, the stretcher gone. Lights on top of the vehicle flashed. "Wait here, ma'am. The EMTs should be along any minute. They'll see to that nasty cut on your cheek."

He waited until she climbed inside the back of the ambulance and sat on a narrow padded bench along one side of the box of the vehicle. "Will you be okay? The sergeant wants me back down at the crash site."

She licked her cracked lips, finally finding her voice. "There's...there's something you have to know. A man—"

He wasn't listening. His body bristled with nervous excitement, and he shifted from one foot to the other, looking over his shoulder at the ravine, as if afraid he'd miss something. "Don't tell me now. The sergeant will want to talk to you. You can tell him everything then."

"But—"

"You'll be fine. Look, ma'am, I gotta go." He spun around and loped toward the ravine, vanishing over the edge in a few long strides.

Chapter 7

Teeth chattering, she scrubbed her hands on her pants, trying to ease the icy numbness that chilled her blood, sinking deep into the marrow of her bones. Her clothes were crusted with dried mud and stained with grass and what she feared was blood. Her running pants were torn, exposing one bruised and battered knee from when she'd fallen.

She peered out of the ambulance, squinting into the bright light. The sun had risen high overhead, but menacing shadows lurked amidst the trees lining the lane. She shuddered and huddled on the seat.

The inside of the ambulance was warm. Four, small recessed lights in the ceiling created a cozy space, but the sharp antiseptic smell reminded her of her too-frequent visits to hospital emergency rooms after Darien had vented his displeasure at something she'd done or hadn't done.

Stop. Don't think of Darien. Not now. Not when two people lay dead at the bottom of the ravine, and a man had tried to kill her. She bit down hard on her bottom lip. Was the man still here? Had he escaped by climbing out of the ravine and even now hid in the forest and waited to finish what he'd started?

She strained to listen, but only the cheerful twittering of birds rustling in the trees and the distant voices of the men in the gully below filled the still air.

A heavy exhaustion settled over her, and she leaned back against the metal side. Her eyes drifted closed as the terror and strain of the past hour took its toll.

"Tough day, huh?"

Her eyes flew open, and she jerked her head up at the familiar, deep, male voice.

Detective Chase Brandon leaned in the ambulance opening. His dark curls hung over his forehead in wild disarray as he studied her, his hazel eyes narrowed. He held a plastic water bottle in one hand.

"You!" She winced at the high-pitched squeak of her voice.

The corners of his mouth quirked. "Yep, it's me."

"What are you doing here? This was an accident, and you're Homicide." A wave of dizziness struck, and she swayed on the bench.

"Here." He unscrewed the cap and handed her the water bottle. "Drink this. You'll feel better."

With trembling fingers, she raised the plastic bottle to her lips and sipped. The cool liquid soothed the agonizing tightness in her throat, but the brackish taste of bile and fear lingered.

He studied her with a hawk-like stare, his face lean and hard. The fine white line of an old scar bisected one dark eyebrow. His jaw was angular, his cheekbones sharp and jutting. "You're bleeding."

He leaned into the ambulance and hoisted a red soft-sided bag with a large white cross emblazoned on the side. Unzipping the bag, he dug through the emergency medical supplies, removed a small paper-covered package, and ripped it open.

He took the water bottle from her and poured water onto the white gauze dressing, and dabbed at the wound on her cheek, his touch gentle. "Looks like the cut's stopped bleeding, but you might need a couple of stitches." The corners of his mouth curved, softening his harsh features. "Wouldn't want to ruin that pretty face."

Their gazes met and held.

She forgot to breathe, forgot she was in the back of an ambulance, forgot the horror of the ravine, forgot someone had shot at her, forgot everything but the unusual green of his eyes—soft, moss green, with golden lights flickering in their intriguing depths.

The wail of an approaching siren broke the spell, and she jerked away. Hands shaking like she had palsy, she grabbed the gauze pad and mopped her damp forehead.

"You reported the accident?" He leaned against the open ambulance door, his long, jean-clad legs crossed at the ankles, his hands stuffed in the pockets of his brown leather jacket. The muscles in his biceps bulged, belying his relaxed appearance.

"I...I was out for a run and saw the tire tracks on the grass on the edge of the bank. I...I didn't think anything of them at first, but I stopped and—" She fought to halt her wild rambling, but the stream of words poured out. "I...I couldn't leave. I had to check to see if anyone was injured. The tires were still spinning, so I knew the accident had just happened."

She sipped another gulp of water and was glad she was sitting. Her legs shook, her knees rubbery as the nightmare returned with vivid clarity. "Something flashed in the sun. I wasn't sure what it was at first, but then...then I saw the car."

"So you called 911, and climbed down into the

ravine and checked the vehicle." His voice was a deep, low rumble, soothing and calming. Just like they were two friends having a conversation.

She nodded.

"What did you see when you reached the car?"

A vision of the dead man with his bizarrely twisted neck and blood leaking from the gash on his forehead floated before her. She shuddered. "The driver...I think he was the one driving...he...he was dead. I saw that right away..." She shook off the image of the dead man's blank stare. "He...he mustn't have been wearing his seatbelt because he was thrown through the windshield when the car crashed into the trees at the bottom of the ravine." She swallowed back a fresh wave of bile.

His gaze didn't leave her face, his eyes unreadable. "Go on."

"I...I..." She wiped perspiration from her forehead and swallowed more water to ease the arid dryness of her throat. "A man. He...he had a gun and...and he shot at me." She swallowed. "I ducked behind the car, but he kept shooting." Her hand grazed the cut on her cheek. "I thought I was going to die." A sob hiccupped in her throat. "I...I thought he'd kill me."

She didn't see him shift, but in the next breath he was beside her, sitting on the narrow bench. His thigh bumped against hers, their shoulders brushing. The warmth of his body seeped through her damp, mud-stained clothes.

He swept back a stray lock of her hair with gentle fingers. "Easy, Natasha. Breathe slow and steady. In through your nose, out through your mouth." He patted her thigh. "You're safe now."

She leaned against his solid bulk, finding comfort and reassurance in his calm presence. The warmth of his hand on her thigh seeped through her running pants to her skin. "He…he tried to kill me." The single stark statement encapsulated her terror, shock, and disbelief.

Chase leaned back and studied her. "Did you recognize him? Had you seen him before?"

She shook her head.

"What about the driver of the car? Did you recognize him?"

A headache built behind her eyes. "I…I don't know. Maybe. I'm not sure."

"Come on, Natasha. Think. This is important." He hunched forward, crowding her. "Have you seen those men before?"

She pinched the bridge of her nose. "Why do you think I know those people?"

"I imagine you know any number of people who own guns." Gone was the compassionate man who'd offered her water and tended her wound, replaced by the hard-eyed, suspicious cop.

His back was to the light, and she couldn't see his face clearly, but the truth hit her like a splash of ice water. He knew. He knew about Darien. Not just about the abuse, but about Darien's other endeavors.

As if reading her mind, he nodded. "I know all about your ex-husband and the people he associates with. Darien McCabe is quite a character."

She clenched her hands, her nails digging into her palms. "What has this to do with Darien? This was an accident."

He cocked his head. "I don't believe in accidents."

"But it was an accident. The car spun off the road

and crashed into the ravine. The driver must have lost control."

He climbed out of the ambulance and jammed his hands in the back pockets of his jeans. "Look, Ms. Hartford...Natasha, I don't want to make this any worse than it has to be, but it's best if you tell me what you know. Don't hold anything back."

"I'm not. I told you everything. Why aren't you looking for the man who shot at me? Why are you questioning me? I didn't do anything wrong."

He blew out a breath. "You heard there was another victim?"

She nodded.

"He didn't die as a result of the accident."

"What?" She rubbed the rising goose bumps on her arms.

"He was murdered." His jaw tightened. "Someone, probably the man who shot at you, put a bullet between his eyes. The man who went through the windshield was shot in the head as well, but that was overkill. He was already dead. Looks like the crash killed him."

The world spun, and she collapsed against the ambulance wall. "What? Oh my God."

"I doubt God had anything to do with this, but your husband might have."

She jolted upright. "What are you saying? Are you telling me Darien's responsible for this? How's that possible?"

His eyes narrowed to slits. "The driver of the car and the passenger are known acquaintances of McCabe."

His words twigged a memory, and her stomach twisted in a painful knot. So that's why the driver looked familiar. She'd seen him before…with Darien.

The man with the broken neck sprawled on the hood of the wrecked car had been in Darien's dark, luxury sedan parked on the street outside her house when Darien visited yesterday afternoon. He'd been wearing dark sunglasses, but it was the same person. She was certain.

"I see you remember." He leaned into the ambulance and grasped her arm. "You'd better come with me."

"Why?" She held steady. "Where are we going?"

"Down to the station."

"The station? The police station? You're…you're taking me to the police station?"

He tugged on her arm. "Come on."

"But—" She tightened her hold on the bench, refusing to allow him to draw her off the seat and out of the ambulance.

"Look, Natasha, this is serious. Two men are dead; another tried to kill you."

"But—"

"I have to ask you more questions and take your statement." He waved his free hand around at the parked emergency vehicles and the thick forest of trees bordering the lane. "This isn't the place. We don't know where the man who shot at you is or what his intentions are, but you aren't safe here." He scrubbed his hand over his chin. "You'll be safer at headquarters."

"But I didn't do anything."

He released her and stepped back. "Okay. If that's what you want. Go ahead and walk home. I'll stop by your house later for your statement."

Relief flooded her, and she climbed out of the ambulance. "Thanks, I—"

He cut off the rest of what she was going to say. "Of course, I can't protect you if the man who shot at you shows up." He shrugged. "You'll be on your own."

Her heart lodged in her throat. That man...the blond-haired man... A vision of his cold, hooded gaze rose before her, the dark barrel of the gun aimed at her, the loud explosions of the bullets ricocheting, the thud as they struck the ground inches from where she hid. "Okay, okay, you win. I'll go with you."

"Smart girl."

Was that a smirk on his face? Before she could confirm her suspicions, he turned and led the way through the swarm of emergency vehicles scattered across the narrow road.

She peered at the ominous, dense forest behind her and hurried after him to a tan, four-door sedan.

Holding open the back door, he gestured for her to climb inside.

She hesitated. "What about the cut on my cheek? The other policeman told me to wait in the ambulance for the paramedics. And his sergeant wanted to talk to me."

"I'll see you receive medical attention." He nudged her another step closer to the car. "Don't worry about the sergeant. This is a homicide. It's my case now."

The pounding in her head increased with each labored breath. She scrambled inside the vehicle. The door slammed with a loud thunk, and she sagged on the hard vinyl seat.

Settling behind the steering wheel, he slammed the car door, and started the engine. He glanced over his shoulder. "Better buckle up. I wouldn't want anything to happen to my prize witness."

Chapter 8

Chase couldn't stop watching her in the rearview mirror. Hell, he'd come within a hair's breadth of clipping a cyclist because he was gawking at her rather than focusing on the road.

She slumped on the seat, her slight body held up by the seat belt, looking as if she was a criminal he was taking to jail.

When he'd gotten the call about the car in the ravine, he'd figured the incident for another MVA. The first uniforms on-scene hadn't bothered to reveal the two victims had a bullet lodged in their brains. That's why he'd told Mike to remain at the station working the Waverley murder. He hadn't thought he'd need him, figured he'd be back at his desk within an hour, tops.

New department policy required a homicide detective appraise a motor vehicle accident scene if the circumstances were the least bit suspicious. The appraisal usually involved nothing more than a five-minute consult with the attending officers.

Not this time.

One look at the car told him this wasn't an accident. Bullet holes peppered the side of the vehicle, and the front tire had been shot out. Closer examination showed both the driver and the passenger had bullet holes in their heads. Whoever did this wanted to make damn sure the men in the vehicle were good and dead.

Once again he glanced in the rearview mirror at the woman in the back seat.

Her face was ghostly white. Silken strands of her long, blonde hair had escaped her ponytail. Her clothes were stained and torn. Blood crusted a cut on her pale cheek, and dark circles underscored her blue eyes. Her hands were clasped on her lap, her knuckles white with the force of her squeezing.

A car horn blared, and he jerked his focus back to the road in time to avoid sideswiping a delivery van.

The van driver glared and shot him the finger as he blasted past.

Chase kept his eyes on the road for the remainder of the trip to the station, but he couldn't quell the chaos in his mind. What the hell had happened at the crash site? Was she telling the truth? Was she an innocent passerby who'd come across the accident scene like she said?

Not likely.

Both men had identification. When he'd called in their names, and Bert ran their IDs through the precinct computer system, alarm bells rang loud and clear. The men had worked as hired muscle for Darien McCabe.

Natasha Hartford had been married to McCabe.

A coincidence? He thought not. As Mike often said…there ain't no such animal.

And what was she thinking climbing down the damn hill? She should have waited for help to arrive. Christ! She could have been killed.

The murders exhibited the rancid stink of a professional hit. The killer had shot at her, but no pro worth his weight in cheap bullets would miss a civilian, not if he wanted to kill her. Was this a warning of some sort? But for whom? And why? It had to be connected to McCabe.

It had to be.

He wheeled the car into the police lot and steered into a parking space. Setting the brake and turning off the engine, he glanced over his shoulder and met Natasha's haunted gaze. "We're here."

Her eyes were bright with unshed tears.

No wonder. Being shot at would freak anybody out. Shrugging off the unwelcome spurt of sympathy, he shoved open his door and stomped around to her side of the car. He yanked open her door and gestured for her to get out.

Like an automaton, she climbed out of the car and allowed him to take her arm and lead her into the two-story brick building and up the stairs to Homicide.

As soon as they set foot in the bullpen, conversation ceased as six other detectives in the room stopped what they were doing and stared at Chase and the woman beside him.

A phone rang, the peal urgent and demanding, but no one answered.

He glared at his fellow homicide detectives, instilling the full force of his anger and frustration into the look.

On any other day, he'd have gotten a kick out of the way the four men and one woman swiveled back to their desks and returned to work, as if their actions were choreographed. The ringing phone was answered, computer keyboards tapped, and conversations resumed.

But not Mike.

He sat in his chair, legs up on his desk and crossed

at the ankles, his gaze fixed on Chase, unfazed by Chase's death stare. Mike lowered his legs, rose from his desk, and strode over. His brows furrowed in a deep vee over his large, crooked nose. "What's this?" He nodded at Natasha. "What's going on?"

"I have to talk to you, Mike. Grab us some coffee and meet me in Interrogation Room A."

Mike's frown deepened, but he nodded and lumbered off to round up coffee.

Chase led Natasha across the room and indicated she should sit in the hard-backed chair beside his desk. "Are you okay with waiting here for a few minutes while I fill in my partner on what's happened?"

She didn't respond, just sat, hands clasped on her lap, staring at nothing.

His gut tightened, and he grabbed the phone on his desk. Maybe she was more injured than he'd thought. Dialing downstairs, he requested a first-aid attendant to look after the wound on her cheek and check her over for other possible injuries. He crouched before her and softened his voice. "I've called for a medic. He'll fix your cut and then we'll talk, okay?"

Fear blazed from the sapphire-blue depths of her eyes. "Okay." Her voice was a thin thread of sound.

He squeezed her shoulder lightly, ignoring the burning weight of five pairs of eyes watching his every move. He'd face some serious ribbing later, but he could handle it. "Relax. It'll be okay."

"Will it?"

"I promise." As soon as the words were out of his mouth, he regretted them. How the hell could he promise her that? If she was involved in this mess, he couldn't help her. No one could. But still he smiled and nodded, and dug the hole of his grave deeper. "I'll do whatever I can to help you."

She must have believed him because the tight thrumming of her body relaxed, and she unclenched her hands. Her full lips curved in a tentative smile.

He swallowed. "I'll get you something to drink." He jerked to his feet and hurried into the break room and poured her a cup of thick, bitter coffee. He added creamer, then tore open three packs of sugar and stirred those into the vile brew.

By the time he returned to his desk with her coffee, the medic he'd called was treating her wound. He set the steaming foam cup on the desk beside her and departed in search of Mike.

"What the hell's going on, Chase? Why did you bring in the Hartford woman?"

Chase winced at the accusation in his partner's gruff voice and closed the door to the interrogation room behind him. He dragged out a chair from the table and plopped down. Running his hands through his hair, he took a steadying breath and proceeded to update Mike on the events of the past few hours.

When he finished, Mike rose and paced around the cramped, airless room, the stub of a pencil clenched between his teeth. "This whole scenario reeks like shit. First Waverley buys it, and then these two goons of McCabe's. And if we believe the lady, someone shot at her this morning."

Chase rolled his shoulders trying to ease the rising tightness. "There's a connection between the murders. That's for damn sure."

Mike stopped his relentless pacing. His gray brows rose. "You think?"

Chase ignored his sarcasm. "We suspect McCabe's involved in Waverley's murder, right?"

Mike nodded.

"And the two guys killed in the car this morning worked for McCabe."

Again Mike nodded.

"So what do you think's going on? A mob hit? A rivalry between gangs?"

Mike shrugged. "Could be. McCabe hangs with some pretty sketchy dudes." The crunch of pencil was loud in the silent room. "Do you think the Hartford woman has something to do with all this?"

"I don't know." Chase spread his hands. "On the surface she seems like another of McCabe's victims, but I don't know. There has to be a connection. The shooter this morning missed her. That was deliberate. It had to be. These guys don't miss."

"Agreed. And?"

Chase puffed out his cheeks. "And...I don't know. This could be a warning. Someone wants McCabe to know he can get to him anytime."

Mike crunched some more, deep in thought. "Okay, then." He rubbed his hands together. "Let's get her statement. Maybe we can catch a break for a change. Maybe she'll crack."

****

Natasha winced as the medical technician smoothed the butterfly bandages over the cut on her cheek.

Detectives bustled around the busy office, typing on computer keyboards, talking on phones, and constantly getting up and down from their desks and refilling coffee mugs.

No one looked at her or paid her any obvious attention, but she caught the odd sly glance and sensed their heightened awareness of her presence.

"All finished, ma'am." The medic rose to his feet and tossed blood-covered gauze and a set of rubber gloves in the biohazard garbage. He replaced the antibiotic ointment and other supplies in his red nylon bag.

"Thank you."

He nodded and strode out of the room.

No more than a minute passed before Detective Brandon and the man he'd talked to earlier strolled into the room, determined expressions on their hard faces.

Chase sat behind the desk, and the other man dragged a rolling chair over and lowered himself with a grunt onto the chair.

Chase pointed at the older man seated beside him. "This is my partner, Detective Mike Podborski. Mike, this is Natasha Hartford."

Mike nodded. "You had quite a day, I understand. Chase, here, tells me you were the first person to come across the crime scene. Wanna tell me about it?"

She drew in a deep breath. The last thing she wanted was to rehash the frightening events, but in order for the police to catch the murderer, she had to tell them everything she knew. "I was out for a run this morning, and I saw tire tracks going off the edge of the bank. When I looked into the ravine, I spotted the car. And the man on the hood…" She bit her lip as a vision of the grisly scene rose before her. "Then…then that guy started shooting at me. I…I didn't know what to do and—"

Detective Podborski interrupted her and leaned

closer. "Did you recognize the man who shot at you?"

She shook her head. "I...I was terrified. I thought he'd kill me."

"Understandable. A gun's pretty frightening, especially when the barrel's pointed at you." He shifted the stub of pencil from one side of his mouth to the other with his tongue. "Do you think you could ID him if we show you some photos?"

"Maybe." She shrugged. "I don't know. I'll try."

The detective rose and threaded through the maze of desks in the busy room to a shelf on the far wall. He rummaged through stacks of large binders piled one on top of the other.

Could she identify the man? She'd only seen him for a few seconds, but his face was imprinted on her brain.

"So you recognized the man who crashed through the windshield." Chase's deep voice broke through the maelstrom raging through her mind.

"Yes. He was sitting in the front seat of Darien's car when Darien came to my house yesterday." The second the words were out of her mouth, she regretted them. She shouldn't have told him about Darien's visit, not after she'd lied the previous day and told him she hadn't seen Darien for weeks.

Chase's eyes narrowed. "You didn't say anything about seeing McCabe when I spoke to you last night." His voice was rife with accusation.

The muscles in her legs twitched, and she struggled to hold them steady. "I...I guess I forgot." She cringed at her lie but faced him, trying not to turn away from his penetrating stare. The last thing she wanted was for him to start asking questions about Darien.

"I'll bet." He didn't bother to hide the fact he saw through her lie. "When are you going to start telling the truth?"

"I am telling you the truth."

A single dark brow arched.

"Okay, so I didn't tell you about Darien's visit yesterday, but everything else I've told you is true."

His brow arched higher.

"Why don't you believe me?"

"Maybe I will when you stop your bullshit."

She reeled back as if he'd struck her. Her mouth opened and closed, but no words emerged. What could she say in her defense? He was right. She wasn't telling him everything. But she couldn't tell him about the briefcase Darien had given her to hide. If she did, Darien would retaliate.

Chase lurched to his feet and towered over her, his hands jammed in the front pockets of his faded jeans. "Why are you protecting him? What hold does McCabe have over you?" He shook his head. "After what that slimy weasel did, I'd think you'd be thrilled to spill the beans."

They stared at each other like combatants in a war zone.

She wilted under the force of his glare. Her earlier bluster vaporized, but if she told him about Darien, Darien would punish her. And if it came to a choice of whom she was more frightened of—the handsome police detective glowering at her or her abusive ex-husband, Darien won hands down. A shudder trilled through her. She was far too familiar with Darien's retribution.

"Here's the mug book." Detective Podborski

plunked a thick binder on the desk in front of her. "Let's hope your shooter's in here."

Her hands shook as she lifted the heavy plastic cover and studied the first page. Row upon row of two-by-one inch mug shots of dangerous looking men covered the large page. All the men had the same dead-eyed, cold gazes and hardened, feral faces of those with nothing left to lose. A seven-digit number was printed below each photograph.

She flipped to the next page, and the next, studying each photograph before moving on. Hours passed. Her eyes grew heavy, and the faces before her blurred.

She closed the cover and sat back and rubbed her eyes. The headache that had threatened earlier was now a full-blown blast of pain. She picked up the foam cup of coffee and sipped, but grimaced at the cold bitter taste and tossed the cup in the garbage. She'd had enough coffee. Exhausted as she was, her body thrummed with a mixture of nervous energy, sugar, and caffeine. She bounced her knee up and down, her foot tapping a rapid beat on the floor.

Chase worked at a computer terminal on his desk, focused on the screen before him. He'd been at his desk the entire time she'd searched through the mug book.

His partner, Detective Podborski, had received a call hours past and headed off somewhere.

The other detectives had come and gone, but the room was still a hub of activity.

As if sensing her scrutiny, Chase glanced up.

Their eyes met, and once again a jolt of awareness arced through her.

"Nothing?" He nodded at the binder before her.

"He isn't in this book. He isn't in any of them."

"I'm not surprised. If the shooter's any good, he hasn't been caught yet."

She blew a strand of hair off her face. "What now?"

"Let me take you home. You've had a long day. I'll set you up with a sketch artist tomorrow and see if we can get a picture of this guy." He pushed his chair back from his desk and stood, placing his hands in the small of his back and stretching. His shirt tightened across his shoulders, revealing well-honed muscles.

She gulped and tore her gaze away.

"Ready?" His blue-black hair gleamed under the harsh fluorescent lights. Golden flecks danced in his eyes.

"Um…yes, of course." She fumbled to her feet and followed him out of the squad room, her legs rubbery.

He ushered her ahead of him along the narrow corridor, down the stairs, and out the back door of the police station to his car. Opening the front passenger door, he gestured for her to climb in.

She hesitated. "What's this? I don't have to sit in the back seat? I guess I'm no longer a prime suspect."

His eyes shadowed. "Just get in."

She sat in the front seat, riding shotgun. A smile tugged at the corners of her mouth. Things were looking up. Oh, yes, they were.

Rush hour was over and they rode in silence along the early evening, quiet streets. Streetlights flickered on, and the last rays of the setting sun lit the sky with a rosy glow.

"Why was your appointment with Waverley so important?"

"My appointment with Waverley?"

He shrugged. "Just wondering."

She thought for a minute and did a mental shrug. "I draw. It's what I do. I've always drawn pictures. I love creating something beautiful on a blank sheet of paper."

"The drawings in your living room"—he set the blinker and steered around a corner—"they're yours?"

"Yep."

"Wow. They're good, really good."

Pleasure flooded her, and for the first time that day she smiled. "Thanks. I'm designing a series of greeting cards, but my dream is to sketch illustrations for children's books." She blew out a breath. "Illustrating books is a hard market to crack."

"And that's why you wanted to meet with Jonas Waverley."

"He's the publisher for the *Turtle Town* series of preschool children's books. You must have heard of them. They're very popular."

He looked blank.

"I guess you don't have any kids."

"Not yet. No wife either."

A spurt of joy filled her. *He isn't married!* She squashed the thought in the next breath. What difference did it make if he was married? He was a police detective. His job was to ferret out criminals. In his eyes, she was a criminal.

"And?"

His question broke into her thoughts. "And what?"

A smile twitched at the corner of his lips. "You were telling me about your illustrations for the kids' books."

She inhaled a deep breath, steadying her ragged nerves. "The…the original illustrator is ill and unable to complete the series. I thought if I showed Mr. Waverley my work, he'd hire me for the book illustrations."

"I'm sure he would have. You're very talented."

Her gaze met his, and she sucked in a sharp breath. The air sizzled between them, and her heart lurched in her chest.

A tinny rendition of a popular country-and-western song pierced the charged atmosphere. The twangy notes clanged again, and Chase mumbled a curse and steered the car to the side of the road and parked. He fished a ringing cell phone out of his jacket pocket. "What?" he barked into the phone.

She remained frozen, struggling to regain her senses. What had just happened? Was he going to kiss her? Did she want him to? Impossible. But, with his tousled hair, and a single dark lock hanging over his broad forehead, how could she not?

His face was all hard planes and angles as he spoke tersely into the cell phone. The golden lights in his eyes had vanished, and once again he was the cynical homicide detective determined to solve a case.

"Something's come up." He slipped his phone back in his jacket, released the brakes, and squealed away from the curb. With his other hand, he flipped a switch and the blare of sirens screamed.

"What is it? What's going on?"

He focused on the road ahead as they sped down the street, sirens shrieking and blew through a red light.

She gripped the edge of her seat, holding tight as they careened around one corner and then another. They raced down her street, and the tires squealed as he skidded into her driveway and jolted to a stop.

"I gotta go." He flicked on the police radio, and the

radio crackled to life with the buzz of excited voices and garbled police speak.

"I guess I'll see you around." She undid her seatbelt and opened the door.

He nodded, but didn't look at her. The second she closed the door, the car reversed, and he blasted onto the street in a blare of sound and a flash of bright emergency lights.

A dull headache throbbed behind her eyes as his car sped down the street and disappeared around the corner.

"Everything all right, Natasha?"

She whirled.

Betty crossed the street, a yapping Taffy leading the way. "That was a police car, wasn't it?"

She grimaced. Betty was the proverbial neighborhood gossip. Every neighborhood sported one. Just her luck the woman lived right across the street. Nothing happened in the vicinity without Betty knowing.

"Why were the lights flashing and the sirens blaring? I near had a heart attack." Betty placed her hand over her heart, edged closer, and peered at Natasha's face. "Oh my, you've hurt yourself. What in Heaven's name happened? Are you okay?"

Natasha backed up a step, avoiding the woman's sharp gaze. "I'm fine. Thanks, Betty."

Betty's brow furrowed. "Wasn't that the same man who visited you last night? I'm sure it was. I'm pretty good with faces. And he's a police officer?" She ignored Taffy's relentless tugging. "Why were the police at your house two days in a row? What's going on, Natasha? In the past few day you've had a lot of strange men stop by."

Taffy chose that moment to squat and relieve his bowels on Natasha's lawn.

"Taffy! No!" Betty's shocked voice pierced the early evening.

Natasha used the opportunity to escape and sprinted to her front door. She fumbled the key out of her fanny pack and slid the key in the lock. In the next second, she leaped inside, and the door slammed shut, Taffy's incessant barking muffled.

She flicked on the hall light and stumbled to the living room, visions of a hot bath and cold glass of white wine filling her head. She switched on the lights in the living room and gasped. Her stomach clenched, and she jammed her fist in her mouth to stop the moan.

Her drawings had been ripped from their frames, some crumpled into balls, others shredded into tiny pieces littering the floor like confetti. The picture frames were broken. Shards of glass covered the floor.

Tears burned her eyes, blurring, but not erasing the vicious damage.

An eight-by-ten color photograph in an expensive gold-plated, metal frame sat on the coffee table, out of place amid the destruction.

She stumbled across the room, glass crunching under her shoes and stared at the portrait of her and Darien taken on their wedding day. Even through her tears, she understood the ominous meaning of the photograph. Betty's words echoed in her brain.

You've had a lot of strange men stop by.

A tear slipped from her eye and dripped on the face of the happy bride, smudging the picture. She collapsed on the floor, her body wracked by soul-shattering sobs.

Chapter 9

Chase slammed the car to a halt with a squeal of brakes and switched off the blaring siren. The flashing red and blue emergency lights of four police cruisers and an ambulance pierced the night sky, creating a carnival-like atmosphere. The crowd of curious onlookers and swarm of reporters added to the festive feel, made all the more macabre by the fact this bustle of activity occurred in a quiet residential district, in front of a white clapboard house typifying American suburbia.

Lights shone from every window of the small one-story rancher, and he imagined a happy family residing inside, safe and secure from fear and harm. Mom and dad watching television, and the kids doing homework or playing a computer game, a large, hairy dog sprawled before a crackling fire.

But this house represented no such ideal. Behind the innocuous white clapboard walls lay not the picture of a happy family, but a scene from Hell. He shook off his morose thoughts. During his years on the force, he'd been at innumerable crime scenes. Grisly murders committed in similar neighborhoods; murders so disturbing they made a sane person question the existence of a just God.

He scrubbed his hands over his face. What was with him tonight? He was a cop, for Christ's sake. He had a job to do, and he wasn't solving any crimes sitting here.

Climbing out of the car, he strode toward the crowd. He flashed his badge at the uniformed officer manning the police line, ducked under the crime scene tape, and crossed the manicured lawn toward the open front door.

Stepping into the warmth and light of the house, he paused and grabbed a pair of paper booties from a cardboard box and fitted them over his boots. He tugged a set of vinyl gloves from his pants pocket and fitted them over his hands. Years ago, Mike had taught him the importance of carrying his own gloves. You never knew when you'd need them.

Half a dozen people bustled in the overheated room in a well-orchestrated dance. Forensic specialists dusted surfaces for prints. Other technicians examined the shiny hardwood floor with infrared lights, another cop took photographs, and still others mumbled into cell phones, relaying information to distant labs and precincts. Adding to the pandemonium, a television in the corner blared an infomercial, the chirpy voice of the saleswoman at odds with the somber scene.

Amid this frenetic activity slumped the victim, Henrietta Kincaid, Jonas Waverley's missing personal assistant. They'd found her, but too late, much too late.

A lone figure hunched over the body in a pose of intense concentration. The salt-and-pepper-haired man took out a pen and pried open the fingers of the victim's left hand. A tiny jewel glistened against the chalky whiteness of the dead woman's palm.

"What've you got?" Chase edged closer.

"About time you showed up." Mike Podborski shot

him a sly look. "I thought you were driving Natasha Hartford home. What took so long? Did you stop in for a quickie? Let me guess, she threw herself at you, and you couldn't refuse?"

Chase's face heated at Mike's jibe, but long experience had taught him the best way to deal with his partner's banter was to ignore the endless ribald jokes. He crouched beside the body. "What's that in her hand?"

"Looks like a diamond earring."

A single, tiny diamond set on a white gold post gleamed in the center of the dead woman's palm. Before Chase could brush her fall of auburn hair off her face and study her earlobes, Mike stopped him.

"I checked. She doesn't have pierced ears. No way this earring was hers." Mike reached in his coat pocket and pulled out a manila envelope. "Take a gander at these. Bert sent them up just before I got this call."

Chase opened the flap on the envelope and tugged out an eight-by-ten color photograph. The picture was taken at a distance, probably with a long-range camera lens, but the photographer knew what he was doing. The images were crystal clear.

Darien McCabe stood beside a black SUV. Another, much larger man held the vehicle's door open for McCabe, and McCabe's left side faced the camera.

Chase held the photograph up to the light. His gut pinged. "Is that a diamond stud in McCabe's left ear?"

"Don't you just love the way that baby gleams in the sunshine?"

A sense of satisfaction swept over Chase. *Gotcha, you asshole.* "So you're thinking she ripped the earring out of her assailant's ear during the attack."

"Out of McCabe's ear." Mike pointed his pen at the diamond stud. "With any luck his DNA'll be on this."

Chase hoped he was right. If the lab detected McCabe's DNA on the earring, they stood a good chance of arresting him for the crime and getting a conviction. The pinging in his gut was now a full-blown clamor. But they couldn't afford to rush to conclusions. Other men wore diamond stud earrings. Hell, the murderer could have been a woman.

His gaze roamed over the body. "What happened? How did the murder go down?"

Mike pointed to an overturned lamp lying on the floor. "Looks like there was a struggle, and her assailant knocked her unconscious and strangled her. She has a bump on the back of her head and bruising on her throat. The autopsy will tell us for sure."

"So not likely a female perp, not with that level of violence." Chase swallowed back the bitter taste of bile. He imagined the attractive young woman relaxing and watching TV, the sudden awareness of an intruder, and the rising terror as she read the intent in her murderer's eyes. "How'd the killer get in?"

Mike shrugged. "No sign of forced entry."

"So she knew him."

"Most likely. Either that or she was one fool of a woman."

Chase nodded. No single woman living in the city would open her door at night to a stranger. The victim had to have known her assailant. She'd trusted him enough to let him in. At least she had until he struck the first blow.

He studied the slight body again, noting the

unnatural sprawl of arms and legs. A few hours earlier she'd been a vibrant human being until one violent act reduced all her energy, all her potential, to a mere husk. Tearing his gaze away, he perused the tidy living room. "This is her place?"

Mike shook his head. "Her sister's. As far as we can figure, she asked her sister if she could stay here for a few days. Said her apartment was being fumigated."

"Where's the sister?"

"Out of town. She and her husband and two kids are in Disneyland for a week."

Chase digested this news. "Lucky for them. Any chance this is related to Waverley's murder?"

"Could be. Her apartment wasn't being debugged. Looks like she was hiding out. Unfortunately, the killer found her before we did."

"I wonder what she knew?" Chase rubbed his chin.

"That, my boy, is what they pay us to find out." Mike groped in his pocket and yanked out the stub of a pencil and stuffed it in his mouth.

"Come on. Let's go. Time we had a little chat with Mr. McCabe." Chase rose and turned to leave, but paused when Mike didn't follow. "What's wrong? Aren't you coming?"

Mike grimaced as he rose to his feet, knee joints cracking. "Can't. Not tonight at any rate. Captain has me riding desk duty. He's pissed I haven't finished the reports from the Mason murder." His lip curled in derision. "Like paperwork's gonna reduce the crime rate in this town."

"How'd you manage to sneak out?"

Mike's lips peeled back in a grin. "I went to the can." His grin widened. "You know that pesky problem with my prostate? Makes me have to pee all the time?" He waved his hand at the crime scene and smirked. "I'm in the can."

"You better hope he doesn't find out you're here."

"I had to come. I mean, when the call came in, and I heard the victim's name, I knew the case was connected to the Waverley murder."

Chase nodded. He didn't blame Mike. He would have done the same. Bodies were piling up, and the finger of blame pointed at Darien McCabe. Long past time they hauled his sorry ass in for questioning. "I guess I'm on my own then. I'll call you and fill you in after McCabe and I chat." He turned to leave, but stopped when Mike called.

"If you're going to confront him on your own, you might want to consider four people are dead. All victims were connected in some way to McCabe. The man's dangerous."

A new realization hit Chase like a fist in the gut. Natasha Hartford! She was connected to the victims and to McCabe. Was her life in danger? The man who'd killed McCabe's two thugs had shot at her. How could he have been so stupid? He'd dropped her off at her house and raced away to the crime scene, not giving a thought to her safety.

Adrenaline coursed through him, and he bolted for the door, ignoring the startled glances of the people he shoved out of the way.

No one else would die. Not on his watch. He had to protect Natasha!

****

Natasha awoke to loud pounding on her front door. She thrust her hair off her face and struggled to sit.

Blinking in the dazzling lights, she focused through gritty, tear-swollen eyes. Why was she on the floor? And in the living room?

Her vision cleared, and her breath whooshed out in a blast as the senseless destruction of her drawings pummeled her like a massive blow. She fell back on the hard floor, fresh tears stinging her eyes.

Darien. He'd done this.

Her gaze settled on the wedding photo lying on the floor where she'd dropped it. He'd destroyed her artwork and left the photo as a reminder of what would happen if she didn't do as he ordered.

She jolted upright at the furious rapping on the front door. A chill coursed through her.

He was back.

No. Not Darien. Showing up in the predawn hours and pounding on her door wasn't his style. She cast a sour look at the surrounding devastation. If he wanted in, he'd proven he didn't have to knock.

Exhausted from hours of crying, she pushed to her feet and crossed to the window on wooden legs. Shoving the curtain aside, she peered out at the dark street. Light from the nearby street light lent an eerie green glow to the chilly night, but illuminated the tan, four-door sedan parked at the curb and the tall, broad-shouldered figure standing on her front porch.

Her stomach knotted. Why was Detective Brandon here? Not to question her again, not at this time of night.

He raised his fist and knocked again.

Her first instinct was to pretend she wasn't home, but the light shining on her front porch revealed the grim determination on his rugged face. She glanced over her shoulder and studied the mess, and her heart rate kicked up a notch. She couldn't let him see what Darien had done. What she'd made him do.

Stepping over the remains of her artwork and broken pieces of glass, she made her way to the door. Unlocking the dead bolt, she drew the door open, careful to block his view of the room behind her. "What is it now, Detective? Can't this wait until morning?" She prayed he didn't hear the quaver in her voice.

He shoved past her and stepped into the foyer, closing the door behind him. His face was haggard, and his hair was rumpled as if he'd thrust his fingers through the dark curls too many times.

"Wha...what is it?" Her voice warbled as her throat tightened. "What's happened?"

He rubbed his hands over his face, the scratch of his unshaven whiskers loud in the close confines of the front hall. "There's been another murder."

"What? Who?" She staggered back a step.

"Henrietta Kincaid, Jonas Waverley's personal assistant. The woman you said you spoke with when you arranged your appointment with Waverley."

Irritation flared at his choice of words. Did he still think she had something to do with Waverley's murder? She wanted to lash out, but the full horror of another senseless death struck her. "She's dead?"

He nodded, and a lock of dark hair fell across his broad forehead, softening his stern features. His shoulders sagged. "God, I'm beat."

She ached at the weariness etched on his rugged face. "I'm sorry."

His tired gaze met hers. "Why?"

"You've had a long day."

He shrugged. "Part of the job." He studied her. "You don't look so good yourself. What happened?"

She stumbled back a step.

His eyes narrowed, and a furrow formed between his dark brows.

She forced a shaky laugh and swiped at her wild tangle of curls. "It's late. I was sleeping. You woke me up."

"You've been crying. Something's happened. Tell me." He strode past her down the hall and into the living room.

With a heavy heart, she trailed after him, dreading his reaction to the disaster in her living room.

"Holy shit!" His curse reverberated off the walls in the small room. He stared at the shards of glass, broken picture frames, and scrunched balls of paper. "What the hell happened?"

"I found it like this."

"And you didn't think to call the police?"

She couldn't meet his probing gaze. "What good would calling the police do? The damage is done."

Bending down, he picked up a scrap of crumpled paper and smoothed it open. "This is one of your drawings, isn't it?" He grabbed another torn paper ball. "Who did this?"

She shook her head, looking anywhere but at him.

"Natasha, I asked you a question." He waved the pieces of her artwork in front of her. "That bastard did this, didn't he? Darien McCabe destroyed your drawings."

She shook her head. "No, I—"

"Why the hell are you protecting him? What hold does he have over you?" He waved his hand at the room. "Look at this. Do you think the bastard will stop here? Do you? Do you honestly believe he'll be satisfied with destroying your artwork? Christ. The next time you piss him off, he'll kill you."

Tears flooded her eyes and streamed down her face.

He clasped her in his arms, holding her close to his hard body. "I'm sorry. I didn't mean to frighten you, but you have to realize what sort of man your ex is. Hell, he may have killed four people in the past few days. And now this. A man like that won't stop. Not unless we make him."

She broke away from his embrace and wiped her tears with the back of her hand. "Don't you think I know what he's like?" She crossed her arms over her chest. "I lived with him for five long years. Every day was a nightmare, every night Hell. I never knew when he'd hit me...or worse." Her breath huffed in and out in a rapid cadence. "I never knew—" The words were lost in her sobs. She collapsed on the upholstered chair, her body shaking.

"I'll make coffee." His calm, quiet voice broke through her upheaval, but she couldn't stop the flood of tears.

Her sobs had eased by the time he returned carrying two steaming cups. She sat up and smoothed her hair off her face.

He handed her a cup. "I hope you don't mind, but I took the liberty of adding something a little stronger I found in your cupboard. I figured we both needed the kick."

Raising the cup to her lips, she inhaled the scent of sweet almonds and strong coffee. She sipped and soothing warmth slipped down her throat, threading through her veins. "Thank you."

He cleared a space and sat on the floor, and leaned back against the chair she sat in and sipped coffee. His shoulders brushed her legs. "I'm sorry I went after you. I shouldn't have."

"You were doing your job." Her legs ached with the need to vibrate, to release her pent-up energy, but she held still, not wanting to break the connection between his broad shoulder and her right leg.

"I'm sorry for what you suffered at the hands of that bastard."

A lump thickened in her throat and tears stung her eyes. She blinked them back, determined not to cry again. "How could you have any idea what my life was like? I didn't tell anyone. Not even my closest friends." She ducked her head. "How could I admit the man I'd married, the one who promised to love me forever, was a monster who beat me until I begged for mercy?" She wiped her damp face with her sleeve. "How could you possibly understand?"

"Because I do."

She spun toward him. "What?"

He stared into his coffee cup. A pulse beat a rapid tattoo in his tight jaw. "I know what you've been through."

"I...I don't understand."

A car drove by on the street outside. A dog barked in the distance. The clock on the wall ticked a steady beat. Tick tock. Tick tock.

"Chase?"

He wouldn't meet her gaze.

Her heart thudded in her chest as realization

dawned. "You've been abused, haven't you? That's what you mean. You, or someone close to you. I'm right, aren't I?"

He shook his head. "Forget it."

"No. Tell me. Please."

He stood and pointed at her cup. "Want some more?"

Okay, so he didn't want to talk about what happened. She wouldn't push him. But now she knew something about him, something important, something that had shaped him and made him the man he was today. The lump in her throat too thick to speak, she nodded.

"How about I hold the coffee this time?" His voice was rough and emanated from deep inside his chest. "I don't know about you, but I could sure do with something stronger."

The corners of her mouth curved. "My thought exactly."

Chapter 10

She jolted awake and shoved off the blankets.

He was here!

Detective Chase Brandon slept downstairs in her guest bedroom. How could she have let that happen? But last night she'd been vulnerable, still reeling from Darien's angry destruction, and she'd needed comforting and the assurance she was safe.

After Chase had returned to the living room with two cups half-filled with the almond-flavored liqueur, they'd sat together in companionable silence, listening to the faint sounds of her neighborhood as night settled in.

There weren't any words to say, but she'd spoken anyway. Not about anything important. Certainly not about Darien and his abuse. She'd probably said too much, and he hadn't said enough. She couldn't remember what the time was or how much they'd had to drink when she'd shown him the way to the spare bedroom and stumbled upstairs to her own bed.

How could she have been so foolhardy? Did she have a death wish? From the minute Chase barged through her front door, her fate was sealed. Darien's spies would report she'd spent the night with the police detective, and Darien would assume she'd revealed his secrets.

She tugged on a pair of jeans and yanked a sweater

over her head, threaded her fingers through her tousled hair, and with heavy steps, plodded downstairs. She passed the door to the living room, but stopped, backed up a step, and stared.

The room had undergone a transformation. She blinked and rubbed her eyes. The living room looked as it usually did…neat and tidy, with no shards of glass, broken picture frames, or pieces of artwork scattered across the floor.

Noises emanated from the kitchen along with the mouth-watering aroma of frying bacon. She shuffled along the hall to the kitchen, her steps halting. A thousand images of their intimate connection the night before flashed before her. What would she say? What could she say? How could she possibly explain? Too much alcohol? Exhaustion? Stress? Fear?

Chase stood at the counter stirring the contents of a bowl. His shirtsleeves were rolled above his elbows, revealing tanned, muscular forearms. He wore one of her aprons tied around his narrow waist. Moving with surprising grace for one so tall, he poured the egg mixture in the bowl into a sizzling frying pan.

She smiled at the incongruity of the formidable homicide detective performing such a domestic task, and happily, apparently, for he whistled a merry tune.

The second he became aware of her presence, his body stiffened, and the easy fluidity vanished, replaced by his more familiar stiffness and reserve.

"Thanks for tidying the living room. I don't know if I could have—"

He cut her off. "Coffee's made." Intent on the task of stirring the cooking eggs, he didn't look up.

Okay, so he didn't want to talk about what

happened the previous night, either. She could do that. Grabbing a mug from the cupboard, she poured hot coffee from the carafe into her cup. She gulped the strong brew, uncaring the hot liquid seared her mouth and burned her throat. If ever she wanted a jolt of caffeine, this was the time. "What are you doing?"

He eyed her with raised eyebrows.

Heat flamed in her cheeks. "I mean I see you're making breakfast, but why?" She swallowed more coffee.

His gaze roamed over her, making her all too aware she hadn't showered or brushed her teeth, and her hair was tangled, her face creased with sleep.

"Why darlin', what sort of men do you usually consort with?" He grinned, dimples dancing in his lean cheeks. "Where I come from, a gentleman makes breakfast for a lady after spendin' the night."

The heat in her face ramped up to a four-alarm blaze. "I...I wouldn't know. I'm not in the habit of having men stay overnight."

His grin widened. "Good to know."

She blinked under the force of his boyish charm. Tearing her gaze away, she swigged her coffee, draining the cup.

He grabbed two plates from the cupboard and dished up fluffy scrambled eggs, adding several strips of crisp bacon to each plate, and a slice of perfectly browned toast.

The food tasted as good as it looked, and she focused on shoveling one forkful after another into her mouth until she pushed her empty plate away and sat back with a groan. "If I eat any more, I'll burst."

"You could do with some fattening up."

"And here I thought a woman could never be too thin or too rich."

He chuckled, the husky tones rolling over her like a warm, cozy blanket. Sipping his coffee, a lazy grin on his all-too-handsome face, he looked comfortable in her sunlit kitchen. Too comfortable.

She was drawn in by his easy charm, forgetting the terrors of yesterday, almost forgetting he was a cop. Almost. Sitting up with a start, she set her cup on the table. "Why are you still here?"

His gaze bore into hers with an unnerving intensity, all pretense of relaxed camaraderie gone. "I'm worried about your safety. People connected to your ex-husband are dying."

"So that's why you're here? To protect a possible suspect? No other reason?" She watched him, hoping he'd say something to prove her wrong. Hoping last night had meant something to him as well.

An uncomfortable silence settled over the room. He coughed and cleared his throat. "What happened last night…" He coughed again. "I was tired. I had too much to drink. I said too much, made this too personal, forgot I'm here to do a job." He licked his lips. "You don't have to worry. It won't happen again."

His words shot at her like a fusillade of bullets, each one striking home. She barked a laugh. "You're a cop. I'm a suspect. You have a job to do. I get it. You've made that more than clear." He opened his mouth to speak, but she cut him off. "Last night you were working, fishing for information. Hoping to loosen me up so I'd talk about Darien." She sneered. "That's all it was." She waved her hand at the empty plates on the table. "That's all this is." She held her breath, praying he'd deny her accusations, hoping he felt the attraction she felt.

His mouth tightened to a thin line, and his eyes shuttered. He banged his fork on his empty plate and swiped his mouth with his napkin, balled up the napkin, and tossed it on the table. "Let's get to it, then. Waverley's assistant, Henrietta Kinkaid was struck on the head and strangled. What do you know about her murder?"

Her body deflated at his harsh, cop tone. "I don't know anything. Why would I? I only talked to her on the phone when I confirmed my appointment with Mr. Waverley."

His gaze drilled into hers.

"You can't possibly"—she inhaled a shaky breath—"you don't think I had something to do with her death?" And there it was. The truth hit like a slap to the head. She was a suspect. He was a cop. He had a case to solve and would do anything to find the person responsible. She'd been a fool to think there'd been anything else between them.

Once again the silence dragged on in the sunny kitchen and hung in the air between them like a weight.

"You're involved in this, whether you know it or not." He lifted his cup and took a long swig. Setting the cup down, he shoved back from the table, stood, and jammed his hands in the front pockets of his jeans. "Your ex-husband's a suspect in the murders of Jonas Waverley and Henrietta Kinkaid. He's also connected to the two men who were executed in the car wreck you found."

A freezing chill settled deep in her bones. "You think Darien murdered those people?"

"McCabe wouldn't get his hands dirty, but he could have hired someone to do the job."

"Darien's no angel, but I can't imagine him resorting to murder." No sooner had the words left her mouth than an image of Darien, enraged, his face flushed, eyes spitting venom rose before her. She rubbed her bruised hip. "If you think Darien had something to do with these murders, why are you here? Why aren't you questioning him?"

"My partner and a team of fellow officers are talking to McCabe as we speak."

"Why aren't you with them?"

He headed over to the coffee maker and refilled his cup. "I told you. You need protection."

Her hand holding her coffee cup jerked, and she yelped as hot liquid spilled over her hand. "I don't need protection from Darien. I have a restraining order against him."

"Worked great yesterday, didn't it?"

She flushed. "Okay, you're right. Darien broke into my house and destroyed my artwork." She grabbed a paper napkin from the holder on the table and dabbed her hand. Her skin was red from the hot coffee. "But that isn't the same as murder. He wouldn't kill me." She choked on the lie, and slurped coffee to wash away the bitterness.

"Come on, Natasha. You don't believe that, and neither do I." His eyes narrowed. "We both know what McCabe's capable of." His jaw tightened. "McCabe knew Waverley. Waverley's dead. Henrietta Kinkaid saw something or overheard something she shouldn't have, and now she'd dead.

"McCabe hired those two muscle-bound meatheads

to protect him. They're dead now too. Are you seeing a pattern here?" He rubbed the back of his neck. "People connected to your ex-husband are winding up dead." He leaned against the counter, arms crossed over his chest.

She fought for breath. "You think Darien's going to try and kill me next?"

"McCabe's not my only worry. Something's going on. I'm not sure what, but whatever it is it's big. Gang trouble, maybe."

"What are you talking about? Darien doesn't belong to a gang."

His brow furrowed. "Believe that if you want, but our intel informs us McCabe runs with the big boys. Has for years." He rocked on his heels. "He may have pissed off some bad guys, and they're cleaning house. The body count's four so far." His hard gaze zeroed in on her. "I'm not willing to risk adding you to the list."

Her head ached, and she rubbed her temples to ease the tightness. She'd known Darien played fast and loose with the law, but she hadn't suspected he was involved with the sort of men who thought nothing of murdering people who got in their way. "Why do you think I'm at risk? Darien and I've been divorced for two years. I'm not involved in his life. Not anymore"

"In his warped way, the creep considers you his property. Look what he did to your drawings. That destruction was personal and originated from a shitload of anger."

"You're right. He's angry with me, but I know how he thinks." She clasped her hands together. "What he did to my pictures…that's his way of punishing me for talking to the police. He's passed on his message, and now he'll cool down and leave me alone." It was a struggle, but she kept her face expressionless in spite of her blatant lie.

Darien would be back. Soon. He'd come to collect his briefcase. But she couldn't tell Chase. Darien would kill her if she told Chase she had the briefcase hidden in her house. Hopefully the detective had forgotten about seeing it in her living room.

Chase gulped coffee. "McCabe's running scared. No telling what he'll do next." His upper lip curled in a sneer. "A cornered rat attacks. I don't want you hurt when that happens."

Her stomach heaved at the frightening scenario he painted. "What…what do you plan to do?"

"Protect you. Keep you safe." He set his cup on the counter. "For the next while, I'm going to be your roommate."

She gaped, for once unable to think of anything to say.

A grim smile flickered at the corners of his mouth. "Don't worry. You'll grow to like me after a few days of cozy togetherness."

****

He couldn't suppress the grin breaking across his face. Her stunned disbelief was something to see.

"You…you're staying here?"

He nodded, fighting back a threatening chuckle. You'd think he'd suggested she spend the next few days in bed with a tarantula. "Hey, you never know. Our arrangement might be fun. Worse case, you'll hate me until you're a feisty old lady living in a nursing home, but at least you'll live."

She leaped from her chair and slammed her hands

on her hips. "You aren't staying here." Her eyes blazed, but not with anger. "No way."

He studied her.

In spite of her bravado, dark, shifting shadows dulled her blue eyes. She was afraid. Of what? Her ex-husband?

Him?

But she hadn't been afraid of him last night. Not one bit. Even though they hadn't so much as touched, they'd shared an easy intimacy that had left him wanting more. So much more.

His gaze dropped to her mouth, and he bit back a groan. He'd dreamed about that mouth. Warning bells screeched in his head, but he ignored them and pushed off the counter and advanced across the room.

He slid his hands around her back and drew her close, breathing in the scent of her hair, her skin. He stroked her cheek...soft, so soft. Placing a finger beneath her chin, he raised it, forcing her to look at him. "You don't have to be afraid. I'll keep you safe. I promise."

She stared into his eyes, her pupils dilated.

Ducking his head, he touched his mouth to hers. As his lips stroked hers, his first thought was he'd been wrong. She didn't taste as sweet as he'd thought; her lips were sweeter, like nectar.

Her lips trembled under his.

He slid his fingers into the silky warmth of her hair.

At first, she held her body ramrod stiff, but as his mouth caressed hers, she softened and melted into him.

He deepened the kiss, reveling in her taste, her feminine scent, drawing her closer. Her soft curves burned his body where she brushed against him. His tongue sought hers.

She stilled and slipped out of his embrace. "This isn't a good idea." A mixture of desire and confusion flared across her expressive face.

He fought to control his rapid breathing. Damn. She was right. No matter how he played this, kissing her was wrong. He was supposed to protect her, not screw her. He'd better get a grip on his libido. Either that or assign one of the other cops in the department to protect her.

He clenched his fists to stop from touching her. "You're right. I shouldn't have kissed you, but I'm not sorry, and I can't promise it won't happen again. I wish I could, but I can't." He clamped down on his bottom lip, halting his bonehead confession. *What the hell?* She was in danger. His job was to protect her. Time to stop thinking with his dick and start using his damn brain.

Her lower lip was swollen and rosy from his stolen kisses. Her hands trembled, and her movements were stiff and jerky as she bustled about the small kitchen, rinsing the dirty dishes under the tap and placing them in the dishwasher. She wiped the counters, avoiding looking at him.

Guilt flooded him. As if she hadn't been through enough with her dirtbag of an ex-husband, he had to come on to her like an out-of-control, horny teenager. He opened his mouth to apologize, but stopped. Words wouldn't make the situation better. Not when every cell in his body demanded more.

She hung the dishtowel on the oven door. "I'm going to have a shower. I expect you to be gone when I'm done."

"Look—" He shook his head in frustration when she ignored him and kept walking. He had to make her realize the seriousness of the situation. According to what Mike had told him when he'd called, all hell was breaking loose at the station.

He jammed his hands into the back pockets of his jeans and raised his voice. "I talked to my partner this morning. Ballistics completed their examination of the bullets used in Waverley's murder and the execution of McCabe's men. The same gun was used to kill all three victims."

Her shoulders stiffened. "What?"

"The same person killed them." He paused and gave her a minute to let his words sink in. "The investigators found the same caliber of bullet embedded in a tree near the crash site. The evidence at the crime scene indicates the man who shot at you caused the crash by shooting at the car and blowing out the front tire. He finished the men off in the ravine." He blew out a breath, hating he was responsible for the fear shadowing her face, knowing he didn't have a choice. She had to know the danger. "We think the shooter was sending a message to McCabe."

"A message? What sort of message?"

He shrugged. "I don't know yet, but we'll figure it out, and when we do, we'll take down this guy. Until then, you need protection."

"But you just said the man wasn't trying to kill me."

He pinched the bridge of his nose. "Don't you get it? This guy's a wacko. There's no predicting what he'll do next." He pinned her with a hard look. "Are you willing to risk your life on the chance he'll miss the next time he takes a shot at you?" He ignored her gasp. This was too important. She had to understand her life was at risk. "Because I sure as hell won't let you be the next victim."

Her shoulders slumped, and she gripped the back of a kitchen chair.

His gut tightened, and he ached to take her in his arms again and comfort her, but he hardened his heart to her distress. Sympathy wouldn't save her life. Hard police investigative work would. "Did Waverley and McCabe know each other?"

Her eyes widened, and she chewed on her bottom lip. "I...I don't know." Her knuckles were white where she clutched the wood on the back of the chair.

His gut pinged. She was lying. "Look, Natasha, don't you think it's time you told the truth?"

Her face flushed red, and her gaze skittered around the room, settling anywhere but on him.

He let the silence build until the weight of his accusation filled the tiny kitchen.

She clasped and unclasped her hands on the chair back and then cracked like he knew she would. "Darien told me Jonas Waverley was a business acquaintance. He claimed that was how I secured my appointment— Darien arranged the meeting."

Bingo. Now we're getting somewhere. Instead of a glow of satisfaction at forcing the truth out of her, he felt like a jerk. He massaged the knot in the back of his neck. He was a cop, and a cop's job wasn't to be popular, but to ferret out the truth and capture the bad guys, no matter what it took.

Waverley and McCabe were connected. Waverley was a respected business leader in the city. His company was a Fortune 500. What would he have to do with a scumbag like McCabe? He sucked in a quick breath and steeled himself for his next round of questions. "Why didn't you tell me this before?"

She rubbed her arms as if she were chilled. "Darien warned me not to talk to the police. He said if I told the police anything about him, he'd…he'd hurt me."

"Why was McCabe so worried about you talking to the cops? What's he hiding?"

She wet her lips. "I don't know."

His irritation spiked with the certainty she was lying. He studied her face, searching beneath the surface beauty for the truth; the full truth, not the sanitized version she wanted him to believe. He wasn't some rookie detective she could bamboozle with her luminous blue eyes and sweep of dark lashes.

She lurched away from the chair and headed out of the kitchen. "It's time you left. You can see yourself out."

He called after her. "You can't get rid of me that easily, Natasha."

She halted in the doorway. "I don't need a stranger looking out for me, Detective. I've survived these past two years on my own. I'll be fine." She fled down the hall, her rapid footsteps growing fainter. A door slammed upstairs, and the house was silent.

A stranger? He was a stranger? After last night? After the kiss this morning? He scrubbed his hands over his face, the scratchy rasp of two days' growth of beard loud. Maybe Mike was right. Maybe he had a problem with women. He sure as hell had a problem with this one. If he had any sense he'd ask—no, he'd beg—to be reassigned.

His cell phone rang, and for once, he was grateful for the interruption. He dug out the small phone from his back pocket. "Brandon."

"Can you talk?" Mike's rough voice was filled with urgency.

"What is it? What did you get from McCabe?"

"Fuck all. He lawyered up the second he saw us. Wouldn't say a damn word without his attorneys present."

"Shit." Chase rubbed his chin. "So you didn't learn anything."

"Oh, we learned lots. McCabe has alibis for the time of death of both Jonas Waverley and Henrietta Kinkaid." Mike's voice was riddled with frustration. "Both airtight. Apparently, he has any number of upstanding Port Hardesty citizens who'll back him up."

"Do you believe him?"

Mike snorted. "Are you kidding? I'd sooner believe the Easter Bunny hopped by the precinct this morning."

The line hummed. Voices echoed in the background, and Chase pictured Mike sitting at his desk in the bullpen, chewing on his pencil stub. "So, what's next?"

"The autopsy results confirm our suspicions. Henrietta Kinkaid was struck on the head with a blunt object and strangled. The lab guys lifted DNA from a fireplace poker and a silk cord used to hold back the curtains in the living room." He huffed out a breath. "The DNA matches the victim's."

"What about the earring?"

"No DNA other than the vic's…nothing."

"Okay, let's think this through." Chase rubbed his

temples in an effort to sort through the case's tangled knot. "We know the same shooter killed Waverley and McCabe's two men, and shot at Natasha."

"Where are you going with this, Chase?"

"Bear with me a minute. We think this guy's a professional, right?"

"Sure looks that way." The crunching of pencil was loud over the line.

"So why didn't he shoot Henrietta Kinkaid? Why hit her in the head and strangle her?"

"Maybe he was worried about the neighbors hearing a gunshot."

"It's more than that. Kinkaid's murder's different from the others. Her death reeks of something personal. This guy wanted to hurt her, wanted her to know he was the one killing her."

"Come on, man." Mike's voice was garbled by crunching wood. "Are you thinking we're dealing with two perps?"

"I don't know." Chase rubbed his eyes. "I don't know what I'm thinking. This case is a real bitch."

"You can say that again." Mike chewed some more.

"What did McCabe have to say about the murder of his bodyguards?"

"Nada."

"That's bullshit. Those men worked for him. He must know something."

"If he does, he ain't sayin'."

Chase reached a decision. "I'm going to talk to him."

"No way, man. He isn't going to talk to you. I told you, he's hiding behind a team of lawyers. They're like a pack of friggin' pit bulls. They won't let you anywhere near the bastard."

"I have a plan."

A long silence resonated on the other end of the line. "What the hell you talking about? What plan?"

"Natasha Hartford and I are going to pay McCabe a little visit."

"What the fuck?" Mike's voice thundered down the line. "You're supposed to be protecting her, not taking her into the lion's den."

"Don't worry. She'll be safe." He rubbed the back of his neck. "If I don't break him, whoever's pissed off at him will continue this vendetta, and more people will die. I don't want Natasha to be another victim. She's been through enough."

Mike's voice deepened with concern. "Shit, man. I recognize that tone. Don't get involved with her. She's trouble with a capital T. I mean it. You don't need the grief."

Chase couldn't agree more, but he feared his partner's words of warning were already too late.

Chapter 11

As soon as she stepped out of the shower, even before she opened the bathroom door, she knew he was still there. His presence filled the house with a vibrant intensity. Her anger flared. Who did he think he was? She didn't need him protecting her like she was a child. She could look after herself.

Ever since she was a young child she'd been on her own. When her mother took off for parts unknown with the latest boyfriend, her father had retreated into an alcoholic stupor. His inebriated ramblings and sudden outbursts of anger had prevented Natasha from inviting friends over to the house.

She'd married Darien right after college, jumping from one nightmare to another. Her new husband had isolated her and discouraged any friendships she might have made, and so she'd been alone then, too.

She'd never told anyone of the abuse. How could she when she was so ashamed? Instead, she'd hidden her bruises and put on a false front of marital bliss. But she'd survived her horrific marriage and escaped his clutches. At least she had until Darien showed up on her doorstep demanding she hide his briefcase.

She drew a comb through her wet hair, wrapped a towel around her damp body, hurried down the hall to her room, and threw on an old pair of jeans and a T-shirt. Dressed, she marched along the hall to her studio.

Perching on the high stool before her drawing table, she opened her sketchbook to a fresh page, selected a pencil from the canister on the desk, and drew. The face took shape with a few sure strokes, and within minutes, she'd filled in the details.

She sat back and studied the drawing, gnawing on her thumbnail as she stared into the cold, hard eyes of the man whose image she'd drawn. Yes, this was the shooter. She'd never forget his face. His cruel blue eyes haunted her nightmares. She tore off the paper, and with the drawing clutched in her hand, hurried out of the room and trotted downstairs.

Chase sat at the kitchen table, coffee cup in hand, reading a newspaper. Her newspaper, and he'd pulled out the sports section and folded back the front page, mixing up the pages. "You're still here." She didn't bother to hide the bite in her voice.

He glanced up from the newspaper. His gaze travelled over her, and he smiled. "Good. You're ready." Pushing back from the table, he rose and carried his cup to the sink and rinsed it under the tap.

His tidiness notched her annoyance to a new level. Gritting her teeth so hard her back molars throbbed, she slapped the drawing on the counter before him.

He glanced at the picture she'd drawn. "What's this?"

"The man who shot at me."

He picked up the paper and studied the drawing. "You drew this?"

She nodded.

"It's good."

In spite of her anger, heat rose in her cheeks at his praise. "I thought we'd save time if we didn't have to wait for the police artist." She jerked her thumb over her shoulder. "Now you can leave. The door's that way."

"Good idea." He folded her sketch and slipped the paper in his shirt pocket. He grabbed her coat from the back of a chair. "Come on."

She planted her feet. "I'm not going anywhere with you."

Ignoring her, he draped her coat over her shoulders, and grasped her elbow in a gentle but firm grip, and steered her toward the back door.

Stunned at his audacity, she allowed him to lead her through the door and onto the back porch, before she dug in her heels. "What do you think you're doing? Let go of me."

His fingers tightened for the briefest millisecond, but then he released her. "Look, the sooner you realize the serious shit you're in, the better."

She opened her mouth to protest, but he tapped two fingers to her mouth, silencing her. The touch of his fingers against her lips set off a clamor of jangling nerves.

"Let's call a truce." He removed his fingers.

"A truce?" She eyed him warily.

"I'm a cop. My job is to protect civilians and solve crimes. You need protection, and I need your help to solve these murders." He smiled, but the light didn't reach his eyes. "Come on. We'll make a great team."

"I've already helped. I drew the sketch of the man who shot at me. What more can I possibly do?"

"I need you to get me into McCabe's office."

"Me? You're using me to get to him?" She shook her head. "No way."

"I won't let anything happen. I promise. You'll be safe."

Their gazes met and held. Once again a frisson of awareness trickled along her spine.

A dog barked on the street in front of the house. The high-pitched yapping broke through the rising tension.

"I won't do it." Just the thought of facing Darien made her skin crawl and her stomach lurch. He'd go ballistic if she showed up at his office with a police detective in tow. She couldn't run fast enough or hide deep enough to escape his retribution. "If you want Darien to talk, get a subpoena or something. Don't involve me. Besides, I thought your partner already questioned him."

His mouth twisted as if he'd bitten into a sour lemon. "McCabe lawyered up. He refused to say a word."

She wasn't surprised. Darien employed a veritable army of lawyers. She was amazed she'd managed to secure her divorce in spite of all his legal wrangling. Her luck had changed when Judge Marilyn Dobson presided over her divorce hearing. The Honorable Judge Dobson didn't take kindly to the attempted bullying by Darien's legal team. She'd granted Natasha her divorce, and for the first time in years, Natasha was free of the monster in her life.

"People are dying." Chase's earnest plea broke through her thoughts. "We have to stop the carnage before anyone else is killed."

"You told me you don't think Darien killed those people."

"He knows who did. I'd stake my Capitals' season

tickets on that."

"He won't tell you anything. He hates the police."

"Most criminals do." He studied her with a probing look. "Will you help me, Natasha? Will you help me stop the killing?"

A chill trickled through her, and the tiny hairs on the back of her neck prickled. Help him? Could she? Dare she? She rubbed the goose bumps on her arms. "I"—she swallowed over the thick lump blocking her throat—"I don't know. If Darien sees me with you, he'll be angry." Angry? She shuddered. An understatement. Darien would go beserk.

"I'll keep you safe. I promise."

"Yeah, you'll keep me safe for now, but what about tomorrow, or the next day, or the week after that?" She threaded her fingers through her hair. "Darien holds grudges. He won't forget I helped you."

"By the time we've finished this investigation, McCabe will be locked tight in a jail cell. If not, you'll enter the witness protection program until this is over. Either way you'll be safe." He scrubbed his bristled cheeks. "You can trust me, Natasha."

She stared into his eyes—green with golden glints—unable to look away. She, better than anyone, knew what Darien was capable of. He'd want revenge. Want her to pay for her betrayal. If he could find her, that is. If she helped Chase catch whoever murdered those people, she'd have to disappear somewhere safe where Darien couldn't find her. Her life in Port Hardesty would be over.

But did she have a choice? Her gut roiled, and she pressed the palm of her hand on her stomach. Her mouth was dry. "Okay. I'll help you."

A grin broke across his face. "Well then, partner, let's get a move on. We have a murderer to catch."

****

Chase tried to keep his attention on the road as he steered the car along the busy streets heading downtown, but he couldn't stop glancing at her.

She stared straight ahead, her face pale, her slim body rigid, her hands clenched in her lap, the knuckles white.

He gripped the steering wheel until his fingers ached. Was he doing the right thing? He was asking her to face the monster who'd beaten the crap out of her for years. The sort of man who thought nothing of punching a woman so hard he put her in the hospital.

A man like his father.

The damning words rattled through him in blazing clarity. He clamped his jaw, and his head throbbed in time to his rapid pulse.

"Pull over." Her voice, a ragged whisper, broke through his turmoil. "I've changed my mind. I don't want to do this."

He jammed on the brakes, ignoring the angry blare of horns ripping the air, and the car skidded to a stop in the middle of the road. "You can't back out now."

"This"—her throat worked as she swallowed— "this is a bad idea. Darien's already furious with me. I don't want to make him angrier. Besides, I don't see how I can help."

A crescendo of horns blasted the air.

"I can't do this without you, Natasha. I need you to get me in to see McCabe without his pack of lawyers present."

She picked at a cuticle. "How can I do that?"

"The people in McCabe's office know you. You're their boss's wife. They won't question you've come to see him."

"Ex-wife."

He nodded. "Ex-wife. McCabe will be curious. He'll want to know why you've shown up in his office with a police detective. He'll meet with us. He won't be able to resist."

"I don't know. I'm…I'm afraid."

Her voice was so quiet he had to lean closer to hear her over the rage of wild honking.

A middle-aged man with an impressive beer gut hanging over his belt pounded on the driver's window. "Hey, mister. You're blocking traffic. Get a freakin' move on."

Chase yanked out the wallet with his credentials, rolled down the window, and flashed his badge at the red-faced, bearded man. "Back off, asshole. Police business."

The man's eyes widened, and he stumbled away from the car. Muttering under his breath about police brutality and shaking his head, he stomped back to his car.

Chase struggled to rein in his frustration. He understood her reluctance to confront her ex-husband. He wasn't playing fair to ask her to do this, but he needed her. Having her with him was his one chance to secure a face to face with McCabe. "Please don't back out. People are dying. We have to stop this murderer before more people lose their lives."

The blare of horns grew louder, and he glanced in the rearview mirror. A long line of blocked traffic stretched behind his stopped car. He stuck his hand out the window and thrust up his middle finger, rammed the car in gear, and sped off.

Three blocks later, still struggling to control his disappointment, he swung around a corner and into an empty parking lot, shut off the engine, and faced her in the sudden silence.

She cowered against the passenger door, her face white and drawn.

Guilt smacked him like a punch to the gut, and he tightened his grip on the steering wheel. She was frightened. In his fervor to solve the murders, he'd come on too strong. The bitter taste of self-loathing filled his mouth. Maybe he wasn't so different from his father after all. "I'm sorry. I have no right to ask you to do this. I understand if you want to back out. No one will blame you."

She edged away from the door, the wariness in her eyes easing.

"Do you trust me to protect you?" He held his breath. Never had an answer been so important.

"I…I don't know." Her lower lip trembled. "I want to, but I don't know."

A jab of pain struck him in the gut. He deserved her wariness, but her lack of faith hurt all the same. "I guess I'll have to live with that."

Her teeth, small and white worried her full, pink bottom lip.

He gulped, remembering how soft that lip was and how sweet she tasted.

"I have a question."

He tore his gaze from her mouth. "What is it?"

"You said I was in danger. Not just from Darien, but from whoever murdered those people. Is that true?"

"I think so."

"And you think it'll help if I go with you to confront Darien?"

"I won't let you out of my sight." His voice roughened. "Not for one second."

"And that's supposed to comfort me?" She arched one perfectly shaped brow, and the corners of her mouth twitched.

A chuckle burst through his lips. "Probably not."

Her mouth curved in a tentative smile. "Okay. I'll do this. But I'm counting on you to keep me safe."

His chest swelled as if he'd won an Olympic medal. He grinned like a ninny, but he couldn't help himself. "That's my girl." His girl? Alarm bells clamored through him. *Whoa, buddy. Slow down. She's a suspect in a homicide investigation. You're a cop. Be a cop. Do your job. Don't get involved.*

Too late. His heart plummeted to his feet as the truth hit. *Too damn late.*

Chapter 12

McCabe's office was located in the heart of the downtown core. Traffic was heavy at this time of day, and Chase circled the block three times before finding a parking space. He squeezed his standard, police-issue sedan into the tiny space between a gleaming black SUV and a flashy red sports car.

He switched off the engine and met Natasha's gaze. "Are you sure about this?"

Her face was pale, and her hands trembled, but she smiled.

A surge of admiration filled him. She'd spent years trying to escape her ex-husband, and now she'd agreed to face the bastard head on. He could only imagine the bravery that took. He climbed out of the car, ducked around the hood, opened her door, and helped her out. "Ready?"

Her eyes were impossibly large, her pupils dilated, but she jutted her chin and squared her shoulders. "Let's do this."

He clasped her hand, frowning at the cold clamminess of her soft skin. "It's not too late to change your mind. You're sure you want to do this?"

She nodded.

"Okay, then." Lacing her fingers through his, he led her across the street toward the towering edifice bearing Darien McCabe's name in large brass letters across the gleaming glass front. The glass-and-steel high-rise dominated the city skyline, a testament to the success of the sleazy crook's questionable business ventures.

Pausing before the double, smoked-glass doors, he brushed back a stray blonde curl from her cheek. Zero hour. Once they passed through these doors, there was no turning back. "Remember, you're not alone. I won't let him touch you."

She nodded.

"Showtime." He yanked open the heavy glass door and ushered her inside.

The lobby was even more impressive than the outside of the building. The room was huge, the floor a vast expanse of gleaming white marble, banked by a wall of floor-to-ceiling, smoked-glass windows. Heavy-leafed tropical plants bearing vibrant orange, yellow, and red flowers grew in thick clusters in tiled containers. Stately palm trees rose from strategically placed garden beds. The air was heavy with the exotic scents of tropical flowers and moist earth.

A spray of water splashed and trickled from an art deco fountain and flowed across the atrium in a man-made, meandering stream. He'd bet a month's salary koi swam in the artificial stream.

A flash of color caught his eye, and he craned his head back and stared up at the ceiling. Tropical birds swooped and dove around the open rafters, twittering and cheeping.

A tall, lean man in a dark gray suit materialized before them out of the jungle-like growth, a smarmy smile wreathing his gaunt face. "How nice to see you again, Mrs. McCabe. It's been a while." He swung to

Chase and inclined his head. "Detective Brandon. Mr. McCabe is expecting you."

Chase's mouth tightened. He glanced at a tall palm tree and caught the red flash of a security camera mounted on its thick trunk. So much for the element of surprise.

"This way, please."

They followed the lanky man across the lobby to a bank of elevators, their footsteps echoing on the marble floor. The elevator doors whooshed open, and their guide ushered them inside. Without pressing a button or giving any indication of a command, the doors swished closed, and the elevator began its smooth, silent ascent.

Seconds later, the doors slid open onto an ocean of dark-blue carpeting and cream-colored walls. A reception area with a couch and two matching chairs was right ahead.

A twenty-something, nubile blonde sat behind a granite-topped desk filing her long red nails. She glanced up from her work, flashed a wide smile, and returned her attention to her nails.

Their escort led them down a wide corridor flanked by museum-quality paintings and framed multicolored tapestries. He halted in front of a smoked-glass door.

Chase slid a glance at Natasha.

A small smile played about her full lips, and she looked relaxed and confident. No one would suspect her trepidation about the upcoming confrontation.

He grasped her cold hand and gave a brief, reassuring squeeze.

The tall man opened the door and ushered them into a large office. "Mr. McCabe will join you shortly." He bowed his way out, closing the door behind him.

Chase strode over to the wall of windows. An awe-inspiring view of the ocean glistening under the noonday sun stretched as far as the eye could see. Ships of varying sizes sailed across the blue expanse, and seagulls wheeled and danced in the air.

He tore his gaze from the mesmerizing view and scanned the room. An oversized glass-and-chrome desk with an executive, black leather office chair dominated the room. Three smaller, hard-backed chairs faced the desk in a semicircle.

Across the room, two black leather couches and a glass-topped coffee table were arranged beside a well-stocked bar. Four bronze statues of human-like figures stood on pedestals around the room. The walls were covered with framed, multicolored textiles. Ceramic pots filled with what looked like dried flowers were set on tables.

He stood in front of a large, stone slab mounted on a metal stand. Rudimentary figures and symbols were inscribed into the worn surface of the ancient stone. He blew out a breath. "So this is how the rich live."

"Don't let the opulence fool you. Beneath all this beauty, Darien's a monster." Her voice was bitter.

He crossed to her and brushed a stray blonde curl behind her ear, his fingers lingering on her satin skin. "Are you sure you can handle this?"

Before she could answer, the door opened, and a short, wiry blond man strutted into the room. He halted when his gaze settled over them, and the self-satisfied smirk on his face transformed to a mask of fury.

As quickly as his anger appeared, it vanished, replaced by cold disdain. "Well, well, well, Natasha. This is a nice surprise." His gimlet gaze settled on

Chase. "And you've come with a protector." His mouth twisted in a parody of a smile. "How nice."

Chase stiffened, struggling to keep his dislike of the other man hidden.

McCabe swaggered over to the desk and sat in the large, black leather chair. Crossing his legs, he leaned back with a studied, casual ease. "And to what do I owe this pleasure? Is this a social call, or do I need to summon my attorneys?"

Chase stuffed his clenched fists in his front pockets. "Don't bother calling in the cavalry. We won't be here long."

McCabe raised his pale eyebrows. He shot a sly glace at Natasha. "Did you like the photograph I left for you, my dear? I thought it prudent to remind you of our happy nuptials."

She gasped and stumbled back a step.

McCabe sniggered.

Chase couldn't help the growl that escaped his clenched mouth. He wanted to kill the arrogant son of a bitch. The stricken expression on Natasha's face hit him like a blow. He had to force himself to remember why they were here. Flying off half-cocked wouldn't get him the information he wanted. He'd get his shot at the slimy little creep. You could take that to the bank.

"Oh my. Where are my manners?" McCabe waved a hand at the chairs facing his desk. "Please, sit. Can I get either of you a drink?" His reptilian gaze swivelled from Natasha to Chase.

Chase strode to McCabe's desk and planted his palms on the thick glass, putting the full brunt of his hatred and disgust into his hard glare. "Who murdered Jonas Waverley and his assistant, Henrietta Kinkaid?"

McCabe's face paled, and he shrank back. "I've already told your coworkers I don't know."

"You're lying." Chase balled his hands, fighting not to smash his fists into McCabe's ferret-like face. "I promise you, I'm going to find out the truth. And then I'm going to put you in a cage where you belong." He reeled back, his chest heaving. So much for keeping his temper.

****

Heavy silence filled the flower-scented air like a thick, cloying blanket.

Natasha clasped her hands behind her back to hide their trembling. She wanted to flee from her volatile ex-husband, but she'd promised Chase she'd see this through. She stole a glance at him.

A vein pulsed in his forehead, his nostrils flared, and his muscular body vibrated with anger as the two men faced off.

She broke the uneasy silence before someone got hurt. "Tell us what you know about the murders, Darien. Please. This is important. More people could get killed."

He brushed lint off the front of his tailored suit jacket. "Lovely to see you, my dear, but I question the company you keep. You know my thoughts on our fair city's men and women in blue." Sarcasm, underlined by hatred, threaded his voice.

She shivered, but held his gaze. "Detective Brandon asked me to come with him today. He has some questions to ask you, and he thought you might be more willing to talk if I were here."

Darien's lip curled in a sneer. "Do you always hide behind a woman, Detective?"

The vein in Chase's forehead pulsed.

Natasha placed a restraining hand on his arm. "Don't do this, Darien. If you know anything at all that can help the police find the killer, I beg you to tell us."

Darien picked up the phone on his desk. "I'll ask my lawyers to join us."

Natasha fought to control her frustration. Once his lawyers arrived, he wouldn't tell them anything. "The man who the police suspect killed your bodyguards and Waverley also tried to kill me. Did you know that?"

He nodded. "So I heard."

"People around you are dying. If you know who's responsible, tell us."

An unnamed emotion flashed across his face and darkened his eyes.

"Come on, Darien. You could be the next victim. Detective Brandon can help you. Just tell him what you know."

His chin set in a stubborn line, and he pressed a button on his phone. "I'm afraid I have no idea what you're talking about, my dear." He rose to his feet. "This visit is over. My assistant will see you out."

Chase lunged at Darien and ripped the phone out of his hand and tossed it across the room onto the leather couch. "Not so fast, McCabe. We're not finished."

Darien's eyes flashed fire. "You'll regret your vulgar behavior, Detective. I know people, important people. I'll have you fired."

"Look, McCabe, this isn't getting us anywhere. You may have the connections to have me fired, but if it isn't me asking the hard questions, it'll be someone just like me. We can have a chat off the record, or I can make this official and haul your ass down to the precinct. The press will love that. You'll be sure to make the evening news." Chase smiled at Darien like a shark that had sighted prey. "Your choice."

Natasha held her breath.

Darien's malevolent gaze drilled into Chase. "Careful, Detective. Accidents happen all the time."

"Threatening a police officer can get you in trouble, big trouble." Chase spoke in low tones, but there was no mistaking the venom in his voice.

The temperature in the room dropped twenty degrees as the two men stared at each other.

The door opened, and the man who'd guided them to Darien's office slipped into the room. Beside him were two muscle-bound hulks, clones of the men who'd been killed in the car crash. "You rang, Mr. McCabe?"

Darien sank back in his chair and crossed one leg over the other. "Escort my wife and her new friend out of the building, Johnson." His gaze swiveled to Chase. "We're done here, Detective."

The two goons advanced on Chase, determined expressions on their brutish faces.

He didn't budge. "I'm not going anywhere, McCabe. Not until we're finished."

The death stares continued, neither man willing to back down.

Her heart raced. The situation was about to explode. She had to do something. She rushed to Darien's desk and grabbed his hand. "Darien, please, let Detective Brandon ask his questions, and then we'll leave."

Darien tore his gaze from Chase and stared at their clasped hands and then up at her. A smile played about his thin lips. Keeping eye contact, he raised her hand to his mouth and pressed a wet kiss to the back of her hand.

She repressed a shudder.

"Anything for you, my dear." He released her hand and turned to his assistant. "I won't be needing you, Johnson."

The assistant nodded and wheeled around and left the office.

The two goons trailed at his heels. The door closed quietly behind them.

She breathed a sigh of relief and resisted the urge to wipe her hand on her coat.

"I'm a busy man, Detective. Shall we get on with this? I have nothing to hide. Go ahead and ask your questions."

"How well did you know Jonas Waverley?"

"Jonas and I were business acquaintances."

"Did you murder him?"

Darien's laughter echoed off the cream-colored walls. "You have quite a sense of humor, Detective."

Somehow Chase kept his composure. "I don't find murder funny."

"Neither do I, I assure you."

"Where were you the night Jonas Waverley was murdered?" Chase's eyes narrowed.

"At home."

"Can anyone vouch for you?"

"Only a dozen of this city's most-prominent citizens." Darien's smile widened. "I hosted a dinner party. I believe Mayor Jenkins was one of my guests."

"What about Henrietta Kinkaid?"

"Didn't she work with Jonas? His assistant, or something? I heard she met an unfortunate end as well."

146

He tutted. "The crime in this city is out of control. Really, Detective, you should be out clearing the streets of dangerous rabble rather than questioning an upstanding citizen like me."

"I suppose you had nothing to do with her death."

Darien's hand flew to his chest. "Really, Detective. I'm offended. How could you think such a thing? I barely knew the woman. Why would I wish to harm her?"

"What about Billy Ray Sandaval or Matty Robinson?"

"They were in my employ." His mouth pursed in a moue. "Your fellow officers informed me they died...something about a car accident, I believe."

"Don't you find it odd people around you are dying?" Disgust filled Chase's voice.

"People die all the time." Darien rubbed his hands together. "Now I believe I've been more than generous with my time, Detective. This interview is over."

Chase huffed out a frustrated breath. "I'll be back, McCabe."

Darien's oily smile was patently false. "I'm always willing to help our boys in blue, Detective."

Chase clasped her hand and turned to leave. "We'll see ourselves out."

They were leaving? She opened her mouth to protest, but held her tongue when Chase squeezed her hand. She flicked a glance at his face, but his expression was impassive and impossible to read.

"Oh, and Detective?"

Chase paused and turned back to Darien.

A smirk twisted Darien's mouth. "Maybe next time you come to visit, you won't bring my wife. A real man doesn't hide behind a woman when he conducts business."

Twin patches of red flared in Chase's cheeks, and a tiny muscle in his jaw twitched. "How long have you sported a pierced ear?"

She shivered at the malevolent glare Darien directed at Chase. If looks could kill, Chase would be dead.

With an obvious effort, Darien regained his control. "Goodbye, Detective."

Chase's hard-eyed gaze raked the smaller man, but he nodded, and with a hand at the small of her back, urged her out the door and along the corridor.

Their guide materialized and escorted them to the elevator, across the vast lobby, and marshaled them through the glass doors onto the sidewalk.

They didn't speak as they crossed the street, and they remained silent while Chase started the car and swerved away from the curb.

She sagged in her seat. The events of the past half hour—had it only been a half hour—left her drained. "Why did you let him off so easy?"

A furrow deepened between Chase's dark brows as he steered the car through the heavy city traffic. "I got what I wanted."

"What did you get? Because from where I stood, you didn't learn anything new."

"We found a diamond stud earring clutched in Henrietta Kinkaid's hand."

"And you believe the earring is Darien's?"

"His left ear is pierced, but he isn't wearing an earring, though the skin on his ear lobe didn't look injured." He shot her a penetrating look. "What do you know about that?"

She frowned. Chase's question about the diamond earring had definitely unsettled Darien. "Darien pierced his ear shortly after our marriage. His stylist at the time convinced him sporting a single diamond stud would add to his mystique. As far as I know, he stopped wearing the stud a few years ago." Her hands twisted, her nails digging into her palm. "I'm sure he didn't have an earring when I saw him the other day. I would have noticed."

He grunted, but focused on the road in front of him.

"Do you think the earring you found in Waverley's assistant's hand belonged to Darien?" Her breath hitched in her throat. "Did...did he kill her?"

"Someone sure wants it to look that way."

"I don't understand."

"Someone's gone to a lot of trouble to make us think McCabe's guilty of these murders. They planted his earring, or one just like his at the murder scene."

Her heart skipped a beat. "Someone's framing Darien?"

"Looks that way." The detective tapped his long fingers on the steering wheel. "We're being played by an expert."

She mulled over what he'd said. Was it true? Was Darien being framed? Was that why he was so on edge? He'd hidden his true feelings beneath a layer of his usual arrogance, but he was rattled. No question.

Chase steered the car into her driveway and turned off the ignition. He blew out a long breath and covered her clasped hands with his large, warm palm.

The motor ticked as it cooled.

The rough rasp of his callused palm, his spicy, masculine scent, and the warm sun shining through the windshield created a cozy cocoon. Inexplicably, tears stung her eyes. She looked away, not wanting him to see how his presence affected her, how long it had been since she'd been this close to a man and not been terrified.

"If you ever want to talk about what McCabe did to you, I'm here."

"I've never told anyone." Her voice cracked. "It's an ugly story, not something I'm proud of."

His callused fingers linked with hers. "You can trust me, Natasha. I'm not him. I'm not Darien McCabe. I won't hurt you."

She wet her lips and stared into his green eyes. And then like a dam breaching, the shameful words tumbled out, one after the other in an unbroken rush of release. "He beat me every day. I never knew when it was coming, but he always found a reason to hurt me. No matter how hard I tried to please him, I couldn't do anything right."

Tears flooded her eyes and slid down her cheeks. "Once he hit me so hard he broke my nose. I can't count the number of times he split my lip and loosened my teeth or kicked me in the gut until I puked blood." She hiccupped a sob. "The hitting wasn't the worst. He called me names...terrible names, and...and he threatened me..." Her voice choked off, the rest of the damning words lost in a wrenching sob.

"He's a monster." Silver flecks ignited in his eyes, reflecting his pain and anger.

She freed her hand and slumped in her seat. "I don't want your pity." Her fingers fumbled with the seat-belt clasp. It released with a metallic click, and she reached for the door handle.

He caught her hand in his again, ignoring her efforts to tug free, and raised her hand to his mouth, and pressed a breath of a kiss to the sensitive skin on her palm. His gaze held hers. "The last thing I feel for you is pity, Natasha. You're the bravest person I know." His voice was a rough husk. "It took a lot of courage to leave that bastard. The woman I saw today, the woman who confronted McCabe, is a woman who isn't afraid of anything or anyone." He brushed his thumb across her lower lip.

She blinked back a fresh wave of tears as his words of support flowed over her like a healing balm. He got it. He understood the nightmare she'd experienced at the hands of Darien. A spurt of hope buried deep inside under layers of hurt and pain, unfurled and flowered to life. "What happened to you? Tell me, please."

And just like that, the silver lights in his hazel eyes faded, and his eyes shuttered. He dropped her hand like it burned, yanked the keys out of the ignition, and wrenched open his door. "Come on. Let's get inside. It's not safe out here." He climbed from the car, walked around to the rear of the vehicle, opened the trunk, and hauled out a small overnight bag. Bag in hand, he marched toward the house.

She sucked in a ragged breath and rubbed her hand where the imprint of his lips on the soft skin of her palm burned. This was the second time he'd hinted he was familiar with what it was like to live in an abusive relationship, and the second time he'd brushed off her probing questions.

She didn't blame him. Confessing to being a victim

of abuse was difficult. Especially for a man. Chase wore the scars like a suit of armor, protection against anyone getting too close to the awful truth. She studied him through the side window.

He stood on her front porch in full-on cop mode, his body braced, his eyes narrowed, his gaze swiveling in all directions. A gust of wind ruffled his dark hair and blew the front flap his jacket back, revealing his gun in the black leather holster.

Grim reality broke through her thoughts. She shuddered. For a moment she'd forgotten there was a murderer out there, watching, waiting.

Chills assailed her, and she rubbed her arms, opened the door, and climbed out of the car and hurried to the house, feeling as if a dozen pairs of eyes were watching her every move.

Chapter 13

Natasha dug in the back of her closet and dragged out an overnight bag. Hurrying, anxious to be gone now she'd made her decision, she tossed an assortment of underwear, socks, jeans, and tops into the bag. She zipped it up, and without bothering to do more than run a comb through her tangle of hair, headed out of the bedroom and tiptoed down the hall.

Creeping down the stairs, she avoided the loose board on the bottom step and stole across the hall to the spare room. She peeked into the dim interior and breathed a sigh of relief.

Chase sprawled on his back on the bed, one long, bronzed arm flung across the mattress. A muted glow from the street light outside shone through an opening in the curtains, illuminating his tousled dark hair and rugged face.

In spite of her hurry, she remained frozen in place, mesmerized by the sight of the sleeping man. A lock of glossy hair had fallen across his forehead, and she had the sudden desire to brush back the wayward curl. Long dark eyelashes swept against the stubble of his lean cheeks, adding a hint of softness to the otherwise stern features.

A gentle snore escaped his mouth, and he rolled onto his side, dragging the blanket with him, exposing his bare back and one leanly muscled hip.

Her breathing quickened at the play of muscles beneath his smooth, tanned skin. She edged closer, drawn to him as if controlled by invisible fingers.

The muted bleating of a distant car alarm on the street outside cut through her trance, and she jerked, guilt heating her cheeks. With one last, lingering glance and a sigh of regret, she crept on silent feet out of the room and down the short hallway to the front door.

Grabbing her coat from the closet, she twisted the dead bolt and unlocked the front door, cringing at the loud metallic click. With a last glance over her shoulder at the dark, silent hall, she slipped through the door and hurried down the steps to her car.

Chase would be furious when he woke and found her gone. He'd laid out the rules last night after they returned from Darien's office. She was to stay in the house. She wasn't to go anywhere without him. He'd issued a host of other decrees, but she'd stopped listening after the first two, knowing even then she wouldn't be around for them to matter.

She scoured the street, searching for prying eyes or unfamiliar parked cars. The street appeared deserted, and she released a breath she hadn't been aware she was holding. Unlocking the car door, she climbed into the car and tossed the canvas overnight bag on the passenger seat. She inched the door closed, wincing at the metallic clunk.

The engine turned over with a roar in the still, predawn air. She gripped the steering wheel and with one last, nervous glance at the dark, silent house, she shifted the car into gear and backed out of the driveway.

Traffic was light, and with little to focus on, her

mind was free to wander. Going to Darien's office with Chase had been a mistake. The second Darien saw them together, his eyes had flashed with fury, and his hands tightened into claws.

He'd denied he murdered Jonas Waverley or knew anything about the murder of Waverley's assistant. Even though he was an accomplished liar, she believed him. He hadn't killed those people. But someone had, and Darien knew who that someone was. That she also knew.

Fear had radiated off him like a bad smell. He hid his panic beneath his usual arrogance, but she knew him too well. He was most definitely frightened. Of whom or what she didn't know. But if Darien McCabe was afraid, she was terrified. The best she could do was get as far away from him and whatever disaster was about to happen as possible.

But where could she hide? Where would she be safe? A dozen scenarios—a sudden trip to Hawaii, staying at a friend's place out of state, running away to Mexico—had played through her mind all night. None of which were feasible. She didn't want to leave an electronic trail either Darien or the police could follow, so she couldn't use her credit cards. Five hundred dollars was all the cash she had in the house. She was lucky to have that much.

When she was married to Darien, she'd slipped into the habit of squirreling away small bills, a dollar or two at a time. He kept a close eye on the money he gave her, but didn't miss the small amounts. The cash she secreted in a shoebox at the back of the closet had been her safe money; money she'd need if she had to flee.

Even though she'd been divorced for two years,

she kept up the habit. The cash in the bottom of her dresser drawer under her socks and underwear provided a sense of security.

But five hundred dollars wasn't enough, not if the money had to last any length of time. One option stood out. The cottage would be a safe place to hide until this mess was settled. As far as she knew, Darien never visited the small, cedar-sided cabin on the forested bank overlooking a fast-flowing river. He'd bought the cottage soon after they married, when for a brief spell, he'd been interested in fly-fishing. He'd wanted to impress his business associates with his ruggedness and love of the outdoors.

He'd taken a client to the cottage once, but the weather had taken a turn for the worse, and it had rained all weekend. The mosquitoes and blackflies had attacked them without mercy, and Darien returned home bug-bitten and suffering from a cold. He'd never gone back.

The cottage was a couple of hours away from Port Hardesty on an old, rarely used logging road. She knew where the key was hidden. Best of all, staying at the cabin wouldn't cost anything. But first she had to pick up supplies. A small general store at the turnoff to the cabin stocked a decent assortment of basic groceries and camping equipment.

Swinging onto a narrow secondary road, she passed thick stands of towering Douglas fir and spruce trees lining the shoulders. Majestic, snow-covered mountains were visible in the distance. She opened her window and let the fresh air, scented with the rich loamy pungency of spring, fill the car's interior. The morning sun crested the ridge and lit the distant hills with a golden sheen. Flocks of black-capped chickadees flitted among the branches in the trees, serenading the dawn and letting the world know spring was here.

A dense stand of trees opened to reveal a small meadow off to the side of the road. Frozen in place in the middle of the clearing stood a statuesque buck, budding antlers jutting from the animal's regal head, watching her with black, expressive eyes.

Entranced, she slowed the car and steered to the side of the road.

The deer quirked its head, its ears twitched, and with a single bound, the animal disappeared into the trees.

She peered into the forest, hoping for one last glimpse of the magnificent creature, but the dark woods provided an impenetrable barrier. A breeze blew in her window and she shivered at the sudden chill. The tiny hairs at the back of her neck prickled at the sense of foreboding, as if unseen eyes spied on her. The trees stood as silent sentinels guarding the interior of the forest. Even the birds were quiet. Nothing stirred in the small clearing.

Rolling up her window, she shifted the car into gear and swerved back on the road. For the thousandth time since she'd driven away from her house, she glanced in her rearview mirror. The road was deserted. No one had followed her; yet, she couldn't shake the unease chilling her blood.

She floored the accelerator, and the car bumped along the rough road. Rounding a sharp curve, she yelped and jammed her foot on the brake.

A vehicle, parked sideways, blocked the road.

Her small car skidded, the rear end fishtailing as

the tires fought for traction on the loose gravel. The sliding momentum slowed, and the car ground to a halt, mere feet separating the two vehicles.

With a shaking hand, she switched off the ignition and sucked in giant gulps of air. She peered through the windshield at the large black SUV. The driver couldn't have stopped in a more dangerous spot. Anyone traveling along the road would have little chance before plowing into the stalled vehicle. It was only due to pure luck and good tires she'd managed to stop.

Why hadn't the driver steered the vehicle to the side of the road? Had the SUV run out of gas? And where was the driver? The vehicle's windows were tinted glass, impossible to see through. Was he still inside?

The chill congealed into a lump of ice in her gut, and her hands tightened on the steering wheel. Was this a trap? Had someone followed her from her house and chosen this remote spot to attack? Was the man with the blond hair hiding in the bushes along the side of the road, even now raising his gun, preparing to shoot? She'd been a fool to ignore Chase's warnings.

Hands trembling, she restarted her car and slammed the gearshift into reverse. Flooring the gas pedal, she raced backward, kicking up a spray of dust and gravel, the engine screaming.

A dark-gray pickup roared up behind her. The gleaming front grille resembled a monster's sharp teeth waiting to devour her tiny car.

She bit back a scream and slammed on the brakes.

The truck driver executed a one hundred-eighty degree turn. The truck's massive tires raised a cloud of dust as it swerved, blocking her escape.

Prying her fingers from their death grip on the steering wheel, she swiped her hair off her face. The engine ticked as it cooled, and the smell of dust and car exhaust hung in the air.

A mammoth of a man dressed in black climbed out of the truck. Mirrored sunglasses covered his eyes, and his shaved head shone in the pale morning light.

She slapped the button to lock the doors and cringed in her seat as he strode over to her car.

He tugged out a gun from the back of his black pants, flashed the deadly weapon before her, and motioned for her to open the door.

Panic clawed at her gut. She fumbled for her purse on the seat beside her. If she could reach her cell phone, she could call for help. Her heart raced, her breath huffing in and out in rapid pants.

He scowled, his face darkening as he stepped closer.

Purse in hand, she fought with the zipper. Shooting a glance at the man looming on the other side of the glass, she screamed again.

The granite-faced man raised the gun and smashed the window. A loud crash resounded, followed by a shower of shattering glass.

She shrieked and covered her head against the flying pieces of window glass.

He leaned in through the broken driver's window, yanked up the door lock, and wrenched open the door. "We've been waiting for you, Mrs. McCabe."

"What do you want?" She scrabbled with the seatbelt latch. The second she was free she scrambled across the seat to the passenger side of the car, yanked the door handle, and opened the door. Heart hammering, she sprang out of the car.

And stopped.

A clone of the man with the gun blocked her escape. Grinning like a shark, he lunged and grabbed her arm in a steely grip. "The boss wants to see you."

"Let go of me, you jerk!" She twisted and yanked, kicking, fighting to break free, but his grip tightened.

His sausage-like fingers dug into her flesh as he dragged her behind him like a plastic doll.

"What do you want? Where are you taking me?" Her chest heaved, and her fists throbbed from punching his rock-hard body.

He wasn't even breathing hard. A terrifying grin was fixed on his brutish face. "Your husband wants to see you, Mrs. McCabe."

Digging her heels deep into the loose gravel, she skidded to a stop. "Darien? You work for Darien?" Ice settled over her, and she shuddered. She should have known.

Her captor's expression remained unchanged, but his hold on her arm tightened, and he dragged her over to the black SUV. He opened the back door, and shoved her into the dim interior.

She landed with a whump, knocking the air out of her lungs.

He slid in beside her and slammed the door.

The sudden acceleration of the powerful vehicle threw her back against the seat. "Let me out!" She plowed her fist into the big man's side, but it was like slamming her fist into a brick wall.

"Stop."

His single command chilled her to the bone. She sank back on the seat, rubbing her sore knuckles and the red skin on her arm where he'd grabbed her. What was going on? If Darien wanted to talk to her, he'd come to her house and force his way in. He didn't have to resort to having his men kidnap her and manhandle her into a vehicle. The icy lump in her throat thickened.

The car swung off the road onto a rutted track leading deep into the forest. Twilight descended over the car as the towering trees blocked the morning light. The vehicle slowed to a halt in a small clearing surrounded by a thick stand of fir trees. A gleaming, black luxury sedan was parked in the clearing.

The driver of her vehicle shut off the engine.

She licked her dry lips. Each second amped up her fear.

The driver's door of the vehicle on the other side of the clearing opened, and a heavyset, brown-haired man wearing a natty, black three-piece suit, struggled out of the car. He smoothed his suit jacket over his protruding paunch and waddled around the car to the back door. With a flourish, he opened the door and stood aside, body stiff, standing at attention.

Darien stepped out, buttoned his suit coat, and faced the SUV, his legs spread, his hands clasped behind his back. Mirrored sunglasses masked his expression, but his mouth was a tight line, and a furrow ridged between his blond brows. Immaculately dressed in an expensive suit and red silk tie, he looked as if he were about to attend a board meeting downtown, not confront his kidnapped ex-wife in the middle of the wilderness.

The man sitting beside her yanked open the door and climbed out. He gestured to her to follow.

She shook her head and gripped the armrest with

her aching hands. "I have no interest in talking to your boss. I'm not going anywhere."

The muscle-bound goon blew out a breath, leaned across the seat, grabbed both her arms, and dragged her out of the SUV and over to Darien.

When he released her, she stumbled a few steps before she found her footing. She met Darien's smirk. "How dare you?" Fury raged through her—outrage at what he'd done, and anger at herself for the fear bubbling beneath the surface. "How dare you drag me out of my car and haul me here"—she waved at the surrounding stand of trees—"to the middle of bloody nowhere. I'll have you charged with kidnapping, and the police will put you in jail where you belong."

He chuckled. "Really, my dear, you're so melodramatic. I wished to see you without your detective friend. This was the most expedient method."

"How did you find me? No one knew I'd be on this road this morning. I didn't even know until a few hours ago."

"I told you I'm watching you." He shrugged. "My men informed me the minute you stepped outside your house."

Damn. She'd checked the street but hadn't noticed any strange vehicles.

"When I heard you snuck out at the crack of dawn, leaving Detective Brandon behind, I knew you were running away." His smile died, and his mouth tightened into a thin line. "You always were a coward, Natasha."

A cold tremor rippled along her spine. "I…I wasn't running away."

"Really?" He tsked. "That's another thing you're poor at…lying." He made a show of inspecting his nails. "My men followed you as instructed. The second you turned onto Gibson Road, I knew where you were going. After that, it was a simple matter of setting the trap and waiting for you to arrive."

He glanced at the sky and released a long breath as if she'd tried his patience to the breaking point. When he looked down, his eyes were flinty. "Did you really think you could hide from me? At the cottage of all places?" He shook his head. "Well, you're here now."

Her control snapped, and she charged at him and slapped him across his smirking face. The smack of her hand against his cheek cracked in the silent forest.

His sunglasses flew off. A red welt in the shape of her hand bloomed on his pale cheek.

The fat man and the gorilla in black raced over. Each man grabbed an arm and jerked her away from Darien.

She shrieked and fought to break free.

The cold, flat light in Darien's pale eyes was reptilian. He raised his arm, his hand clenched in a fist, his knuckles white.

She tensed and squeezed her eyes shut waiting for the worst. She'd never dared hit him before.

Time hung suspended.

She pried open her eyes.

He'd lowered his arm, but his eyes spat venom. The toes of his polished leather shoes mashed against her sandals. He leaned into her face, the stench of his coffee-laced breath gagging her.

She struggled to back away, but the men held her steady.

"Don't ever do that again." Spittle sprayed from his mouth and splattered her face. "Ever. Is that clear?"

She swallowed hard.

He gripped her cheeks in a vise-like grip, his fingers squeezing, hurting. "Is that clear, Natasha?"

The men holding her jerked upright on her arms.

She yelped and rose on tiptoes to ease the agonizing pressure. "Yes, yes, okay, I won't hit you again." Her voice was a thin, terrified squeak.

He nodded at the men, and they released her.

She fell to her knees, hating herself for being so weak, for cowering before him like a frightened child. "What do you want, Darien?" Tears filled her eyes and slipped down her cheeks.

He nodded at his men. "Give us some space."

The two men strode around the car to the other side of the clearing. They were out of earshot, but they were alert, and they kept their hard gazes pinned on her.

"You're disgusting. Stop sniveling in the dirt and get up."

She winced at his harsh words, but struggled to her feet. Unable to witness the gloating triumph on his face, she kept her face averted and swiped at her tears. He was right—she was disgusting. Why couldn't she stand up to him? She deserved whatever punishment he doled out.

No! The single protest was almost lost in the riot of self-castigation. She was stronger. She'd stood up to him. She'd slapped him. And then fell to the ground and groveled at his feet. But this wasn't over. He didn't have the right to hold her against her will.

She slid a glance at his men.

The two who'd held her were out of earshot. They'd been joined by three other men dressed in black and wearing mirrored sunglasses. All the men stood with their backs to her and Darien, facing the forest. Each man held a large pistol in his hand.

Sucking in a deep breath, she straightened her shoulders. Okay. Time to show Darien she wasn't a mouse. He and his gang of muscle-bound goons could force her to stay here, but she didn't have to make her imprisonment easy.

The sharp tang of cigarette smoke stung her nostrils, and she swung back to Darien.

A thin trail of smoke curled from a cigarette in his hand.

"You're smoking?"

"A bad habit I've recently taken up, I'm afraid." He slipped the cigarette between his lips and sucked in a deep breath. His lips pursed as he blew out a long plume of smoke. "Where's my briefcase?"

"Safe at the house. I hid the case like you asked."

He inhaled another drag and glanced at the ring of men guarding them. "I want you to forget this foolish idea of running away and return home."

"You want me to go back? Why do you care?"

He puffed on his cigarette. "You and Detective Brandon are becoming quite chummy."

She opened her mouth to protest, but he cut her off.

"Save it, Natasha. I don't care who you sleep with." His gaze fixed on her with a sudden intensity. "Why did Brandon ask if I had a pierced ear?"

"What?"

His mouth tightened. "Answer the question.

"The police found a diamond earring at Waverley's assistant's house. They…they think the earring is yours."

He tossed the cigarette on the ground and crushed

the smoldering stub beneath his shoe, grinding the ash into the forest litter.

She sucked in a sharp breath. "It's your earring, isn't it? You used to wear a diamond stud in your left ear. You killed that woman."

"Don't be ridiculous." He kicked a pebble. The small stone skittered into the trees. "Go back home. Keep me informed. If Brandon learns anything new about the murders, I want to know."

"I won't spy for you." She sucked in a shaky breath.

His eyes transformed into icy splinters. "Of course you will."

Anger mixed with fear rose anew. "We're done here. Get your thugs to take me back to my car." She spun on her heel and strode toward the waiting SUV. Her back tingled under the weight of his furious glare. Her knees quaked, but she kept walking, terrified if she stopped, she'd give into the bone-chilling fear and once again collapse on the ground.

"Natasha."

She didn't want to witness his rage, but years of obeying took over, and knees knocking, she turned.

His face was pasty and drawn, his expression as hard and unyielding as ever, but something flickered in the depths of his pale blue eyes.

"What do you want?"

"I need your help."

She stared nonplussed. "You want me to help you?" She fought against the conflicting emotions rioting through her. She'd adored this man once, but he wasn't the same person she'd married. The handsome, dashing man she'd wed had morphed into a monster who beat her, a beast who enjoyed inflicting pain and watching her suffer. "I can't help you, Darien."

"Not even if you could save my life?" The shadows filled his eyes again.

She staggered as the truth rammed home. He was afraid. The man who'd terrorized her for years, the one who controlled legions of thugs by the threat of his violence, was frightened. The thought terrified her more than anything he could have said or done.

"The man after me is dangerous, Natasha. He won't stop at hurting just me. He'll go after everyone close to me."

She shuddered at the fervor in his eyes. "What are you talking about? Who's after you?"

"Careful, Natasha, you almost sound like you care." His eyes narrowed. "Stay close to your detective. He's a hotheaded jerk, but he'll protect you."

She blinked, struggling to make sense of his confusing words, but then she shook her head. Whatever he was afraid of was his problem. With a last glance, she climbed into the SUV.

The driver got in, started the powerful vehicle, and the car rolled out of the clearing.

She glanced back.

Darien stood alone, his eyes bleak, his face expressionless. A gust of wind flapped against his suit jacket, molding his pants to his thin legs.

Chapter 14

Her car had been moved and was now parked on the shoulder of the road, the smashed driver's side window gaping, the keys dangling in the ignition. The truck that had blocked her escape was gone.

Exhaling a shaky breath, she stared after the vanishing SUV. She couldn't believe they'd let her go. After she'd slapped Darien, she was certain she was doomed. He hadn't liked her hitting him in front of his men, but for some reason, he hadn't retaliated.

Yet.

Her hands shook as she opened her car door and brushed tiny cubes of glass from the driver's seat onto the floor mat. The sooner she left this isolated spot, the better. At any moment, Darien could change his mind and come looking for revenge for her act of defiance.

The roar of an engine filled the air, and she jumped. Too late.

But instead of the large, black SUV, a beige, police-issue, four-door sedan rounded the corner and skidded to a stop, sending up a cloud of dust. Chase glared from behind the wheel, a fierce frown on his handsome face.

She raised a hand in greeting, but her heart thudded in her chest.

He leaped from the vehicle. "What the hell do you think you're doing? I told you not to go anywhere without me." He scanned the empty road. "And why are you stopped here in the middle of godforsaken nowhere?"

He marched over and his eyes widened. "What the hell happened to your window?" His gaze switched from her car to her face. "Holy Christ. Are you okay? Are you hurt?"

She covered her mouth to stifle a sob.

He advanced another step and gentled his voice. "What happened?"

Her desperate desire for comfort overrode her innate fear of his anger, and she fell into his arms, burrowing into his solid warmth. "Hold me, please."

He wrapped his arms around her, encircling her protectively.

She snuggled against the hardness of his chest, finding solace in the strong, steady beat of his heart. A freezing wind kicked up swirls of dust and tangled in the loose strands of her hair. But she wasn't cold, not nestled in his arms with his masculine scent surrounding her.

Her fear eased, replaced by a more powerful, but equally disturbing emotion. The embrace transformed from a reassuring hug to something more, much more. Her belly quivered as a wave of liquid warmth rushed through her. She snuggled deeper into his arms and smoothed her hands along the planes of his back, reveling in the rippling muscles beneath his firm, warm skin.

He made a noise deep in his throat and his mouth sought hers, ravaging the flesh of her lips.

A dart of excitement found its target and she caught her breath, thrilling at the taste and texture of his questing tongue.

His hands followed the curve of her waist and cradled her hips, fitting her against him. "Natasha." His husky voice rumbled like a purr through his chest.

"Kiss me again." Her voice was a hoarse demand.

His lips crushed hers, his tongue probing and seeking, unleashing a fresh onslaught of overpowering sensations.

She couldn't breathe, couldn't think; could only ride the wave of heat washing over her, devouring her.

****

Biting back a groan, he ripped his mouth from hers. He swore under his breath and released her.

Her eyes were dazed with passion, her mouth red and swollen from his kisses, her cheeks flushed.

His heart rate kicked up a notch. He was a fool to stop. But he couldn't ignore twelve years of training. He was a cop…first and foremost. He rubbed his whiskers, hard, anything to distract him from her passion-glazed eyes. Kissing her was wrong in every sense of the word.

As if to further test his resolve, her small pink tongue slipped out, and she licked her swollen bottom lip.

He sucked in a breath. The passion fogging his brain made it hard to think; it was almost impossible to do what was right. "No." The single word exploded out of him. He said the word again, louder this time, hoping he'd believe the desperate command. "Look, Natasha"—he pointed at his chest and then hers—"this…us…it isn't right." He ground down on his back teeth. "I'm a cop."

She nodded, but the wounded hurt in her eyes

struck him like a blow.

"Your life is at stake, and I've sworn to protect you. I've done a crappy job of it so far, but that has to change." He scrubbed his chin.

She ducked her head, avoiding his gaze, but not before he noticed the fresh sheen of tears in her eyes.

Shit. Now he'd made her cry. What an asshole. Seconds ago he'd been all over her, only thinking of how he wanted to rip off her clothes and make love to her right here on the goddamn road.

He blew out a breath and dug deep to retrieve the anger that had driven him here—the shock at discovering she wasn't in the house when he woke up this morning, and his outrage when her car wasn't parked in the driveway. Fury swept in, thrusting aside his lust.

If it weren't for his old buddy, Sergeant John Fredericks, he'd still be searching for her. John was out on a routine call, following up on witnesses to a poaching incident. He'd found the small red car, with the driver's side window smashed, parked on the side of the road, and called it in, requesting an ANPR on the license plate.

The Automatic Number Plate Recognition kicked out Natasha's name and her connection to the Waverley murder investigation. Chase was contacted as the lead detective on the case.

He'd jumped in his vehicle and switched on the sirens and flashing lights, and broken ground speed records to get here. Visions of Natasha lying dead, her body riddled with bullets, played through his mind in an endless nightmare.

His relief at finding her unharmed only increased

his anger. "Do you mind telling me why you snuck out of the house this morning? Where were you going? Why are you parked here? And what the hell happened to your window?"

She huddled into her coat, drawing the collar close. "Darien's men followed me. They stopped me here. I...I couldn't get away. One of the men broke my window and dragged me out of the car. He drove me to Darien."

Anger, threaded with fear, blazed through him, but he tamped down the rage. She was already scared. No reason to frighten her any more. "What did the bastard want? Did he hurt you?"

She shook her head.

"What did he do?" He held up his hand, stopping her before she could speak. "And don't tell me he didn't do anything, because I won't believe you. Fear's plastered all over your face." A headache throbbed somewhere behind his eyes. "I'll run his ass in."

"On what charge?" She arched her eyebrows. "Blocking a highway?"

"Kidnapping, breaking the restraining order, littering, being a jerk..." He rubbed the back of his neck. "I'm sure the little creep's committed any number of indictable offenses."

The corners of her mouth twitched, and her lips trembled in a smile.

A wave of happiness flooded him as if he'd been awarded the Medal of Honor. He searched for something to say to keep her smiling, but the situation wasn't the least bit humorous. And so he narrowed his eyes and shot her a penetrating cop look. "You haven't told me what he said."

She chewed on her bottom lip.

Heat seared through him as he remembered how he'd kissed that lip mere minutes earlier, how soft her flesh had been, how sweet she tasted. He tore his gaze from her mouth. "Tell me what McCabe said."

"He wanted to know what you knew about the murder investigations."

He nodded, not surprised. When they'd gone to see McCabe at his office, he figured the asshole would be anxious to find out what the police knew. And he figured he'd try and get information from Natasha. But he hadn't counted on her having to face McCabe alone. Damn it! He was supposed to protect her. Why hadn't he heard her leave the house this morning?

"Chase?"

Her voice, barely a whisper, drew him out of his recriminations. He swallowed over a sudden lump at the fear shadowing her eyes. "You shouldn't have had to face him alone. I should have been with you."

"This wasn't your fault. I left the house without telling you."

"Damn right you did."

She smoothed a hand over her tangle of curls. "You were right."

"About what?" He raised his eyebrows. This was a first.

"The earring is his." Her slim throat worked as she swallowed. "I'm sure of it." She hunched her shoulders. "Does this mean he killed that woman?"

"It's a bit too convenient his earring ends up clutched in the victim's hand. That sort of thing only happens in B-grade movies."

The wind gusted, blowing dried leaves and raising

dust swirls on the road.

"He's afraid."

"Of what?" He stared at her. "Ruining his thousand-dollar suit?"

"I don't know why he's so frightened, but whatever he's afraid of, his fear is real." The ghostly pallor of her face emphasized the delicate ridges of her high cheekbones. She shivered and huddled deeper within the folds of her coat. "I've never seen him afraid of anything."

Desperate to ease her worry, but uncertain how she'd react to his touch, he traced a finger across the softness of her cheek. "I'm sorry you had to face him alone."

She stiffened and drew away.

His breath whooshed out. "Are you going to flinch every time I come near you?"

"I didn't flinch." Her denial was too quick, her lie all too obvious.

"The hell you didn't." He opened his mouth to demand she tell the truth, but stopped. *Focus on the job!* The words blazed through him like a command from above. He shoved down his hurt. "Did McCabe say anything else?"

"There were several men with him...bodyguards, I think. They carried guns, and their eyes never stopped moving, scanning the forest, as if they were expecting an imminent attack."

"They probably are."

Her eyes widened. "Is that why his two men were killed?"

"Being connected to McCabe's a death sentence these days." The second the words were out of his mouth, he regretted them.

She clapped a hand over her mouth, and her face lost what little color remained.

"You don't have to worry. I won't let anything happen to you." His words hung in the air, all the worse because they were a lie. Look at the piss-poor job he'd done so far. McCabe had been able to kidnap her without any problem, thanks to Chase's incompetence.

"I messed up today. It won't happen again." He clasped her chilled hands in his and met her gaze with a fierce one of his own. "I won't let anything happen to you. I promise."

She stared at him as the wind whipped around them, tugging at her long, blonde hair. "I'm sorry I left the house without telling you."

He tightened his grip on her hands. "So, we're good?"

She nodded.

"You won't sneak out on me again?"

The corners of her mouth twitched. "No, I won't."

"You'll follow the guidelines we talked about last night?"

The twitching morphed into a grin. "You mean the rules you set out?" Her grin widened. "Not on your life."

He chuckled. "Okay. Maybe I was a bit autocratic."

Her brows arched. "You think?"

"Only one rule now. You don't leave the house without me." He pinned her with a hard look. "Can you live with that?"

"Probably."

"Okay." He blew out a breath and released her hands. "Let's go. I'll follow you back to your house."

She climbed inside her car.

Before she closed the door, he grabbed the handle and bent down, leaning close. Her perfume wafted around him, and he inhaled lavender, roses, and something elusive, yet eminently feminine. Smoothing a lock of her silky hair behind her ear, he brushed his lips against the soft skin of her cheek. "Just so you know, this thing between us isn't over. Not by a long shot."

Chapter 15

He swerved into her driveway and parked behind her car, blocking her exit. She'd promised she wouldn't run away, but his mama hadn't raised a fool. Better safe than sorry.

She climbed out of her car, carrying her purse and an overnight bag, and strode up the sidewalk to the front door.

He hurried to catch up and grabbed the bag from her as she fumbled in her purse for the key.

He studied the front door lock, his gut tightening.

Small scratches marred the shiny brass faceplate of the keyed, single-cylinder lockset. The edge of the door and the strike plate were gouged, and the door hung ajar a half inch.

Shoving past Natasha, he ignored her outraged gasp as he drew his gun from the shoulder holster under his coat.

"What is it? What's wrong?" She crouched beside the steps, her face white.

He motioned for her to stay put and pushed open the door and slipped inside, his gun held before him. The house was dark, the curtains closed from the night before. He eased ahead, watching the shadows, searching for the intruder.

An echoing, empty silence settled around him, and he released his breath. Whoever had broken into the house was gone. He flicked on the light switch.

The hall light blazed, revealing the carnage. Chairs were upended, their upholstery ripped to shreds. Long slashes marred the couch cushions. Books had been dumped from the shelves and scattered across the floor, their pages torn. Both lamps were broken, the shades crushed. The room looked as if a tornado had twisted through, destroying everything in its path.

Crunching through shards of broken glass, he peered into the spare bedroom where he'd slept mere hours earlier. The blankets and sheets had been ripped from the bed and tossed on the floor, the mattress shredded; the closet was emptied of clothes and boxes of shoes.

Behind him, a sharp inhalation of breath sounded, and he spun, gun ready.

Natasha stumbled into the room, her eyes wide. "What…what happened?"

"I thought I told you to wait outside. I could have shot you." He swept his hair back from his forehead. Why was he surprised she hadn't listened?

"I…I can't believe this mess." She shuffled out of the bedroom, her gait stiff. "My house…it's ruined. Everything I own is wrecked."

She followed him as they checked out the rooms on the main floor and the ones upstairs. With each room, his fury increased. The place was a disaster. The house had been trashed with a chilling thoroughness.

"Why would someone do this?" Her voice was a croak.

"You don't think your ex is responsible?"

She shook her head. "Darien wouldn't do this."

"He didn't have a problem destroying your artwork

the other night."

"This is different." She nodded at the surrounding chaos. "Darien would never go this far."

The certainty in her face unsettled him. The metal lock faceplate had been scratched and the doorframe gouged. Whoever searched the house had broken the lock to get in. "Does Darien have a key to your house?"

"I don't think so." Red patches flamed on her pale cheeks.

"Come on. He must have a key. Isn't that how he got in the other night?"

She heaved a deep breath. "If he did this, he'd leave a sign. Like he did when he left our wedding photo on the table when he wrecked my drawings. He'd want the credit."

He rubbed the bridge of his nose and studied the kitchen. Cupboard doors were open, their contents removed and tossed. A bag of flour had been slashed, and white powder coated the tile floor. He headed to the bathroom.

She followed.

Shattered pieces of the toilet tank lid lay on the floor. The shower curtain was ripped from the hooks. Even the bathtub drain had been removed. His gut curdled. No question. A pro had searched the house. "Okay, let's say you're right and McCabe didn't ransack this place."

"He didn't."

He gave a half shrug. "Whoever tore your place apart was looking for something."

She nodded. "Valuables to steal."

"Not a chance."

Her brow furrowed. "How can you be so sure?"

He tugged out his cell phone and punched in Mike's number. "Because your television, stereo, and laptop are still here. These guys were looking for something specific."

Mike picked up on the first ring. "Yep?"

"I have something you should take a look at. Bring some crime scene techs with you to Natasha Hartford's place. I'll be waiting." He hung up before Mike could ask questions. Judging by the scope of the destruction, whoever had trashed Natasha's house hadn't found what they were looking for. They'd be back. And when they returned, the house might not be the only thing they destroyed.

Natasha clutched the bathroom counter.

His gut tightened at the raw fear on her face. "Grab your bag."

"Wha…what?"

"We're leaving." He fought to soften his order, but judging by the way she flinched, he'd failed.

"Leaving? But the police will be here in a few minutes."

"As soon as they arrive, we're out of here. This place is a disaster. You can't stay. Besides, the investigators will be working here for hours."

"But what about this mess?" She waved her hand at the surrounding destruction. "I can't leave my house like this."

"Don't worry. After the investigators are finished, a cleaning crew the department uses will come in and straighten things up."

"But where will I go?"

He stuffed his hands in the front pockets of his jeans. Here was the part she wasn't going to like. "To a friend of mine's apartment. We'll stay there."

Her eyes widened. "We? You're going with me?"

He nodded, fearing if he said anything he'd spook her even more.

The doorbell pealed.

"Get your bag. We're leaving." He strode out of the room and marched down the hall.

Two uniformed police officers tromped in, followed by four crime scene investigators, and trailed by Mike.

Mike's thinning gray hair stuck out in wild spikes, and a fierce frown furrowed his craggy face. "What the hell's going on, Chase?"

"Someone tossed this place like a pro. They were looking for something, but I don't think they found what they wanted." Chase kept his voice brisk, laying out the facts, ignoring his partner's irritation.

Mike nodded. "You're leaving?"

"Yep."

"You and the broad?"

"Yep."

"Mind telling me where you're going?"

"Marina's place."

Mike chewed the pencil stub stuck in his mouth. "Ms. Hartford's gonna love that."

Natasha headed down the hall toward them. She carried her overnight bag, her purse strapped across her shoulder. "Detective Podborski." She nodded at Mike.

"Ms. Hartford."

Chase jerked his thumb at the open door. "Ready to go?"

"I…I'm not sure." She looked at Mike with pleading eyes. "Detective Podborski, do you really think it's unsafe for me to stay here? Chase is determined I go with him."

Mike's gaze sawed between Chase and her. "I'd trust Detective Brandon. He'll look after you."

She nodded as if reassured by Mike's words.

Mike leaned close to Chase and muttered so only he could hear, "Keep your mind on the job, partner, and your dick in your pants."

Chase frowned. What the hell? He took Natasha's arm, ignoring the tensing of her muscles, and led her through the door and outside before Mike could say anything more.

"Y'all take care, you hear?" Mike's sardonic voice followed them down the steps to the driveway. "I'll call and let you know if we find anything."

****

Neither Chase nor she spoke on the drive to his friend's apartment. Tension filled the air, creating a thick barrier between them. Images of her devastated house flickered before her like a horror movie on endless rewind. Her possessions were destroyed; everything she held dear, ruined.

And it was her fault.

The people who wrecked her house were searching for Darien's briefcase. She was sure of that, but they hadn't found her hiding place. Before she joined Chase and his partner at the front door, she'd slipped into the kitchen and checked under the sink. The bottles of dish soap and cleaning products had been tossed on the floor, but nothing else was disturbed. The secret hole where she'd hidden Darien's briefcase was untouched.

Her stomach knotted, and she pressed her hand to her chest in a futile effort to slow her racing heart. *Tell*

Chase about the briefcase. The words bubbled up and she almost blurted out the truth, but she bit hard on her bottom lip, halting her confession. How could she tell him about the briefcase now after everything they'd been through? She slid him a glance.

His features were set, his mouth a firm line, his eyes narrowed as he focused on the road.

He'd be furious if he knew she'd held back. But she wasn't lying. Not really. She'd tell him…eventually. First, she wanted to see for herself what was in the briefcase. And then she could decide what to do.

He steered the sedan onto a busy street in the east end of town and parked along the curb before a two-story, brick building with a flashing neon sign depicting a larger-than-life nude dancing woman and the words Girls Girls Girls covering the front of the building. Smaller neon signs proclaimed the club featured Topless and Cheap Drinks. The sign above the striking red door flashed Leggz.

"Your friend lives here?"

He undid the clasp on his seatbelt. "She has an apartment upstairs."

She? What sort of friend lived above a strip club? Before she could ask any more questions, he climbed out of the car and slammed the door.

He strode around the hood of the car and opened her door. "Ready?"

She stepped out, clutching her purse to her chest.

He opened the back door and grabbed her bag. "Let's go." Gripping her elbow, he steered her toward the red door. The purple glow from the giant nude woman, lit in all her neon beauty, sputtered and crackled, pulsing across his face as he opened the door.

A rush of rock music and loud conversation blasted out, and she staggered back a step.

Two men spilled out of the club and shoved past them onto the sidewalk, their voices loud and slurred.

One man's bleary gaze swept over her from her head to her toes and zeroed in on her breasts. "Whoohee!" He smacked his lips. "What a rack." Leering, he stumbled toward her. "Lookin' for some action, honey?"

She shrank against Chase.

The drunk advanced. His sour, alcohol-laced breath washed over her. "Come on, babe." He swatted a clumsy hand at her butt.

Chase growled and lunged at the man, grabbing him by the collar of his coat and shoving him into the street.

The drunk landed on his back in the gutter with a loud explosion of air.

"Hey, man. Leave him alone." His friend lumbered toward Chase, fists raised.

Sparks shot from Chase's eyes. "Do you really want to go there?" Each word was encased in ice.

The drunk lowered his hands and staggered back a step. "Take it easy, man." He grabbed his friend by the arm and hauled him out of the gutter. "Come on, Joe, let's get outta here."

They stumbled down the sidewalk, arm in arm.

"Are you all right?"

Chase's concerned voice jolted her out of her immobility. "I…I'm fine."

"It's better inside.

"I bet."

He grinned and clasped her hand in his before leading her into the dark, noisy club.

A haze of smoke filled the air in a dense fog. The floor vibrated from the blare of loud rock and roll music. A single bright spotlight shone on a stage in the center of the room where a woman, clad in a sequined, skintight minidress, swung around a pole, her long brown hair flying.

A ring of ogling men seated in chairs at small circular tables, drinks in front of them, cheered and whistled.

The roar of music, the suffocating cloud of smoke, the leering men, the sickly sweet aromas of sweat and alcohol was overwhelming. Natasha clung to Chase's hand.

He leaned close, his lips brushing her ear, his warm breath fluttering wisps of her hair. "The apartment's upstairs."

Crossing the crowded room, they weaved between groups of hooting men, then walked down a dimly lit hallway to a set of narrow stairs leading up into darkness.

Chase led the way as they climbed the stairs. A motion-activated light flared to life, and he stopped before a door painted the same garish red as the front door of the strip club.

Fishing in the pocket of his jeans, he withdrew a small key, inserted it in the lock, and opened the door. He reached inside and flicked a switch. Soft light glowed to life, and he released her hand and motioned for her to enter the room.

The apartment was a pleasant surprise. A navy-blue upholstered couch and matching chair faced a big-screen TV mounted on the wall above an electric fireplace. Tasteful prints in black frames were on the walls. A bar separated the tiny kitchen from the living room.

She crossed the room to the single window and peered outside at the street. Traffic noises and the steady thump of music from the club below filled the room. The light from the purple neon sign flashed on and off, pulsating like the beat of a heart. She turned. "What sort of friend lives here?"

His eyebrows quirked. "A good friend."

"Must be if she doesn't mind us staying here."

A dimple danced in his cheek. "She's a real good friend."

A spurt of unexpected jealousy hit her like a blow and took her breath away. She forced what she hoped was a bland expression on her face. "She won't mind we're here? That I'm here?"

He shook his head. "She lives with her boyfriend." His chuckle raised the heat in the room by several degrees, letting her know he'd seen through her pretense. "Come on. I'll give you the fifty-cent tour."

He led the way down a short hallway to a bedroom filled with a massive king-size bed covered with a black silk comforter and matching pillowcases. A lamp, with a pink, gauzy scarf draped over the shade, was on a small table beside the bed.

She stepped into the room. "This is nice..." Her voice trailed off as she spied the floor-to-ceiling mirror covering the wall at the end of the bed. She glanced up. Another mirror hung suspended from the ceiling. Heat surged up her neck and flared over her cheeks as she imagined how the all-seeing mirrors would reflect any movement on the giant bed.

She caught Chase's image in the mirror.

The knowing smirk on his handsome face inched the heat up another notch. "Where's"—she swallowed, her mouth arid dry—"where's the bathroom?"

He tossed her overnight bag on the bed and pointed out the door. "Across the hall."

She nodded, keeping her face averted, afraid he'd read the panic in her eyes.

"McCabe won't think to look for you here. You'll be safe."

He was right. She couldn't imagine Darien going to a strip club. If he wanted to see naked women, all he had to do was call up the prettiest call girls in town, and they'd come running.

"I'll see you in the morning." His gruff voice cut into her thoughts.

"Where...where are you sleeping?" Her gaze settled on the bed, and flicked to the mirror on the wall, and up at the one on the ceiling. She gulped.

The corners of his mouth twitched. "Is that an offer?"

Her heart raced. How had she not noticed the dimple in his right cheek? Or the way his teeth gleamed against his swarthy skin when he flashed his devilish grin?

His laughter filled the room. "Don't worry. Your virtue's safe. I'll sleep on the couch."

"Thank you." Her voice was a high-pitched squeak.

Still laughing, he headed out of the room, closing the door behind him.

She sank onto the bed. What was she? An eighteenth century virgin with a serious case of the vapors? What was she afraid of? He was sleeping on the couch. A door and several feet of space separated them.

With shaking hands, she opened her bag and jerked out her nightgown, wishing she'd thought to pack her flannel pajamas instead of the sky-blue wisp of silk. When she packed her bag, she'd planned to be alone, not sharing an apartment above a strip club with a cop.

Not just any cop, but a hard-nosed, opinionated cop too good-looking for his own damn good.

Chapter 16

She didn't sleep. Couldn't. Closing her eyes, deep breathing, focusing on pleasant thoughts, counting sheep...nothing worked. She tried listing all the places she wanted to visit in the world. Number one hundred and thirty-six, and she was still wide-awake.

Earlier, footsteps had sounded in the hall outside her closed door. The bathroom door opened and closed, the toilet flushed, and water ran as Chase prepared for bed. But the tiny apartment had been silent for the past several hours. Well, not silent, exactly. The bass from the club below pounded through the floor, beating in time with the incessant flicker of purple neon light alternately lightening and darkening the room.

Cursing, she sat up and thrust her hair off her face. She switched on the bedside lamp and peered at her watch in the rosy glow. Catching a flicker of movement in the mirror on the wall at the foot of the bed, she grimaced. Her hair was wild, her face puffy from lack of sleep. Dark circles rimmed her eyes. She groaned and flopped back on the bed, squeezed her eyes shut, and ordered herself to sleep.

After a further ten minutes of lying in bed staring at her image in the mirror above, she gave up. Her mouth tasted like dust. Maybe a drink of water would help. She threw off the covers and slipped out of bed.

Walking on silent feet, she opened the door to her

room and peered into the dark hall. Casting a furtive look in the direction of the living room, she hustled out of the room and tiptoed across the hall to the bathroom.

The door swung open, and the hallway flooded with light.

She blinked in the sudden brightness.

Chase stood in the doorway, a towel wrapped around his narrow hips. His hair was damp, and dark curls fanned around his face.

She swallowed, and her mouth dried as her gaze dipped lower.

His chest was bare. The sheen of dampness on his smooth, tanned skin highlighted the definition of muscles and the intriguing swirl of dark hair. Below the towel, his muscular thighs and calves led to long, narrow feet.

He cleared his throat, and her gaze flew back to his.

A wide grin plastered across his face. "Couldn't sleep?"

"I…I wanted a glass of water. I was thirsty. I thought a drink of water would help." She tried to stop the inane rambling, but the words spewed out. "I didn't know you were still awake. I thought you—"

He placed two fingers over her mouth, stopping her. "I couldn't sleep either, so I had a shower." He leaned against the doorframe, his long, lean body glistening. An arrow of dark hair disappeared beneath the scanty towel.

The temperature in the hall ratcheted up to an inferno. Sweat broke out under her arms and between her breasts.

"Since neither of us can sleep, why don't I make a

cup of tea? That might help." He rubbed his chin, and his gaze roamed over her. "You might want to put something else on." He faked a leer. "Not that I'm complaining, but you'll be cold."

Another wave of heat flooded her as she realized what she wore. She crossed her arms over her breasts, spun around, and raced back to her room, slamming the door behind her.

****

He forced his legs to unlock and stumbled away from the bathroom. His chest heaved as if he'd sprinted five miles. Man, oh, man. He was in trouble. Big trouble. The image of Natasha clad in the wisp of blue silk was branded on his eyeballs. The thin material had clung to her curves like a second skin, revealing far more than it covered.

He shouldn't have looked. Hell, he should have turned around and slammed the bathroom door shut. But he wasn't that strong. One glance at her near-naked body and all he could do was stare.

He wiped his chin, surprised his skin wasn't wet with drool.

He glanced down at the towel wrapped around his hips and grimaced. If he didn't want to embarrass himself, better get dressed before she made another appearance. Hurrying down the hall, he grabbed his jeans from the chair in the living room and struggled into them. He tugged his shirt over his head, smoothed his hand over his hair, and heaved a breath.

The bedroom door opened, and a rush of desire flooded him. His legs weakened, and his heart hitched in his chest. Wheeling toward the kitchenette and ignoring the trembling in his hands, he filled the kettle

191

with water and set it to heat on the hotplate.

He smelled her before he heard her. Her perfume—what was that scent anyway?—wafted in the air.

"Thank you for making tea. Maybe it'll help me sleep."

Her soft voice settled over him like a warm summer breeze. "No problem." *Phew*. He sounded normal. Turning, he sucked in a breath as if struck by a blow to the gut. Dressed in baggy, gray sweatpants, a bulky sweater, her hair scraped back into a ponytail, and her face bare of makeup, she was stunning.

A tentative smile flickered on her full lips.

Their gazes met and he stared, drawn into her luminous blue eyes. The room around him dissolved. The furious beat of the music from the strip club matched the racing of his heart.

He advanced, his bare feet silent on the linoleum floor, and touched her arm, a mere brushing of his fingers against her soft skin.

She glanced down at his hand, but didn't pull away.

Their gazes connected again, and the heat between them thickened and writhed like a living, breathing entity.

The frantic booming of his heart filled the room. He caressed her arm, never releasing her gaze as he lowered his head. A high pitched whistle rent the air, but he ignored the sound, focused on her and her alone.

Her breath mingled with his.

And then she tensed.

He jerked his hand back.

The infernal whistling continued.

"Aren't you going to get that?"

"Get what?" His voice was guttural.

"The kettle. The water's boiling." She pointed behind him.

The kettle. Of course. Scrubbing the whiskers on his chin, trying to clear his head, he turned to the hot plate. A plume of steam poured out of the kettle's spout. He lurched over and switched off the burner, lifted the kettle, and poured boiling water into the teapot.

Without looking at her, afraid of what he'd do if he did, he filled two mugs with tea. "Take anything in your tea?"

"No. That's good, thanks."

He handed her a cup, and careful to keep his distance, slid past her into the living room and sprawled on the chair.

The raucous music from below pulsed in a primal beat through the room. He gulped his tea, breathing in the woodsy scent of chamomile, uncaring the hot liquid burned his mouth.

"The tea's good." She perched on the couch, looking like a prim schoolmarm from days gone by. Her knees were pressed tight together, her feet crossed at the ankles. Her posture screamed, "Do not touch."

"Don't you think it's time you came clean about McCabe?" *Damn.* Why the hell had he opened that can of worms? Why couldn't he have asked her how the Braves were doing, or about the upswing in the Market, anything but her ex-husband and his abuse?

"What?" She jerked and spilled hot tea on the cushion. Her hands shook as she grabbed a handful of tissues from the box on the coffee table in front of her and scrubbed at the wet stain.

He blew out his cheeks. "Why did you stay with him? I mean, after he hit you the first time, why didn't you leave?"

Her eyes filled with shadows, her motions jerky and stiff.

The seconds ticked. Music throbbed. Purple neon light flashed on and off, on and off.

She shrugged. "I don't know. I guess I thought the abuse was my fault. I tried to do better, tried to do what he wanted, but nothing I did was ever good enough."

Hatred for McCabe flooded him. He gripped the arms of the chair so he wouldn't go to her and comfort her like he was so desperate to do. "It wasn't your fault. You know that, right?" He gripped tighter, his nails digging into the soft fabric. "That's what these jerks do. They keep at you, and at you, until they've destroyed your self esteem."

She wiped her eyes. "He was always full of remorse after he"—she swallowed—"after he hit me. He drove me to the Emergency room himself, begging me to forgive him. Each time he promised he wouldn't hit me again, told me he how much he loved me." She squirmed on the cushion, and her sweater loosened and slipped off her shoulder, revealing a small, thickened knot on her collarbone. "I guess I believed him, or hoped he meant it."

The walls of the small room shifted inward, crushing him, removing all the air. He stared at the lump on her delicate bone. He'd seen the same knitted bone after his father broke his mother's collarbone the first time. His hands balled into fists, and he wanted nothing more than to pummel the shit out of Darien McCabe.

He forced his hands to relax, his fingers to uncurl. "My father beat my mother. Afterward, he was always sorry. He hadn't meant to hit her, but she'd driven him to hurt her. His violence was her fault." He rubbed the back of his neck. *What the hell? Why was he spilling his guts?* Only Mike knew of the abuse Chase's mother had suffered at the hands of her husband.

Until now.

The rhythmic beat of music vibrated across the void separating them.

Her warm, probing gaze fixed on him. "Did your mother leave him? Did…did she get away?"

A familiar tightness filled his chest. He smoothed a hand over his damp hair. How could he put into words the horror of his parents' marriage? How could she possibly understand? He halted and stared at her. Of course she understood. She'd lived through the same hell. She knew the terror of being beaten just because you were there. She'd suffered the same vicious assaults and the even worse barrage of constant verbal abuse.

Shadows shifted in her sapphire eyes, revealing remnants of the pain she'd suffered.

He blinked back a sudden sting of tears. "My mother didn't leave. At least, not until the old man beat her so bad, he killed her."

Chapter 17

She spluttered, stunned at his shocking revelation. In the next breath, she banged her cup on the coffee table and darted across the room. Crouching before him, she clasped his large, callused hands. "I'm so sorry, Chase, so very sorry." Her voice was thick. "How old were you when"—she swallowed hard— "when she died?"

He wiped his eyes, but the tears streamed unabated down his rugged cheeks. "Old enough. I was twelve. I should have stopped him. I should have—" His voice cracked.

"You should have what? Come on, Chase, tell me. What is it you think you should have done?" She kept her voice low, but she knew her words were like a needle lancing a wound.

His reddened eyes sought hers. "I…I should have saved her. I called the police, but they got there too late." He sniffed. "Don't you see? I didn't save her." He buried his face in his hands as his shoulders shook with a broken sob. "I let her die."

Her heart lurched, and matching tears filled her eyes. "You were a child." She wrapped her arms around his knees and laid her head on his lap, wishing she could ease his heartache.

He uttered a low, guttural groan, filled with acres of pain.

"It wasn't your fault," she whispered.

Time passed. The incessant beat of the music quieted, and the flashing light went dark. Her arms ached from holding him, but she didn't let go. Wouldn't. Not until he believed her. Not until he understood he wasn't to blame for the actions of his father. How could a child be expected to stop an enraged, grown man?

His tears eased, and the muscles in his thighs relaxed beneath her head.

She sat back on her heels and swiped at the damp tendrils of hair that had escaped the confines of her elastic band.

Expelling a ragged breath, he scrubbed the moisture from his face with his hands. "And that's why I never talk about my past." He attempted a weak smile.

"I'm glad you told me." The silence in the small apartment settled between them. "You do know you aren't to blame."

His eyes were bleak. "I should have stopped him."

"Your mother was the only one who could have ended the abuse. She should have left." She met his reddened gaze. "You know that, right? She should have taken you and left."

"Like you did."

Their gazes connected, and the air sparked between them.

He reached for her at the same time she rose from her knees and slid onto his lap.

A sense of rightness stole over her as she inhaled his familiar masculine scent. She wanted this man, wanted his taste, his touch…wanted him.

His eyes, fringed by dark lashes, smoldered with

golden lights. He tugged the band from her hair and threaded his long fingers through the strands. Lowering his head, he dipped his mouth to hers, a mere brushing of lips, a tasting.

Her lips softened and she opened her mouth.

He deepened the kiss, adjusting her in his arms so she sprawled across his lap, her chest pressed to his, their hearts beating together in a thunderous rhythm.

The taste of him, and the play of his tongue against hers, had her squirming and desperate for more. She slipped her hands under his shirt and traced the smooth warmth of his flat belly. Sliding her hands over his firm chest muscles, she toyed with the whorls of soft hair and glided her fingers over the nubs of his nipples.

"I'll never hurt you, Natasha. Never." He kissed a trail of fire along the sensitive skin of her neck and across her collarbone, lingering on the small knot of healed bone.

The sweet words uttered in a husky rasp tore a low groan from her, and she arched toward him as he traced a callused finger along the gentle rise of her breast, circling the swollen mound. Her blood liquefied and pooled low in her belly.

His mouth engulfed her nipple, dampening the soft cotton of her sweater.

Moist heat surrounded her. Her senses flamed, and she writhed beneath him.

He stopped the delicious torture and lifted his head, his brows raised. "Trust me?"

Surging through her was a rush of passion that couldn't be contained. She opened her arms and drew him closer. "Don't you dare stop."

Relief flooded his handsome features, and he

kissed her, crushing her mouth under his.

She sucked in a sharp breath as he smoothed his hand under the waistband of her sweat pants along her stomach, seeking lower, and lower still, setting off rocket blasts of sensations. A wave of heat and light engulfed her, and she cried out, his name sweet on her lips.

Tightening his arms around her, he rose from the chair and carried her across the room and down the hall to the bedroom. He lowered her onto the satin-covered, king-size bed. "Are you sure?" His voice was a hoarse croak.

"Are you?"

The dimple in his cheek danced. "I've never been more certain of anything in my life."

Her hands were clumsy as she fumbled with the tiny buttons on her sweater, undoing first one and then another until the heavy garment slipped from her shoulders and slid down her arms. A breeze wafted over her bare breasts, and she shivered.

The passion in his hungry eyes impaled her and fired her blood to boiling. A flood of pleasure rushed through her. Her skin tingled under his torrid gaze.

He stared, his eyes hungry, as he ripped off his T-shirt and tossed it on the floor. His jeans came next. And then he stood before her with nothing between them but a few feet of bed and a whole lot of sizzling heat.

Her breath caught in her throat.

Well-defined muscles rippled across his chest. His broad shoulders narrowed to slim hips and a flat stomach.

Her gaze dipped lower, and she bit back a gasp.

The need to touch him and feel the ripple of his warm skin beneath her questing fingers overwhelmed her. His name husked on her lips like the sweetest nectar. "Chase." She lay down on the satin sheet and crooked her finger, beckoning. "Come here."

He climbed onto the bed and stretched out beside her, his lean, hair-roughened thighs tickling her soft skin. He smoothed the palms of his hands with aching slowness up and over her breasts, cupping them as if they were precious fruit. The callused pad of his thumb brushed against her nipple, and she whimpered, begging for more.

Her breath huffed in and out in rapid pants, her chest heaving. She couldn't breathe, couldn't think, couldn't… "Please." Her body burned. She wanted him, needed him. Now.

As if reading her desperate yearning, he gripped the waistband of her sweatpants and yanked them over her hips and along her legs until she was free of the concealing cotton.

She shivered, naked on the black satin sheet.

"Cold?" His voice was rough.

She shook her head, unable to form words.

He grinned, slow and sexy, his eyes heavy-lidded with passion as he trailed his fingers along the sensitive skin on the inside of her thighs in an agonizing, slow parade, inching closer to where she ached for his touch.

"Please." The single word spilled from her as she writhed beneath him. "Please."

He chuckled deep in his chest and continued his erotic torture.

She caught a glimpse in the mirror above of their sweat-dampened bodies moving in a sensuous dance. A rising swell of excitement coursed through her. She sucked in a ragged breath at the enticing flex of the muscles in his back and shoulders, the firm swell of his butt, the contrast between his long, tanned limbs and her pale body. For the first time she understood the appeal of the mirrors.

In the next breath, she forgot the mirrors, forgot he was a cop, forgot everything but the touch of his skilled fingers and the play of his muscles beneath her hands. Crying out, she gripped his arms, nails digging deep, riding the wild sensations in wave after exquisite wave.

In a single smooth motion, he grasped her hips and eased into her moist warmth.

She arched against him, drawing him deeper and deeper.

His groan was primal as his hips bucked.

Once again she rode a wave of desire, clutching him, hanging on as the storm roiled. Brilliant light flashed behind her eyes, her body heaved. She cried out his name in a guttural, primitive groan.

****

Chase drove deeply one last time. Her name burst from his lips on an explosive gasp. Chest heaving, he rolled onto his side, drawing her warm body against him, holding her close. He smoothed damp tendrils of golden hair from her flushed face and nuzzled her temple where a tiny pulse beat a frantic pace. "Wow!" *Not cool, definitely not cool. But how else to describe such an earthshattering experience*?

In his next breath, the world tilted on its axis and everything changed.

She stiffened and lurched up, shoving his arm away. Her face was closed, her mouth set in a tight line.

Scrambling across the massive expanse of bed, she grabbed her sweatpants and struggled into them.

He sat up. "What is it? What's wrong?"

She shook her head and wheeled around, reaching for her sweater, but not before he glimpsed the tears glistening in her eyes.

"Why are you so upset? I thought you…" He grasped her arm, but she jerked away as if he'd burned her, and his words died on his lips. He opened his mouth to demand answers but his cell phone rang.

Damn. Not now.

She yanked on her sweater, clutching the soft cotton between her breasts, not bothering with the buttons.

Again, he reached for her, and again she flinched. Something inside him crumbled, and the euphoria of seconds ago vanished.

The piercing wail of the ringtone penetrated the tension in the room.

He had to answer. He was on duty. He cast a look at her pale, distressed face, and with a loud curse, lunged across the bed and grabbed his jeans from the floor, and fished in the front pocket for his phone. "Brandon."

Mike's voice was tinny and distant in his ear. "Hey, man, you don't have to snap my head off."

He scrubbed his chin, his gaze never leaving Natasha's pale, stricken face. "What's up?"

"What the hell do you mean, what's up? I've been trying to get hold of you for the past hour."

He grimaced, glad his partner couldn't see what he'd spent the last hour doing and with whom he'd been doing it. "I've been…um…busy."

Natasha finished dressing and stumbled out of the room. The door to the bathroom slammed shut, and the lock clicked in place with a decisive snap.

"Are you still there?" Mike's voice, mixed with static, echoed from the phone.

Chase threaded his fingers through his hair. "Yeah, I'm here. What's going on?"

"The boys didn't lift any unexpected fingerprints from Natasha's house. Looks like the guys who tossed her place wore gloves."

Chase wasn't surprised. Too many criminals watched crime shows. They knew how to avoid detection. The only hope the cops had was if the crooks were stupid. Most were.

But not the ones who'd hit Natasha's house. They were pros. Pros didn't make mistakes.

"Any idea what they were looking for?" Mike's brisk voice drew him back. "Has she spilled?"

"Nope." He scratched his whiskers. "She hasn't said a word."

"Try some of the famous Brandon charm. That should soften her up."

Chase grunted and eyed the rumpled sheets. The musty scent of sex hung heavy in the air. Yeah. He had charm, all right. He'd charmed her right out of the room, and now she was locked in the bathroom hiding from him.

"That'll have to wait." Mike's teasing banter ceased, replaced by his gruff, no-nonsense cop voice. "There's been a new development in the case. You'd better get your ass over here. The chief wants to meet with us ASAP."

"I can't leave Natasha. She could be in danger."

"Already taken care of. Samuels is on his way. He should be at Marina's apartment any minute."

"Okay. I'll see you in fifteen." Chase ended the call, grabbed his jeans, and yanked them on. He marched out of the bedroom and tapped on the bathroom door. "Natasha?"

Silence.

Light shone from under the door.

He knocked again. "Something's come up. I have to leave." He raised his voice so she'd hear him through the closed door. "Officer Samuels is going to look after you while I'm gone."

The floor in the bathroom squeaked, and he pictured her huddled in the corner of the tiny bathroom, quaking in regret at what they'd done.

Damn.

He needed time, time to figure out this mess, time to fix things.

A loud knock sounded on the door to the apartment.

Too late. "He's here now. I'm leaving. We'll talk about this when I get back. Okay?"

The silence hung in the air like the aftermath of an explosion.

He blew out a breath. Turning, he hurried into the living room, grabbed his socks and shoes, and finished dressing. He opened the door and let in Samuels. "She's all yours."

Samuels, a young rookie dressed in regulation blue, removed his cap and smoothed the palm of his hand over his light brown hair cut in a military-style buzz. He nodded and sauntered into the apartment. "Where is she?"

"In the bathroom." Chase dragged on his coat and brushed by Samuels, but paused on the top of the stairs. "Any idea what's going on?"

Samuels shrugged. "All I know is the shit's hit the fan. Everyone's running around like crazy."

Chapter 18

Natasha swallowed the last dregs of cold coffee and grimaced at the bitter taste. The dull throb from the club below once more vibrated the floor. She cast a sour look at Officer Samuels sprawled on the couch where he'd sat, unmoving, for the past several hours. The television was tuned to yet another baseball game, the sound on low.

After Chase had run off in the middle of the night, she'd crept out of the bathroom, said a quick hello to Samuels, and climbed into the king-size bed, determined to sleep. The rumpled sheets, the faint smell of sex in the air, and the all-too-vivid images rattling through her brain made sleep a fantasy.

Memories of how she'd thrown aside her last remnants of restraint and given in to Chase's expert caresses, how her body had sung with rippling sensations, flowed through her mind in a never-ending spool of torrid images.

She punched the pillow and flipped onto her side, snuggled under the black satin sheets, and thought of the contract she'd secured with Casemont Greeting Cards for their upcoming Valentine's Day collection, her mortgage payment due the next day, how she hadn't been to the gym for days…anything to distract her, but her mind kept going back to what had happened in this bed a short time ago.

Making love with Chase was a mistake, but when he'd revealed the tragic events of his mother's death and his overriding guilt, she'd yearned to comfort him, to somehow ease his pain.

In his vulnerability, he'd forgotten he was a cop, and he'd sought out her warmth, her comfort, her femininity. She hadn't been able to refuse him, even though she knew he'd regret his actions in the morning, and that was something she couldn't bear.

And so, still damp from his kisses, her heart thudding from her release, she'd leaped out of his arms, run into the bathroom, and huddled on the cold tile floor, tears streaming down her face.

She'd covered her ears, blocking out the confusion and hurt in his deep voice as he pleaded with her to open the door. But what was there to say? How could she explain her abrupt exit from his arms? How could she tell him that after what Darien had done to her, after all the abuse, she couldn't trust another man, certainly not one in a position of power.

First and foremost, Chase was a cop. He was keeping her in the safe house for her protection, but he didn't trust her. Beneath all his charm, he still thought she was involved with Darien and the murders.

Oh, he liked her all right. He hadn't made a secret of his attraction to her. He'd wanted her, and he'd enjoyed having sex with her. He spoke all the right words, did all the right things, but every once in a while she caught a flicker of doubt in his eyes when he looked at her. And that frightened her more than anything, especially since he was right not to trust her.

She hadn't told him about Darien's briefcase.

While he'd sought comfort and release with her

body, she'd bared her soul and made love. She sat up with a jerk, heart hammering. Love? She didn't love him. Of course she didn't. How could she? She was tired. That's all this was. The anguish on his rugged face, torment she identified with all too well, had breached the barriers guarding her good sense, and she'd succumbed to his kisses. But it wasn't love. No way.

She didn't know what time she drifted off, but beams of sunlight striped the floor beside the bed when she next opened her eyes. The pillow beneath her cheek was damp. She wiped her face, surprised at the tears on her cheeks.

She crawled out of bed and stumbled into the bathroom. The shower didn't help. Nor did the six—or was it seven?—cups of coffee she guzzled during the long hours she sat on the chair in the living room with Officer Samuels and waited for Chase's return, dreading the coming confrontation.

A quick tap at the apartment door jolted her to her feet.

Samuels' earlier lethargy vanished, and he lunged across the room, beating her to the door. He held a gun in his hand, his lean body stiff with tension. "Who is it?"

"Brandon."

Samuels peered through the spy hole in the door and stood back and opened the door.

Chase shoved past him into the room. His presence filled the small apartment with a new vibrancy.

Samuels closed the door, locked the dead bolt, and slipped his gun into the leather holster attached to the thick nylon belt hanging around his slim hips. "Any news?"

Chase's face was haggard and his hair was a wild tangle of curls. His mouth was set in a stern line, and deep grooves scarred the skin between his dark eyebrows.

Her breath hitched in her throat. "What is it? What's wrong?"

"Someone tried to kill McCabe."

The breath whooshed out of her, and she collapsed on the chair. "What? How?"

A small pulse throbbed in his jaw. "A bomb exploded in his car."

"Oh my God. Is he"—she swallowed over a thick lump stuck in her throat—"is he okay?"

A thin white line rimmed his tight lips. "You care what happens to him?" And there it was again...the glimmer of doubt in his hazel eyes.

She blinked away the sting of tears. "I don't want anyone else to get hurt."

He studied her for another heartbeat. "Well then, you'll be happy to know that other than a few scratches, he's fine. He'd just stepped out of the car when the bomb exploded." He met her gaze. "His driver wasn't so lucky. He's in Intensive Care. They aren't sure he'll make it."

She tugged at her shirt collar in a futile attempt to ease the tightness in her throat. "Who did this? Who set the bomb?"

"That's the six million dollar question now, isn't it?"

She recalled the fear dulling Darien's pale eyes. "Did you ask Darien?"

A tight smile lifted the corners of Chase's mouth,

but no hint of humor lightened the storm in his eyes. "He doesn't have any idea who'd want to kill him. To hear him tell it, everyone loves him."

"But he must know. I mean, he was frightened of someone when I talked to him yesterday."

"He's not talking. Whoever did this has him scared. He's refusing to say a word." He rubbed the back of his neck. "McCabe's house was ransacked, but apparently, he's in the midst of renovations." He made air quotes around the last word.

She fought to swallow, but the lump in her throat was too thick.

"The same pros who tossed your place did his." He stalked toward her. "Why do you think that is?"

She shrank into the chair. The briefcase! The thought blazed before her as if lit by neon lights. Whoever had searched her house and Darien's wanted the briefcase Darien had given her and would stop at nothing to get it.

"Isn't it time you told me what they were looking for?" He fixed her with a hard-as-diamonds stare.

She chewed on her bottom lip. People were dead. More would die if she didn't tell the truth. "Darien"— she swallowed—"Darien gave me a briefcase the other day." Her voice faded at the furious frown on his face, but she dug deep for courage. "He...he wanted me to hide it for him."

The room stilled, the air thick and heavy.

He blew out a long breath and jammed his hands in the front pockets of his jeans. His eyes blazed. "Are you telling me the briefcase I saw in your living room is the one McCabe asked you to hide?"

She nodded.

"And this is the first I've heard of this?" His voice was cold, the words clipped as if chipped from ice.

"I—"

He held up his hand, stopping her. "I don't want to hear your excuses. Tell me where this damn briefcase is."

She winced at his fury, but she didn't blame him. She'd lied. Not outright, but by omission. She opened her mouth to tell him where she'd hidden the briefcase, but then he spoke, and the words died on her tongue.

"I thought so. You're involved in this mess. That's why you're hiding McCabe's briefcase, why you've kept it a secret all this time."

His suspicions, finally out in the open, struck like a knife to her chest. At the same time, outrage bloomed. After what happened between them last night, he still believed her capable of murder. A chill settled over her. "The briefcase is safe."

"Tell me where it is."

"No."

His eyebrows rose. "No?"

"No."

He stared, his eyes fierce. "What sort of bullshit is this? If you know where the damn briefcase is, you'd better tell me."

She surged to her feet and slammed her hands on her hips. "Or what? You'll run me in? Arrest me? Use your questionable charms to persuade me to reveal my secret? Is that what you were doing earlier?" She nodded in satisfaction as his cheeks flamed at her not-so-subtle reference to their lovemaking.

An ominous silence settled between them. The air sparked with anger. She glared into his furious gaze, hoping hers was as fierce. A loud cough startled her, and she spun toward the sound.

Officer Samuels' gaze flitted between Chase and her as if he were watching a tennis match. When he noticed them looking, his face flushed, and he retrieved his uniform coat from the back of the couch and strode to the door. "Well, I guess I'll head back to the precinct." He unlocked the door and slipped out of the room, closing the door behind him.

She swung back to Chase.

His frigid gaze settled on her. "Are you going to tell me where the damn briefcase is?"

She quaked at the warning in his hazel eyes, but hung onto her fury. "I'll show you where it is."

"No way. This is too dangerous. You're not leaving the safe house." He advanced a step.

She held still, even though her instincts screamed to run. Forcing a casualness she was far from feeling, she crossed her arms over her chest. "Well, then, I guess you don't want the briefcase." In other circumstances she would have laughed at his shock at her rebellion.

He stomped over to the couch and slammed his fist into the back cushion with such force the heavy couch bounced a foot across the floor. His back was to her, his shoulders stiff, the muscles in his arms rigid. He inhaled several deep breaths, and when he turned, his face was expressionless, but fire raged in his eyes. "Okay. Let's go."

She stared, dumbfounded. *Okay*? She fought back a smug smile, but knew she'd failed when he glowered and marched over to the door.

Her smugness vanished, replaced with a jittery

nervousness.

She'd poked the bear. She prayed he wouldn't exact vengeance.

Chapter 19

He gripped the steering wheel as he shifted from staring through the windshield at the road ahead to checking the rearview mirror to make sure they hadn't been followed. His nerves were on edge, and he struggled to stay focused. He couldn't afford to let his exhaustion, his anger at her for not telling him about the briefcase, or his fear for her safety, distract him.

Her mutinous silence made matters worse. Jammed against the passenger door, she stared fixedly ahead, her slight body bristling with anger.

He searched the rearview mirror again and rechecked the view in the side mirrors. Why hadn't she told him about the briefcase? He understood she hadn't trusted him at first, but after last night, after their lovemaking?

"You don't think we're being followed, do you?" Her quiet voice broke into his thoughts.

He shot her another glance. In spite of her earlier bravado, she was scared. Good. Fear would make her more vigilant. "Pays to be careful. The people after McCabe could target you next."

"I have nothing to do with Darien. Not anymore. I haven't for years."

"You didn't have anything to do with him until he asked you to hide his briefcase. Now you're involved up to your pretty neck in this mess."

She worried her bottom lip. "Once I show you where I've hidden the briefcase, what happens?"

He shrugged. "Depends on what's inside."

"What happens to me?"

He scanned the road ahead for anything suspicious. "I'll take you back to the safe house. Samuels will watch over you. You'll be safe with him."

"You mean I'll hide while you figure out who's killing all these people?"

"Of course." He risked a glance and shuddered. *Shit. Wrong thing to say.*

Her mouth was set in a stubborn line, and her eyes flashed fire. "If I give you Darien's briefcase, I want to be involved. I want to help. I won't sit in a safe house and twiddle my thumbs."

Damn. Couldn't she see the danger? People had died. She could be next. "Come on, Natasha, don't be a fool." The second the words left his mouth he regretted them. *What the hell*? Couldn't he keep his damn mouth shut?

The temperature in the car dropped a dozen degrees. She crossed her arms over her chest. "Well, that's the deal, Detective. I show you the briefcase, and you let me help." Her jaw set in a stubborn line. "Take it or leave it."

He gritted his teeth. She was serious. If he didn't agree to her ridiculous terms, she wouldn't tell him where she'd hidden McCabe's briefcase. Well, two could play her game. He fought to fix an earnest expression on his face. "Okay. I don't like this arrangement, but you've got a deal."

Her eyes widened. "Really? You mean it?"

He bit back a smirk. He had her—hook, line, and

sinker. "You bet. You give me the briefcase, and I'll let you work with me."

"You promise?"

He nodded, hoping she couldn't see through his lie. "I promise."

She grinned, her eyes lighting up. "That's great. We'll be partners. You'll see. I'll be a big help."

Swallowing back a prickle of guilt, he forced a smile. "We're here." He swung the sedan into her driveway and switched off the ignition. Studying the house through the windshield, he peered up and down the street. He was pretty sure they hadn't been followed, but the men they were dealing with had shown they'd stop at nothing to get what they wanted. And they wanted McCabe's briefcase. Real bad.

He slid his gun out of his shoulder holster and opened the door. Before he climbed out, he turned back to her. "Do you have your key?"

She nodded and rummaged in her purse and withdrew a key on a small fob.

He stepped out of the vehicle, checked the surroundings, and strode around the front bumper and opened her door. He grabbed her hand. "Let's go. Stay close."

They hurried to the front door. He plucked the key from her, unlocked the door, opened it, and stepped into the dim interior.

For once she did as he asked. He stopped, and she bumped into him, her soft breasts grazing his back. An image of those full breasts with the turgid nipples flashed before him, and blood pooled in his groin.

Focus!

They progressed from room to room, flicking on

lights, checking to ensure the house was empty. The cleaning crew had done their job. The house was as neat and tidy as the first time he'd seen it.

She stayed close. Too close. Her perfume floated in the stale air.

Each step he took, her arms, hips, or breasts brushed against him. The slight contact was enough to fire his senses. He ached to take her in his arms and kiss her. *You're a cop. Act like one.* "Where's the briefcase?"

"In the kitchen." She skimmed past him and headed down the hall.

The enticing sway of her hips heated his blood. *Down, boy.* He followed her into the kitchen and over to the sink. "You hid the briefcase in the kitchen?"

She nodded and crouched to open the cupboard doors under the sink. Shoving aside bottles of cleaning supplies the maintenance crew had replaced, she leaned into the back of the cupboard. The screech of wood against wood filled the room. She sat back on her heels, an aluminum briefcase in her hands.

He made a grab for the briefcase, but she reared back, clutching it to her chest.

"What the hell?" Once again he reached for the briefcase.

She stood and backed away.

He blew out a breath. "Come on, Natasha. We don't have time for games. Give me the briefcase."

Her fingers tightened on the metal case. "How do I know that once I give this to you, you won't go back on your word?"

He ground his teeth. "I could take the briefcase from you. I'm bigger, stronger and"—he lifted the flap

of his jacket and revealed the gun in a leather holster—
"I have this."

Her face paled, but her blue-eyed gaze remained fierce. "You could, but you won't."

He scowled. Of course he would. The briefcase was too important to the case. One way or another, he'd have the damn briefcase.

They glared at each other.

She'd been through a lot with McCabe, but the bastard hadn't crushed her spirit. Suddenly he wanted to be that man, the one who stood up for her, the man she could trust, the one who didn't let her down, who kept his word.

He blew out another long breath. "Okay, you win. Give me the briefcase, and you can work with me on the case."

Her eyes were skeptical, and she didn't budge, her grip tight on the briefcase.

He raised his right hand, palm out, and made a three-finger salute. "Scout's honor."

She arched her eyebrows.

Blowing out a ragged breath, he ground on his molars and caved. "Okay, okay. I promise on my mother's name I'll let you help me." *Man, oh, man, Mike was going to have a field day with this latest development.*

Chapter 20

Five days later, he regretted his decision. Tension ratcheted up to an unbearable level in the far-too-damn-small apartment above Legzz. The incessant beat of the music all day and most of the night, the pulsating purple neon light, the strained smile on Natasha's pale face, coupled with the stilted conversation, drove him over the edge.

The case was at a stalemate. Had been for days. He and his new *partner*, Natasha, had taken McCabe's briefcase to the precinct.

The tech crew had jimmied the lock and returned the briefcase to Chase and Natasha to open.

Chase hadn't known what to expect inside the metal briefcase. His thoughts had run the gamut from illegal drugs, to a prohibited weapon, to bundles of cash. He sure as hell hadn't expected a stolen, jewel-encrusted dagger worth millions.

Not wanting to touch the ancient artifact, he'd called in an art expert from the museum and Natasha, Mike, and Chase had stood around a well-lit table in an interrogation room and watched as Doctor Antoine Fortese, the museum's antiquities expert, unwrapped the dagger.

"Where in Heaven's name would Darien find something like this?" Natasha's voice was breathless.

"If this is what I think it is, this dagger is a very

rare find." Using tweezers and wearing nitrile gloves, Fortese eased the muslin wrapping off the dagger. Sweat beaded his brow as he worked with slow, steady fingers.

A communal inhalation of air filled the room when the dagger was revealed in all its jeweled splendor.

Mike blew out a whistle. "Pretty fancy knife."

Fortese's lip curled. "This is no mere knife, Detective."

Mike gave a mirthless laugh. "You can say that again."

Natasha's shoulder brushed Chase's as she leaned closer to the dagger. "It's beautiful." She pointed at the short, curved blade. "Is that ivory?"

Fortese nodded. "Indeed it is." He lifted the dagger and held it in the palm of his gloved hand. "The hilt is crafted from gold, and look at these. He pointed at the jewels inset in the golden hilt. "These are diamonds. And this is an emerald." He pointed to a red stone. "Here's a ruby." He set the dagger down on the thick velvet cloth he'd draped over the tabletop.

"I'll bet that fancy blade's worth a bundle on the black market." Mike crunched on the pencil stub stuffed between his teeth. "No wonder McCabe didn't want it found."

Fortese picked up a magnifying glass, adjusted the overhead light, and examined the hilt. "Just as I thought. These engravings are lions, a very common motif found in artifacts from Fourth Century BCE in the Middle East."

"Fourth Century what?" Mike rubbed his temples. "Speak English, Doc. I'm getting a headache."

The scientist's lips tightened, his frustration at

dealing with ignorant laymen all too obvious. "BCE, Detective, refers to Before the Common Era, a numbering system used to designate the date of an object. It's from the Julian and Gregorian calendars and refers to the years before the start of this era."

Mike blinked, his eyes glazed.

Dr. Fortese blew out an aggrieved breath. "In other words, Detective, this dagger is more than two thousand years old.

"Holy shit," Mike said. "That old, huh?"

Dr. Fortese set the magnifying glass down and removed his glasses. "Do you have any idea what you have here?"

Chase shook his head. "You're the expert. What's it worth?"

Fortese blew out his lips. "Of course, I can't be certain. A number of factors come into play with rare objects such as this."

"How much?" Mike's gruff voice revealed his impatience.

"Five to six million on the black market, I should think."

A collective gasp settled over the room as everyone inhaled at the same time.

"Six million dollars?" Natasha's voice rose. "Are you telling me I hid something worth six million dollars under my kitchen sink?" She collapsed on a chair and fanned her hand in front of her face.

Chase stared at the stunning dagger. "How the hell did McCabe get his hands on something like this? Is it stolen?"

Fortese rubbed his chin. "I can't be certain, but most likely this dagger was looted from a war-torn, third-world country's museum." He shook his head. *"Thefts like this happen all the time."*

Mike's gaze met Chase's, and Mike grinned. "So, we have McCabe on art theft. That's a start. Now we can bring him in. No way can he hide behind his pack of lawyers after this."

Fortese gathered his tools and packed them into a small, leather case. "Good luck, gentlemen. Please contact me if you find any more treasures."

They'd asked the D.A. for, and received, a warrant for McCabe's arrest. One problem with the plan— McCabe was nowhere to be found. He'd disappeared. Chase's lip curled. Probably cowering in a bolt-hole like the rat he was until the whole mess blew over.

Maybe that's why the bodies were piling up. Whoever McCabe had stolen the dagger from wanted the priceless artifact back. Six million bucks was nothing to sneeze at. Men had been murdered for far less.

They'd uncovered a link between Jonas Waverley and McCabe. On closer examination, they discovered some of the art objects in Waverley's extensive collection didn't have the proper provenance. The prevailing theory was that McCabe supplied Waverley with stolen, priceless artifacts for Waverley's collection. McCabe must have ripped someone off and Waverley got caught in the crossfire and got popped.

His assistant was killed because she saw something she shouldn't have, knew too much, or outlived her usefulness. Someone in Waverley's organization had to be involved. How else would Waverley's murderer have known the security codes for Waverley's building and the location of the security cameras?

They still didn't know who the killer was, and the strain wore on Chase. He grimaced. He hardly recognized the man in the mirror in the morning when he shaved. His face was pale and haggard, his eyes bloodshot, and he'd lost weight. Even worse, his short-tempered impatience made him surly, and he snapped at anyone who dared get too close.

He'd argued with Mike, bickered with the other detectives, and sulked at the captain's impatience with the progress of the investigation.

But Natasha bore the brunt of his ill temper. She was an easy target. She was beside him every minute of the day and down the hall at night. He wasn't proud of the way he acted, but he couldn't stop.

If a break in the stalemated case didn't happen soon, they'd all go crazy.

****

Natasha slammed down her mug, uncaring that tea slopped over the rim onto the table. She had to get out of the apartment. If Chase snapped at her one more time, she'd lose what little restraint she had on her temper.

The man was a veritable curmudgeon. He spent his time on the phone pacing around the tiny apartment, yelling at his colleagues, demanding they find answers. When he wasn't grousing at his beleaguered partner, he bossed her around.

She couldn't survive one more minute of the enforced confinement. Fresh air was what she needed, and exercise. She glanced out the window. Dark clouds lay swollen and heavy with rain, and a strong wind blew newspapers and dried leaves around the gutters in the street below. A storm was on the way. Good. She enjoyed walking on the beach in the wind and rain. Facing a fierce wind head-on and braving the elements would clear her mind.

She changed into jeans and a sweater and donned sturdy walking shoes. Chase would be against her leaving, but she was past the point of caring what he thought. Besides, he'd gone downstairs to the club to meet with a possible informant. Or so he'd said. For all she knew, he was drinking beer and ogling the strippers as they performed their sensuous dances on the spotlighted stage.

She grabbed her coat off the hook and hurried across the living room to the door, anxious to leave before he returned.

Heavy footsteps sounded on the stairs outside the apartment.

Her heart sank, and she froze in mid flight.

The door opened and Chase stood framed in the doorway, his narrow-eyed gaze sweeping over her, taking in her hiking boots and warm coat. "Where do you think you're going?"

She stiffened. Who was he to tell her whether she could leave the apartment or not? She wasn't under arrest. Squaring her shoulders, she stuck out her chin. "I'm going for a walk." She held her breath, waiting for the explosion. No matter what he said, no matter how much he protested, she was doing this.

He nodded. "Okay. I'll go with you."

She blinked. "Okay?"

He grabbed his coat off the back of a chair and shrugged into the soft leather jacket.

She opened her mouth to tell him she wanted to go alone, but victory in one battle was enough. Careful not to brush against him, she marched past him onto the small landing and down the narrow stairs, through the noisy, smoke-filled club to the street outside. The wind whipped her hair in her face, and she shivered and huddled into her coat.

Chase stepped in front of her, blocking her progress, and scanned the street. He nodded, as if satisfied they were unobserved, grasped her hand, and led her across the road to his police-issue sedan. He held the passenger door open.

She climbed inside and buckled her seatbelt.

Leaning into the car, he smoothed windblown strands of hair off her face. "Where are we going?"

"To my favorite place." Her breath hitched in her throat as she breathed in the spicy, pine-forest scent of his aftershave. Their gazes met, and a jolt rushed through her. The moisture in her mouth evaporated.

He backed away, slammed the door closed, strode around to the driver's side, opened the door, and settled behind the wheel. Starting the car, he steered onto the busy street.

Once they arrived at the turnoff to Germanson Point, he drove into the deserted parking lot and turned off the vehicle. "Stay here until I check this place is safe." He slipped out of the car.

His barked order irritated her. She was tired of being told what to do, tired of hiding, tired of being afraid. *Well, to hell with that.* She opened her door and stepped out into the wind and cold. The gale tore at her hair and flattened her coat against her. She faced the wind and breathed deep, sucking in long draughts of fresh, salt-tinged air.

"I told you to stay in the car." His voice carried

over the scream of wind, crash of waves, and screech of gulls.

Ignoring him, she followed the narrow, scrub-lined trail leading to the beach. Blood sang through her veins. She loved storms. Something in the unbridled fury of a raging tempest struck a chord. She'd discovered this deserted stretch of sand a few years ago, and ever since then Germanson Point was her favorite walking spot.

A long finger of rippled sand and waving sea grass stretched into the ocean for several miles. Huge rock outcroppings at either end acted as a barrier and limited access to the beach beyond. The Point was exposed to the ocean and difficult to traverse at high tide, but right now, the tide was low. The crashing seas and howling wind were the ticket to settle her ragged nerves. She glanced over her shoulder.

Chase scrambled along the trail after her, slipping and sliding in the damp sand. His face was red, but whether from anger at her disobeying his orders, or the force of the wind, she couldn't tell. Nor did she care. Not when for the first time in days, she was free.

"Come on." She grinned at him and took off running, exhilaration overtaking her endless days of confinement.

Chapter 21

She loped along the narrow, sandy trail, her long, lean legs leaping the barnacle-covered rocks blocking the entrance, her blonde hair streaming behind her like a golden flag. Her joy at being out of the safe house was infectious, and a weight slipped from his shoulders.

The past days had been a nightmare, the tension in the apartment unbearable. They spoke, and yet said nothing, refusing to speak the one thought on their minds. As if pretending they hadn't made love made the fallacy true. Touching her satiny skin, kissing her sweet lips, her breath mingling with his—He cut off the torrid images. Making love to her had been a mistake, one he wouldn't repeat. *Liar*. The word mocked him on a blast of wind. He couldn't look at her without wanting her.

To make the situation worse, the case had stagnated—not a single break in the past week. He'd worked countless criminal investigations, but never one so dead in the water so early in the investigation. This case had stymied them from the beginning. Not one of the murder scenes had yielded tangible clues. What little evidence they had led to dead ends.

Take the earring they'd found clutched in Henrietta Kinkaid's lifeless hand. The proverbial smoking gun. Not so. There'd been no trace of DNA other than the dead woman's on the earring. The killer must have wiped the small jewel clean before placing the stud in the poor woman's hand.

Even finding the multi-million dollar dagger in McCabe's briefcase hadn't helped. Dr. Fortese reported the ancient dagger had been stolen from a small museum in Yemen several months back. Though McCabe was guilty of possessing illegal contraband, they hadn't arrested him. The slime bucket had disappeared, and so far he'd managed to evade the manhunt out looking for him.

While Chase had been keeping an eye on Natasha, Mike had done the footwork, running down every useless lead. They were no further ahead than they'd been a week ago.

His gut warned him Natasha was in danger. Whoever had tried to blow up her ex, would come after her. The killer would strike again. And when he did, Chase intended to catch the son of a bitch.

Natasha glanced back, her cheeks flushed from the rising gale, her long, blonde curls dancing. She opened her mouth and called something, but the wind snatched her words away. She laughed, displaying a flash of even white teeth.

He staggered as if he'd been punched in the gut.

She laughed again, the musical notes carrying on the wind.

Again a kick deep inside stole his breath, followed by an all-too-familiar surge of excitement. A fierce blast of wind buffeted him, and he stumbled. *You're a damn fool standing here in the middle of a gale mooning over her.*

She clambered up a rocky bluff and vanished over the top.

What the hell? Anyone could be waiting on the

other side of those rocks. With a growl, he leaped into action, racing across the rocky ground toward where he'd last seen her.

He crested the bluff and scanned the beach below. Eyes watering, he squinted into the tempest.

The vivid blue of her coat and her flag of blonde hair caught his eye as she emerged from behind a sand dune.

Relief surged through him. Refusing to make the same mistake twice, he scrambled down the rocks and jogged across the expanse of smooth sand to her side. His chest heaved as he struggled to catch his breath, but he managed to gasp, "What the hell do you think you're doing? I told you to stay with me."

The light in her eyes faded, and he regretted his harsh words. He wasn't mad at her. He was angry with himself for forgetting the principles of his job, but he hadn't meant to take his anger out on her. In an effort to make up for his sharp rebuke, he forced a smile. "This is a beautiful spot. No wonder you like walking here."

Her smile built until she grinned, and her sapphire eyes blazed. "I knew you'd like the Point." She grabbed his hand and tugged. "Come on, I've something I want to show you."

The second her small hand grazed his, the kick in his gut once again felled him. He glanced at her excited face and soft creamy skin, and for the second time in his life, he ignored his gut and acted on his heart's desire and stumbled after her.

****

She'd never felt more alive. Wonderful to be out of the stuffy, cramped apartment. The exercise, combined with the fresh air, was a reprieve from the unbearable tension of the past days.

Chase explored the shoreline, picking up beach rocks and hurling them into the raging ocean. A wave crashed onto shore, splattering his pants with seawater. The wind tore at his hair. The harsh light of the gray day outlined the rugged lines of his face. As if sensing her gaze on his, he turned and grinned, a lone dimple dancing in his cheek.

Her heart lurched, and she sucked in a breath.

He loped across the sand and clasped her hand in his. "The storm's getting worse. We should head back before the rain starts."

A shock of awareness surged through her at the contact of his warm, callused palm against hers. She barely heard him as she struggled to come to terms with the sensations his touch evoked.

"Natasha, did you hear me? We should leave."

Tearing her gaze from their clasped hands, she took a deep breath and studied the beach. The sky had darkened as angry clouds massed overhead. Immense rollers crashed onto shore like wild horses driven by the keening wind.

He was right. They should leave, but she wasn't ready to return to their earlier stilted awkwardness, and she had one more place to show him. "Come on." She tugged on his hand. What was a little rain and wind compared to a few more minutes of this easy intimacy? "There's a cove beyond those rocks." She pointed further along the beach where a line of dark rocks gleamed through the mist. "You can't come to Germanson Point without seeing the cove."

He hesitated, scanning the massing dark clouds.

She smiled her most winning grin. "Please?"

"Okay, but we'll have to be quick." He squinted into the rising wind. "This storm looks like it's going to be a doozy."

Hand in hand, they scrambled along the beach, pursued by the freshening squall.

They clambered over a rock outcropping and dropped down into a small, sandy cove protected on two sides by a towering pile of gray rocks covered with mussels, barnacles, periwinkles, and limpets. The rock barricade jutted into the roiling ocean, and the air was several degrees warmer in the lee of the sheltering rocks. Massive breakers crashed onto shore, but without the howling wind, the tiny cove was a welcome respite from the fury of the oncoming storm.

"What do you think?" She waved her arms at the secluded cove.

"Nice." His smile widened. He wasn't admiring the pristine cotton candy sand, or the stark, jagged rocks. He watched her, his green, gold-flecked eyes burning with fire. "Very nice."

She gulped as a rush of heat raced up her neck and flooded her face.

"You're so beautiful."

His husky voice washed over her like a warm bath. Her knees quivered, and she leaned toward him as if drawn to a magnet, and slipped into his welcoming arms. The peaceful cove and the distant crash of waves disappeared as his lips sought hers. His scent, his warmth, his hard body surrounded her. She moaned, sinking deeper under his spell, helpless, caught in something beyond her control.

The kiss deepened as his hands roamed, seeking and finding the buttons on her coat.

She shuddered with rising desire. Her fingers covered his, helping him with her buttons. First one, and then another, until her coat opened, revealing her soft, pink sweater.

He smoothed his hands under her sweater, caressing flesh, raising goose bumps in his path.

A fierceness seized her, and she kissed him again, reveling in his taste and the sensations his touch aroused.

A loud crack rent the air.

He jerked back and shoved her to the ground.

Her scream of surprise was cut off as he threw himself over her, the force of his body knocking the wind out of her. Gasping, fighting for breath, she shoved against his crushing weight. "What are you doing? Let me up."

"Stay down!

"This isn't funny, Chase. Let me up. I can't breathe." She shoved the hard wall of his chest.

"Stop!"

She froze, stunned by his harsh tone. "Wha…what is it? What's wrong?"

"Keep down. Someone's shooting at us."

"What? Are you sure?"

Another loud crack resonated in the small cove. A nearby rock splintered.

She cringed, trying to sink into the soft sand. Someone was shooting. She'd never forget the terrifying sound. Was the man with the blond hair shooting at them? Or someone else? Another loud retort, and a spray of sand scored her face.

"We can't stay here. We're too exposed. We have to find cover."

A shudder rippled along her spine. "Who—?"

He cut her off. "When I tell you, I want you to run toward the rocks. Squeeze as close to them as you can and stay hidden until I tell you to move." He grabbed her shoulders, his fingers bruising through her rumpled clothing. "Do you understand?"

She nodded, fear making her mute.

"Okay, then…now! Go!"

In one motion, he rolled off her and sent her stumbling to her feet.

She sprinted toward the wall of rock, at any second expecting the burning pain of a bullet. A popping sound and a spray of sand off to her left had her digging her legs deeper into the sand, fighting for leverage, running faster. Skidding to a halt, she flattened against the cold solidness of the bluff.

She spotted an indentation in the rock a few feet away. Pressing her back against the hard stone, she slid along the rock face, ignoring the sharp scrape of crustaceans, and squeezed into the tight niche.

She glanced at Chase, expecting to see him running toward her, seeking the cover of the rocks, but he remained where she'd left him, crouched, gun in hand, his body exposed.

Fresh terror overtook her.

An expectant hush hung over the cove. The howl of wind quieted, the crashing of waves muted by the buffering wall of rocks.

She held her breath, waiting for the next shot, praying Chase would be safe, praying she wouldn't lose the love of her life.

He lurched to his feet and fired a shot at the bluff above her temporary refuge. Then he bent low, and weaving back and forth, he sprinted toward her.

She dragged him into the fissure and wrapped her arms around him. "Thank God you're okay. What were you thinking? You could have been killed."

He returned her embrace for a brief second, but then thrust her away, his face grim. "I have to find the shooter." His hazel eyes flashed steel. "Stay here. I'm going after him."

She grabbed his arm, gripping him tighter. "Don't go."

His eyes softened to gold. "Don't worry, you'll be safe here." He drew out his cell phone. "Call 911." He thrust the phone in her hand.

Tears blurred her vision. "Please don't go. I couldn't stand if—"

Crushing his mouth to hers, he silenced her with a scorching kiss. He ripped his mouth from hers and stepped out of the small hollow. Crouching low, he raced along the lee of the rocks and clambered up the face.

A shot rang out, followed by a second, louder pop.

With shaking hands, she dialed 911.

Chapter 22

Hot liquid slopped over her hand as another bone-shaking shiver rattled through her. In spite of the blanket wrapped around her shoulders and the steaming cup of coffee in her hand, Natasha doubted she'd ever be warm again.

Rain pelted the windshield, and wind buffeted the vehicle. The storm had broken with a fury seconds after Chase had raced after the shooter. She'd flattened her body into the overhang, but the pounding rain had slanted in and drenched her hair, soaking through her coat and clothes to her skin. She'd closed her eyes and prayed for help to arrive, prayed Chase was safe.

After an eternity, a uniformed police officer, clad in a yellow rain slicker, had materialized like a phantom out of the storm and escorted her to a waiting police cruiser. He'd offered her the wool blanket and shoved the hot coffee into her shaking hands before joining his fellow officers in the storm.

In spite of the rain streaming against the outer windshield and the condensation on the inside glass, she made out the flashing red and blue emergency lights of three police cars and the dark shapes of cops swarming over the rocks and along the beach, scouring for evidence left by the shooter.

Using a corner of the blanket, she wiped the moisture off the windshield. Chase stood amid a small group of uniformed officers and men in yellow rain slickers, his legs braced against the rain attacking him in horizontal sheets. His coat hung on him in a sodden, misshapen mass. Water streamed off his dark hair and dripped into his eyes. His mouth was a thin, hard line.

The car door flew open, and a gust of wind and rain blasted in as Detective Podborski lowered his bulk into the seat behind the wheel. He slammed the door shut, blocking out the tempest. Rainwater dripped off his yellow raincoat and pooled on the floor mat. He tugged out a handkerchief from his pocket and wiped the rain from his face. "Man, what a storm. What in blue blazes were the two of you doing in this godforsaken place on a day like this?"

"We...I had to get out of the apartment," she offered lamely.

His grizzled brows quirked. "Chase is a trained professional. He should have noticed the gunman long before you two became sitting targets. What in the hell was he doing?"

She blushed at the probing intensity in his intelligent blue eyes. What could she say? Chase had been distracted. Her face flamed as she recalled what they'd been doing when the first shots were fired.

An uneasy silence settled between them as the rain pounded on the roof of the car.

She licked her dry lips. "Did you find the person who shot at us?"

"He got away." He blew out a breath. "We followed his tracks to the other side of the Point. He had his vehicle parked on an old fire road ready for a quick getaway." He rubbed his hands together. "From the looks of things, the attacker stalked you guys for a while before he started shooting."

She shuddered at the frightening image of the gunman spying on them, waiting for the opportunity to kill. "Do...do you think it was the same man who killed Darien's bodyguards and shot at me?"

His shoulders lifted in a half shrug. "Don't know yet, but we'll find him. Don't you worry." He patted her knee. "We're pretty good at our job." Strapping on his seatbelt, he inserted a key in the ignition, started the car, shifted the cruiser into Drive, and steered the vehicle across the muddy parking lot toward the exit.

She sat up with a start. "Where are we going?"

"I'm taking you back to the safe house."

"What about Chase?"

The creases between his brows deepened. "He's a big boy. He can take care of himself."

"But—"

"He has to file a report about this incident at the precinct." He patted her knee again. "Don't worry, I'll keep you safe. I may look ancient, but I can still handle a gun like the best of them."

His words washed over her in a blur as the reality of what happened sank in. She bit her bottom lip to stop the trembling. She hadn't believed Chase when he'd warned her someone wanted to harm her. She'd just wanted to escape the cloying atmosphere in the apartment. Her selfishness had nearly gotten him killed.

"Ms. Hartford, are you okay?"

Blinking, struggling to control her emotions, she managed to stammer, "I...I'm just...just cold."

"You've been through a frightening experience."

She bit back a sour laugh. She was frightened, all right. Terrified. But not because once again someone had shot at her. That was terrifying enough, but her new reality was worse. Much worse. She was in love with Chase. Her heart skipped a beat.

In love with Detective Chase Brandon.

Oh my.

****

She opened her eyes, going from sleep to wide-awake in a single heartbeat. The room was dark, but light from the streetlight on the road below seeped through the gauzy, pink curtains. Rain pelted the bedroom window hard enough to drown out the keening of the wind and the incessant thumping of rock and roll music.

Scrubbing her hands over her face, she struggled to clear the fuzziness from her brain. Glancing at the bedside clock, she noted the time and blinked. Midnight.

When Detective Podborski had escorted her back to the tiny apartment above Leggz, she'd followed him through the raucous strip club crowd and up the narrow stairs. She'd staggered down the short hall to the bedroom, changed out of her wet clothes, and collapsed on the massive bed, falling asleep the second her head hit the satin-covered pillow.

But now she was awake, and she was thirsty. Climbing out of bed, she tugged on jeans and a top and opened the bedroom door. The hall was dark, but a dim light shone from the living room. She stepped into the hall, but paused at the rumble of angry male voices.

"What in the hell were you thinking?" Chase's partner's deep baritone was raised in anger. "Christ, man, you aren't a damn rookie. You know better."

Chase's response was lost in a gust of wind

blasting the front of the small building and rattling the windowpanes.

But no amount of storm drowned out Detective Podborski's fury. "Come on, man, don't give me that crap."

Not wanting to eavesdrop on a private conversation, she tiptoed back into the bedroom, but halted at the older detective's next words.

"I don't give a damn. You almost got her killed today. Hell, you almost got both of you killed."

Guilt overwhelmed her. Chase's partner was upset because Chase had let her go to Germanson Point. She was the one who'd insisted. Detective Podborski should be reading her the riot act, not Chase.

A chair clattered on the floor as if someone had shot up, knocking it over. "Don't you think I know?" Chase's anguished voice tugged at her heart. "Christ, it's all I can think about."

"Too bad you weren't focused on the job when the shooter snuck up on you." Detective Podborski's voice lost some anger, and she strained to hear his next words. "Hell, man, this isn't like you to let your defenses down, especially when you're on a case. What the hell's going on with you?"

She edged into the hall and tiptoed closer to the living room, careful to keep to the shadows.

Chase spoke in a harsh whisper, his voice ragged, laced with exhaustion. "I don't fucking know."

"Well, you damn well better figure it out and soon before you get her killed and yourself as well, in the bargain." Ice cubes clinked in a glass. "You're lucky I covered for you with the captain. He'd fire your ass if he knew what you've done."

"I know." Chase's hoarse voice cracked "You don't have to cover for me anymore, Mike. I'll hand in my badge when this is over."

The springs on the couch squeaked as someone stood, and she spun and fled down the hall. Bad enough Chase had to suffer his partner's dressing-down; worse if he knew she'd been listening.

Once in the bedroom, she sat on the bed and ruminated over what she'd heard. Detective Podborski blamed Chase for what happened at Germanson Point. Guilt burned like a sizzling coal in her belly. It was her fault their lives had been in danger. She'd been desperate to get out of the safe house. She took Chase to Germanson Point and led him to the tiny cove where the shooter had attacked.

Bile rose in her throat as images of what had happened in the cove assailed her. No sooner had they escaped the full fury of the wind than they were in each other's arms, too intent on their rising passion to pay any attention to their surroundings. A battalion of gunmen could have driven up in tanks, and they wouldn't have noticed. It was a miracle neither of them had been hurt, let alone killed. They'd been sitting ducks for anyone watching from the rocks above.

Chase was a hero. He'd thrown his body on top of hers and remained in the open, protecting her retreat to the protection of the rock bluff. He drew the gunman's fire while she scurried to safety. A sob tore at her throat, and she jammed her hand over her mouth to stifle the sound.

And now he was in trouble. She winced as she recalled Detective Podborski's scathing accusations. Chase hadn't defended himself. He'd taken the cutting insults the older detective had thrown at him and said nothing in his own defense.

He was in trouble with his partner and his captain. He said he'd quit the force. Her heart lurched. She couldn't let him. He loved being a cop. She had to do something to make this right. He shouldn't be punished for her actions.

Chapter 23

Not until the gray light of dawn filtered through the curtains did she figure out a plan. She'd promised Chase she wouldn't sneak out again.

So much for keeping her word.

He'd be furious, but leaving was the right thing to do; the only way she could repair the damage she'd caused and make things right. She climbed out of bed and dressed.

She'd go. Now. Before she had second thoughts.

Strapping her purse across her shoulder and carrying her shoes, she crept across the room on sock feet. After opening the door, she peered into the dark hall. The apartment was silent. Even the constant thump of music had stilled. She tiptoed down the hall.

Chase slept on the sofa, huddled under a thick blanket.

Holding her breath, she padded across the room, slid the deadbolt, and opened the front door. With a last glance at Chase's sleeping form, she eased onto the landing and closed the door behind her.

She crept down the narrow stairs and slipped into the silent club. A thick pall of stale smoke, spilled beer, and sweat permeated the air, and she wrinkled her nose. The light emanating from the red exit sign above the door lit her way, and she slid on her shoes and hurried across the room to the door. Huddling into her jacket, she tugged the hood over her head and stepped outside.

She scanned the empty street. No one loitered in recessed doorways; no cars were parked on the street with the drivers sitting inside watching the club. Heaving a breath, she stole off into the early morning, careful to keep to the shadows. Jogging down the sidewalk, she crossed the street when she reached the corner and traveled six more blocks before she stopped at a busy bus stop.

The morning rush hour had begun, and traffic was piling up. By taking the bus, she hoped to blend in with the morning commuters. Most passengers were too sleepy and too wrapped up in their cell phones to pay her any attention.

She stayed on the bus, taking note of each glance cast her way and each new passenger, until she reached the downtown core and transferred to another bus that took her across the city. From the west side of town, she hailed a taxi and directed the driver to take her to a major hotel near the airport.

She was certain she hadn't been followed, but the man who'd shot at her and Chase had to have been watching the safe house yesterday and followed them to Germanson Point. Since the attack had failed, she assumed he'd try again.

Careful to keep the hood of her coat pulled low over her face, she boarded the crowded airport bus and squeezed into a seat beside an overweight woman with an atrocious case of body odor. Trying to breathe through her mouth she let her thoughts roam to the safe house. By now, Chase would be awake.

Not wanting him to panic and think she'd been abducted, she'd left him a note explaining her disappearance. She grimaced as she pictured how his brow would furrow and his hazel eyes blaze when he read what she'd written.

Her subterfuge was worth inciting his anger. By the time she next saw him, she hoped to have found the person responsible for the attacks. He'd be so happy she'd solved the case his anger would be forgotten.

Maybe.

"Where y'all off to?"

The nasal voice cut through her thoughts, and an elbow nudged her in the side. She turned and met the bright gaze of the woman on the seat beside her.

"Hey, y'all right?" The woman's eyes were wide with curiosity. "I'm headin' for Los Angeles. Got a flight booked and everything." Her gray curls bounced around her full, round face. "Off to see my gran' kids, all four of 'em, the little darlin's. Haven't seen 'em for a good long time. Lord love 'em, I bet they're tall as oaks now."

Natasha let the woman drone on, not really listening to what she said, but nodding every now and then as if she were. Her mind was on other, more urgent matters. She had to find Darien. He'd disappeared, but he hadn't fled the country. The police had found his passport when they searched his house. Besides, he wouldn't go far, not when he thought she still had his briefcase.

That was the glitch in her plan…if Darien found out the police had his dagger, he'd vanish, and she'd never find him. As long as he believed she possessed the briefcase, she had a chance. But first she had to find a safe place to stay while she contacted him.

The bus stopped at the departure zone at the

airport, and the passengers climbed off, retrieved their luggage, and trudged into the bustling airport. She waved goodbye to her chatty seatmate and hurried along the concourse to the airport arrivals area. Flagging down a taxi, she headed back into town, hoping her circuitous route had thrown off anyone following her.

The driver let her off at a bus stop on the side of a busy road, and she walked three blocks to the Blue Bay Motel, a small roadside inn located in an industrial section of town beside a major freeway leading from the airport to downtown. It was the type of motel frequented by tourists and businessmen traveling on a tight budget.

The motel wasn't much, but the manager didn't ask prying questions when she registered under an assumed name and paid cash. She inserted the key card in the lock and stepped into the dark room. The stench of stale smoke hung in the air, and she grimaced. So much for requesting a non-smoking room.

Stepping inside, she closed the door behind her, switched on the light, and locked the door. The lurid brightness of the orange-and-yellow floral bedspread draping the double bed bruised her tired eyes. Matching curtains covered the window. Cheap, paint-by-number paintings of mountain scenery were nailed to the beige walls, adding to the desolate décor. The carpet was an unrecognizable shade of gray and had seen better days. A battered desk with a small, flat-screen television on top of the scratched surface sat against the far wall facing the bed. A door led into a tiny bathroom. In spite of the air of decay, the room was clean and there were plenty of towels.

She shrugged out of her coat, hung it on a hook beside the door, and kicked off her shoes. Removing her jeans, sweater, bra, and underwear, she folded them and placed the stack of clothing on the desk. Stepping into the bathroom, she climbed into the tub and twisted the tap on the shower. Hot water gushed out of the tap, sending a welcome plume of steam into the chilly air.

Refreshed, she turned off the shower, grabbed a towel from the rack, and dried off. Her wet hair hung in tangled ropes to her shoulders. She wrapped the towel around her, snugged the ends between her breasts, and stepped into the bedroom.

A man lounged on the bed.

She screamed and stumbled backward, clutching at the towel.

****

"Well, well, well. So this is where you ran off to." In spite of his anger, Chase couldn't help but stare as the white terrycloth towel slipped, exposing the creamy tops of her plump breasts. He shouldn't look. A gentleman wouldn't. But then again, he was no gentleman. That was for damn sure.

"You?" Two bright patches of red blossomed on her cheeks as she grabbed at the drooping towel and dragged it up to her neck. "What are you doing here?"

His mouth dried as he looked his fill. *Nice legs. Long, lean, and tanned, just the way he liked them.* The torrid thoughts flashed through his brain before he remembered why he was here. "I've been on your tail since you snuck out of the club. You should be quieter when you break a promise."

He smirked at the stunned expression on her face. Once again his gaze dipped, and he gulped. Her smooth, creamy skin was flushed and damp from her shower. She was naked beneath the towel. That was obvious. He shifted on the bed, his jeans suddenly too tight. Rising, his gaze roving over her near-naked body again and again, he stepped toward her as if drawn by an irresistible force.

She paled and backed away.

Lust fled, replaced by his earlier fury. "Get dressed. We have to talk."

Her spine stiffened, and she scuttled back into the bathroom and slammed the door.

He scowled and rubbed the knot in the back of his neck. She wasn't the first beautiful woman he'd worked with, but she was the first who'd driven him to such distraction he'd cast aside his integrity and professionalism and broken the rules. Broken them? Hell, he'd shattered them.

There were no excuses for his behavior. He hadn't defended himself against Mike's accusations, even though every reproachful word had struck like a knife to his gut. He meant what he'd said. Once this case was solved, he'd turn in his badge and quit.

For as long as he could remember, he'd wanted to be a cop. His father had been one, and his father before him. Getting accepted into the academy had been the easy part. He'd sailed through cadet training, finishing at the top of his class. The hard part had come once he graduated and earned the right to wear the blue uniform and carry the shiny badge.

Once out on the streets, a myriad of temptations assailed him, countless opportunities to cut corners, to give some lowlife a break and accept a payback for his efforts. Some of his fellow officers succumbed. Some got caught and were drummed out of the force.

Many had not.

He hadn't wanted to be one of those who bent the law. The one tenet he held firm, the belief that made the pain and suffering he witnessed every day on the streets bearable, was his absolute confidence in the sanctity of the badge he carried.

For twelve years he'd held true to that belief. Until now. His mistakes the past few days had nearly cost Natasha her life. For that, he wouldn't forgive himself. He didn't deserve to be a cop.

Not anymore.

He'd forfeited the right the second he broke protocol and made love to Natasha Hartford. And then she'd run away.

He'd awakened to the sound of the door closing in the small apartment and fury, fueled by a deep-seated hurt, raged. She'd left. Again. Didn't she realize the danger? The safest place for her was the apartment above Leggz.

With him.

His first reaction had been to stop her. But what if he was wrong? What if she was involved in the recent murders and the attack on her ex-husband? She had more reasons than anyone to harm McCabe. Motive was evident, all right. Plenty of motive.

Sickness roiled in his gut. Had she deceived him all this time? Maybe, but he refused to allow his personal emotions to cloud his judgment. He'd done enough of that. So he let her think she'd escaped, and he'd followed her.

Her attempts at losing anyone tailing her were pathetic. The fact she didn't notice he was on her tail added to his fury. She was an easy target. Too easy. Fortunately for both of them, no one had been waiting outside the strip club, and no one, except him, had followed her.

He'd been surprised when she stopped at this cheap motel and disappeared into one of the rooms on the second floor. Within minutes, he'd sprinted up the stairs, picked the flimsy lock, and broken into her room. He'd settled back on the bed, his anger simmering as he waited for her to finish her shower.

And now he waited…again. What the hell was taking her so long? He glanced at his watch. She'd been in the bathroom fifteen minutes. How long did it take to get dressed?

He jumped to his feet and paced across the floor. Then he spotted the clothes folded in a neat pile on the desktop. A white, lacy bra peeked out from under a pair of faded jeans and a blue sweater. Ignoring the heated image of her cowering naked in the bathroom, he gathered the clothes and knocked on the bathroom door.

"What?" Her voice was muffled.

He knocked again.

The door opened a sliver, and she peeked through the crack. "What is it?"

He held up the clothes. "Looking for these?"

Her face flushed, and she snatched the clothes out of his hands and slammed the door.

He couldn't help chuckling. Backing up several steps, he faced the door, arms crossed over his chest, stern expression in place, and waited.

Five minutes later, the door opened, and she stepped out, her face shiny and free of makeup, her eyes wide and luminous. Her snug-fitting jeans and tight blue sweater didn't hide her soft curves any more than the skimpy towel had.

His mouth dried, and his heartbeat kicked up a notch.

She didn't look at him, but stood before him, hands at her sides like a penitent child awaiting punishment.

He grimaced at the twinge of guilt cramping his gut over the way he'd scolded her, but then he recalled her deceit, and he glared. "You promised you wouldn't leave. I trusted you. I guess your word doesn't mean shit. Tell me, what else are you lying about?"

She clasped her hands in front of her. Her lower lip trembled.

His resolve weakened, and he opened his mouth to apologize, but stopped before he made a complete fool of himself. He'd nearly gotten her killed by letting his guard down; he wouldn't make the same mistake again.

He was a cop, for God's sake. He had a job to do. *So do it!*

Chapter 24

"Well?" He was furious. A fiery gleam flashed in his eyes. The muscles in his arms bulged as if he barely restrained himself from throttling her.

Her first thought was to escape once again to the relative safety of the bathroom with the lock on the door. How many times had Darien scowled with the same anger moments before he lashed out?

She breathed, slow and steady, willing away the numbing terror. "Well, what?" She gripped her hands tighter to hide their trembling.

His gaze drilled into hers, the pupils golden brown with flecks of green. "I want the truth, Natasha. Why the hell are you here?"

Relief he hadn't struck her was so profound she didn't trust her quivering legs to support her, and she stumbled to the sole chair in the room and sank onto the hard surface. "Didn't you see the note I left? I'm not running away from you, I'm…" Her voice broke under his unwavering glower. "I'm trying to protect you."

"Protect me?"

"You were almost killed yesterday."

His face didn't change expression. He didn't blink.

"Don't you get it? If I hadn't demanded we go to the Point, nothing would have happened, and you wouldn't be in trouble."

"You overheard Mike and me talking, didn't you?"

He was silent for several heartbeats. "The attack wasn't your fault. I knew what was at risk when I let you leave the safe house."

"But—"

"Forget it." He waved her concerns aside.

She studied the rigid lines on his grim face. "How did you find me?"

"I followed you. I was curious to see what you were up to."

"So you really don't trust me."

He shrugged, and she read the truth in his eyes.

A rush of outrage, as hot and heady as a wildfire, flashed through her. "You've never trusted me, have you? Not even after we…after what happened between us." In spite of her anger, tears stung her eyes.

He spread his hands in front of him. "Look, I'm sorry, but what do you expect? The second my back was turned you snuck out of the safe house."

"Believe what you want, but I'm here to find out who murdered those people."

He sniggered. "The entire Port Hardesty Police Force can't solve this case, but you're going to? What's your plan?" He sat down on the edge of the bed and crossed his arms over his chest. "Come on. Fill me in. I know I'm gonna love this."

Her face flushed. "I'm going to talk to Darien. He knows more than he's saying."

His snort of laughter filled the room. "Don't you think you've forgotten one little flaw in your brilliant plan?"

She studied the painting above the television set—a log cabin nestled on the side of a mountain, surrounded by a thick forest. The brushstrokes were awkward, the artist unskilled, but anything was better than looking at him and seeing the ridicule on his handsome face.

"Have you forgotten McCabe's missing?"

She whirled around. "Of course I haven't." The words were a shout. She clamped her mouth shut, her chest heaving as she fought to restrain her fury. "You really don't think much of me, do you?"

The smile faded, and he flinched as if she'd struck him. "You're wrong." His voice was raw. "I think of you too damn much." He lunged to his feet and stormed out of the motel room. The door slammed behind him with such force, the paintings on the walls rattled. His footsteps thudded on the landing outside the room.

I think of you too damn much. His cryptic words echoed in the small, stuffy room, reverberating from one beige wall to the other. Tears stung her eyes. *I think of you too damn much.*

Her tears had dried, and her eyes were raw and scratchy when a knock sounded on the motel room door.

"Open the door, Natasha. It's me."

"Chase?" She gripped the edge of the chair, her heart racing. Staggering to her feet, she stumbled over to the door, opened it, and peeked outside.

Chase stood on the dimly lit landing, a sheepish grin on his face. He held up two paper bags. "I bring a peace offering."

The delicious smell of fried onions and melted cheese wafted into the tiny room. Her stomach growled, and in spite of her misgivings, she heard herself say, "Come in."

The tense lines striping his forehead relaxed. Brushing past her, he placed the paper bags on the desk.

He shrugged out of his coat and hung it over the back of the chair. Opening the bags, he lifted out two cheeseburgers and a massive pile of fries, and set the food on two paper plates. "Look, I'm sorry." His jaw worked as he gnawed on his bottom lip. "I shouldn't have said what I did."

She closed the door, but remained still. "I get it. You don't trust me." He opened his mouth, but she held up her hand, stopping him. "Let me finish. I understand. Really, I do. Why should you trust me?" She rubbed her eyes. "I lied to you about Darien coming to see me, I didn't tell you about the briefcase he asked me to hide, and I ran away."

"Twice."

"What?"

"You ran away from me twice."

She bit the inside of her mouth. "Look. This isn't doing any good. Arguing and sniping at each other isn't getting us anywhere. We have to trust each other."

"Agreed."

"What?"

"Agreed. You're right."

She narrowed her eyes and searched his face for artifice. "Do you mean that?"

He threaded his fingers through his hair. "I trust you. Maybe I didn't at first, but I do now."

A weight lifted off her chest, and for the first time since she'd tiptoed out of the safe house she inhaled a deep, cleansing breath. "I think I know how to contact Darien."

His eyes widened. "And you're just now telling me this?"

"I didn't think of it until last night."

He watched her for a long minute. "Let's say you find McCabe, why do you think he's going to tell you anything? We've questioned him, and he hasn't said a word."

"He'll talk to me."

"Why's that?"

"Because he wants his briefcase. If he's in hiding, he needs money. A lot of money."

He stuffed his hands in the front pockets of his jeans. "You may be on to something. We've frozen his bank accounts and stopped his credit cards. He must be desperate for cash. McCabe could survive a hell of a long time on the money he'd get if he sold that dagger."

She nodded, her heart racing. "You see? This'll work. I'll refuse to give him the briefcase until he tells me what he knows."

He rubbed his chin. "Not bad. Not bad at all." He grinned. "It could work."

A flush heated her cheeks. "Okay. Let's get started. I'll—"

"Whoa. Not so fast." He picked up a paper plate of food and held it out. "Let's eat first. I'm starving."

She hesitated, but then she accepted the plate and sat on the corner of the bed. "All right, but we have a lot to do."

He chuckled. "Slow down, Dick Tracy. Even cops have to eat sometimes."

Chapter 25

Chase wiped his mouth with a paper napkin before rolling it into a ball and tossing it in the plastic trashcan beside the desk. His grease-stained, empty paper plate followed.

Natasha stood on the far side of the room, her back toward him, her shoulders hunched. The hand holding the cell phone to her ear was clenched, her knuckles white as she spoke in low, urgent tones.

He couldn't hear what she said, but the stiffness of her body indicated the conversation with McCabe wasn't going well.

Earlier she'd made dozens of calls to McCabe's cell phone, leaving messages saying how important it was for her to speak with him. The jerk had taken his sweet time getting back. The plan was to get McCabe to meet with her and reveal what he knew of the murders if he wanted to retrieve his briefcase with the priceless dagger inside.

Chase leaned over and picked up her plate from the bed and tossed a mound of cold fries and most of the burger he'd given her into the trash.

She ended the call and stumbled over to the bed and sank onto the soft surface. Rubbing her eyes with her fingers, she inhaled several deep breaths. "He knows the police have the briefcase."

He stilled. "How could he know?"

"I don't know, but he's upset." Her voice hitched on a sob. "He…he knows I betrayed him."

Chase slid closer until their thighs brushed. "He can't touch you. I won't let him." His throat tightened. He'd do anything to take away her fear, to erase the dullness in her blue eyes.

She dipped her forehead to his chest and leaned into him.

Tightening his arms around her, he drew her into his embrace. Anger at her shit of an ex-husband surged through him like a raging river. He wanted to kill the bastard.

She sat back and wiped her face with her sleeve. "He said"—she swallowed—"he said terrible things."

Cursing under his breath, he slammed a fist into the mattress, wishing it were McCabe's weasel-like face.

Her body tensed, and she flinched.

Cursing again, he called on all his strength of will to tamp down his outrage, and softened his voice. "Hey, it was worth a try."

"I don't understand how he found out the police have the briefcase." She rubbed the palms of her hands on her thighs.

"I don't know." He sat back. She'd made a good point. How the hell did McCabe know about the briefcase? They'd taken care to keep the discovery of the dagger under wraps. Only a few key people knew. He rubbed the back of his neck in a futile attempt to ease the painful tightness. "Maybe he has someone on the inside." The second he said the words aloud he discarded them. No one would have blabbed. He trusted his men.

She blew out her cheeks. "He wants me to bring

him something from Waverley's office. He says if I do, he'll forgive me and answer my questions."

"Waverley's office? What are you talking about?" He laughed a harsh laugh. "Don't tell me the bastard wants you to replace the dagger he lost with one of Waverley's antiquities. Because that sure as hell isn't happening."

She shook her head. "He wants me to find an envelope."

"An envelope?" Christ, he sounded like a parrot. "What sort of envelope?"

"I don't know, but whatever's in the envelope must be important or he wouldn't ask me to get it."

"The police went over Waverley's office with a fine-toothed comb. Hell, Mike told me he came close to tearing the place apart. He didn't find anything unusual."

Her mouth set in a stubborn line, and a determined glow lit her eyes.

Surging to his feet, he stomped to the far side of the small room. "Forget it. You aren't going anywhere near Waverley's office." He strode over to the chair and jerked his cell phone from his coat pocket. "I'll send Mike and a team of investigators over. They'll run another search, this time for this mysterious envelope. If it's in Waverley's office, they'll find it."

She crossed her arms over her chest. "Please don't do that."

"What are you talking about?" He punched in Mike's number.

She flew across the room and snatched the phone from his hands and tossed it on the bed.

He stared in stunned disbelief. "Why the hell did

you do that?"

She grabbed his hand. "You and I have to do this. Together. Just the two of us. He'll know if you involve other police officers. Please?"

The warmth of her fingers lacing with his seared him as if he'd been burned.

Her blue eyes were fathomless pools.

Under their power, he melted like a chocolate bar left in a hot car. "Okay. Explain this to me."

"Darien wants this envelope. I don't know what's in it, but he sounded desperate." She released his hand and ran her delicate fingers through the shiny strands of her hair. "If we find the envelope, he'll come out of hiding to get it. In exchange, he promised he'd tell me who's behind the murders." She met his gaze. "Isn't that what we want?"

He rolled his shoulders. *Damn. She was right.* McCabe was the key to this whole mess. If they could get him to talk, they might be able to solve the case. "How do you plan on finding this particular envelope? Waverley's office must have hundreds of envelopes."

"We won't know until we try."

"There's a big hitch in your plan." A wave of relief blasted him. They wouldn't be able to follow through on her crazy idea.

"What's that?"

"I don't have access to Waverley's building. We released the crime scene a week ago. There's no way we can get inside."

"We don't need a key. Darien told me a secret way to enter the building and get into Waverley's office."

His brows arched. "Really? That's interesting." McCabe knew of a secret entrance into Waverley's office? Is that how the killer gained access to the building without being seen? Had they been wrong all this time? Was McCabe the murderer?

"So are we good now? Can we go and look for this envelope?" Her body vibrated with rising excitement.

A sense of impending doom blasted him. *Man, oh, man, was he in trouble.* Fishing out his car keys from his coat pocket, he turned toward the door and spoke the words that guaranteed the end of his career, "Okay, let's get this done."

She hesitated. "Are you going to call your partner at the precinct?"

"Mike wouldn't understand." His gut tightened at his understatement. Mike would be furious when he found out what Chase was up to. Breaking and entering, interfering with a crime scene, consorting with a wanted suspect, and obstruction of justice were just a few of the laws he was about to break.

If he had any doubts regarding his future career on the force, his next actions would seal his fate. After tonight's shenanigans, even if they solved the case, his career as a police detective was flushed down the toilet.

****

Puffing, Natasha climbed the last step in the metal stairwell. She used her small penlight to sweep the thick darkness. Unpainted gyp rock walls covered both sides of the narrow hallway extending into the gloom. The cement floor was covered with a thick layer of dust broken by the scuff of footprints. A stale, musty smell filled the air.

A large hand settled against her back, and Chase's comforting masculine scent subdued the sour stench. His warm breath blew over her as his voice husked in her ear. "This is the right floor. If McCabe told the truth, the hidden door panel should be down the hall."

"Darien said the panel wouldn't be easy to see." She inched ahead, setting one cautious foot in front of the other.

When they'd first entered the building by the small, recessed door in the back of the office building hidden behind the dumpsters, they'd passed two security guards patrolling the floors below. Other than that, the office building appeared deserted, but they couldn't risk getting caught. Chase had gone along with her plan, but she was under no illusions as to the consequences he'd face if they were caught sneaking into Waverley's building.

So far, everything was as Darien had described. He'd given her the passcode for the building's exterior back door and told her where the entry panel to the hidden staircase was located.

What sort of illicit activities had Waverley been up to? No normal businessman required a secret entrance and hidden stairwell to access his office.

Twenty-nine, thirty, thirty-one, thirty-two steps.

She halted and shone the light on the wall on her left. A small indentation with a metal ring in the center painted the same color as the gyp rock was at waist height. She ran her hand over the ring and pressed the button.

A portion of the wall slid open, revealing Waverley's luxurious office. Ambient light from the street below streamed in through the large glass windows on the far wall and illuminated the elegant office furniture and Waverley's collection of antiquities.

She stepped through the opening onto the plush, cream-colored carpet.

Chase motioned for her to wait and walked on silent feet across the room to the door leading to the receptionist's desk and the outer lobby. He edged the door open and slipped out. He was back in seconds and returned to her side. "It's okay." His voice was hushed. "The guards must be on another floor. But let's be quick. We don't want to get caught."

Chase had explained that since Waverley's murder, his offices had remained closed. The employees, except the security guards, were on an extended break as the lawyers determined what would happen to his estate.

She shone her light and studied the room. Nothing had changed since she was last there. The extensive collection of priceless art objects was displayed either in glass cases or set out on the antique wooden tables. Original oil paintings hung on the walls.

Her gaze lit on the jagged pieces of the wood carving she'd broken, and she grimaced, guilt flooding her. Only a short time ago she'd been excited at the prospect of meeting the great Jonas Waverley and securing a position as book illustrator in his company. Then she'd broken the carving, and Chase had appeared and told her about Waverley's murder.

Chase's suspicious scowl had made her so nervous she'd barely been able to string together two coherent thoughts. He'd accused her of being involved in Waverley's murder, and now he trusted her enough to put his career on the line. And she... She gulped. Well, she loved him. Really loved him.

"Here. Put these on." He handed her a pair of blue vinyl gloves.

"What are these for?"

He shoved his hands into his own gloves. "In case we find anything. We can't risk contaminating evidence with our fingerprints." Hands covered, reminding her of a doctor about to perform surgery, he nodded. "Let's get started." He placed his hand on the small of her back and nudged her onward. "The security guards will be checking this floor soon." He arched a dark brow. "I don't suppose McCabe told you where this so-called envelope was hidden?"

She slipped on the gloves. "No such luck. We're going to have to search the entire office."

"That's what I was afraid of." He pointed across the room. "We found a safe hidden behind that painting, but the safe contained publishing business papers and author contracts. I don't remember any mention of a special envelope."

He blew out a breath and crossed to Waverley's desk. "I'll look here. Why don't you check the area by the exercise equipment?" He used his flashlight to point toward a corner of the large office where a treadmill stood on the floor in front of a large, flat screen television mounted on the wall.

She made her way across the room to the state-of-the-art treadmill. The front console of the exercise machine possessed every possible feature. Rows of dials and buttons resembled the cockpit of a fighter jet. She slid a glance at Chase.

He was on his hands and knees examining the underside of a drawer from Waverley's desk, an expression of intense concentration on his handsome face. As if sensing her watching him, he glanced up and grinned, his white teeth flashing.

Warmth flared deep in her belly and spread throughout her body like molten fire. Her fingers and toes tingled. A frisson of awareness electrified the air.

He grinned again and turned back to his inspection of Waverley's desk. Crouching lower, he reached inside the desk. A puzzled look crossed his face. A faint click filled the silence. "Well, well, well, look what I found."

"What is it?" She hurried over. "Did you find the envelope?"

He shone the beam of his flashlight under the desk in the space left by the missing bottom drawer to a small plastic switch. He nodded at a discreet security camera set in the ceiling above the desk, its lens pointed at the visitor chairs arranged before the desk.

A tiny red light flashed.

"Watch this." He flicked the switch on the drawer, and the light on the camera went dark. He flipped the switch again, and the red light blinked to life.

"I don't understand."

"How the hell didn't we find this switch before? Mike said he checked the desk." He blew out a breath. "This explains how the killer was able to enter Waverley's office and make his way to his assistant's office undetected. The assailant knew about the secret passage. Once he broke into the office, he switched off the security cameras, made his way down the hall to Henrietta Kinkaid's office and shot Waverley."

"This switch turns off all the cameras on this floor?"

"That's what I figure." His face broke into a grin. "Looks like we're finally getting somewhere in this damn case."

She blinked, dazzled by the power of his smile.

264

"That's good, real good." Desperate to kiss him, but knowing it was wrong, she backed away. "I guess we'd better keep looking for the envelope." She smacked into the treadmill and stumbled. Her face flamed.

The corners of his eyes crinkled. "Yeah, I guess we'd better."

She hid her burning face behind a fall of hair, and forced her attention to the treadmill. The base was unusual, wide enough for two people to run side by side. The tracks of the treadmills at the gym she trained on three times a week were narrower, allowing room for the placement of one foot in front of the other. This machine was different.

Stepping onto the track, she studied the control panel and pushed a large green, glowing button.

A slight whirring emanated from the motor, and a row of buttons, dials, and gauges lit up. Start scrolled across the LED screen.

She poked the green button again.

The rumbling increased to a hum as the machine revved to life, and the tread advanced.

She yelped and grabbed the handrails and broke into a jog as the rubberized belt picked up speed. In seconds she was sprinting full out as the belt revolved faster and faster.

Chase slapped a hand on a glowing red button, and the thrum of the motor ceased, the tread slowing to a stop. Lifting her off the machine in one smooth motion, he set her on her feet on the carpet, but didn't release her. "What the hell are you doing? This isn't the time to get some exercise."

She opened her mouth to defend herself, but stopped. A narrow metal drawer protruded from the wide base of the treadmill. Freeing herself from his arms, she crouched before the open compartment. "What's this?"

He knelt on the floor beside her and shone the beam of his flashlight on the small, open compartment set within the base of the treadmill. A thick brown envelope was stuffed inside. "Eureka!"

With shaking fingers, she picked up the envelope and handed it to him.

He turned it over in his hands. "Waverley carried an envelope just like this the night he was murdered."

"What was in it?"

He shrugged. "We never found it. The security video shows him carrying a large, brown envelope to his assistant's office, but when his body was discovered, the envelope was missing."

"Do you think this is the same envelope?" She scratched her head. "But that would mean the killer murdered Waverley in the other room and then came back here and replaced the envelope in its hiding spot in his office. Why would he do that?"

"He wouldn't." He held up the envelope. "I don't think this is the same envelope. The killer knew a lot of details about the secrets in this office, but it's hard to believe he knew about this hidden compartment."

He helped her rise and led the way to the desk where he placed the envelope on the gleaming mahogany surface. "Do you want the honors?"

She picked up the envelope, and peeled off the flap. Five black-and-white, eight-by-ten photographs were tucked inside the envelope. Hands shaking, she drew out the photos and set them on the desk one on top of the other.

Chase shone the beam of his light on the top photograph.

The photo was grainy and slightly unfocused, but the scene depicted sent chills through her heart. She leaned closer.

Chase's warm breath rustled her hair as he too bent forward.

Three young men holding guns stood in a semicircle, facing another man who stood behind a counter of some sort. A cash register was on a shelf beside the man behind the counter. His face was blurred, but his grimace of fear was clear.

Her breath rushed out in a gasp as she recognized one of the men holding a gun. "That's Darien! He's a lot younger, but it's him."

Chase tapped his finger on the image of another man. "And this guy looks like Jonas Waverley."

"Are they robbing a store?"

"Looks like it." His voice hardened. "These photos were taken by a store security camera." He slid the first photo aside, revealing the one beneath. "Let's see what else is here."

She stared at the shocking photo as her heart beat double-time. Darien and Waverley pointed guns at an elderly woman. The third, unidentified man had moved behind the counter and held a gun to the terrified clerk's forehead.

The final photograph revealed a scene from Hell. The old woman sprawled on her back, a small, black hole in her forehead, her eyes fixed and staring at the camera. The clerk slouched facedown on the floor, a dark pool of what must be blood beneath his head.

Her stomach roiled, and she swallowed the rush of

bile threatening to erupt. She squeezed her eyes shut, but the nightmare images were imprinted on her retinas. Two innocent people dead…murdered in cold blood.

Darien had been in the convenience store holding a gun. Jonas Waverley, too.

She lunged to her feet and grabbed the small metal garbage can beside the desk and vomited, her guts heaving again and again.

"Easy. Breathe. Slow and steady." Chase gripped her arm, supporting her. Drawing her close, he held her in his arms as he rubbed soothing circles on her back.

His quiet voice eased the horror clamping her stomach, and she gave in to his comforting embrace, letting her body relax, melting against his muscular strength, but as the horror of the damning photos flashed before her eyes, she stiffened and pulled back. "Those pictures"—she swallowed and tried again—"Darien…he murdered those people."

His jaw tightened. "You, of all people, should know what McCabe's capable of."

"I never expected he'd do something like this." She pointed to the photographs on the desk, but the truth was evident. The man who'd beaten her time and time again had murdered those innocent people. She'd known Darien was involved in shady ventures, but she hadn't imagined he'd stoop this low. She'd married a murderer. Shame clogged her throat.

"I remember this case." Chase's eyes took on a faraway look. "The murders happened before I started with the force, but Mike was the lead detective. He talked about the crime all the time. A convenience store on the East Side was robbed. A customer and the store clerk were both shot in the head." He pinched the bridge of his nose.

"The senseless brutality of the murders shocked the city. People were up in arms. The cops assigned to the case worked their tails off trying to find the suspects, but the videotapes from the security cameras inside and outside the store were missing, and the only witnesses were dead." He blew out his cheeks. "No one was ever charged with the crime."

"Now we know who's responsible."

"Now we know." He chewed on his bottom lip. "But McCabe wasn't the shooter." He lifted one of the photographs and held it before her. "If you look close, you can see Waverley and McCabe standing back guarding the female customer." He jabbed his vinyl-clad finger at the next photo. "This man's the killer. Look...here he's shooting the woman, and here he pops the clerk."

She stared where he pointed. He was right, but the knot in her stomach didn't loosen. "Darien may not have shot anyone, but he was there. He robbed the place at gunpoint. That makes him just as guilty, doesn't it?"

Chase nodded. "Doesn't matter if he did the actual shooting. Those people died while he committed a felony. He's looking at a first-degree murder charge."

She swallowed down a fresh surge of bile. "Do you recognize the man who killed the people?"

Chase shook his head. "Impossible to tell. He's wearing a ball cap and sunglasses."

"Look at his hand." She pointed with her index finger. "The one holding the gun. What's the mark above his wrist? Is it a tattoo?"

Chase leaned closer, the pinpoint of his light zeroing in on the gruesome scene. "You might be right." He opened the top drawer of Waverley's desk and scrambled through a tangle of paperclips, pens, sticky notes, boxes of staples, cough candies, tape rolls and other office detritus. Grunting with satisfaction, he fished out a small, handheld magnifying glass. Leaning over the photograph, he peered through the magnifying glass. "It's blurry, but it's definitely a Celtic cross. If we find this guy, this tattoo will nail his ass."

"I don't understand why Jonas Waverley was involved in something like this. He was a respected businessman. Last year, the mayor awarded him 'Man of the Year', and he sat on the boards of several large charities."

Chase shrugged. "Maybe he got involved in a gang. Lots of young men do." He shrugged again. "We know he was involved in buying stolen art objects, so he wasn't the law-abiding citizen he portrayed himself to be."

"Darien told me Jonas Waverley owed him some favors, but I had no idea they'd known each other so long."

His mouth twisted. "I imagine McCabe has lots of secrets."

"But why did Waverley keep the photos all these years? I mean, they incriminate him as well as the other two men. Wouldn't he want to destroy any connection to a double murder?"

"If I had to guess, I'd say Waverley held onto these pictures for blackmail."

"Blackmail?" The knot in her gut tightened yet again. "Waverley blackmailed Darien? But I thought they were friends."

"No honor among thieves. Waverley was probably

blackmailing the shooter as well." His mouth tightened. "No doubt that's what got him killed. The guy got tired of paying." He slid the photographs back in the envelope and slipped the envelope in his jacket pocket. "These photographs prove McCabe and Waverley, and the man with the tattoo on his wrist were robbing the convenience store at the time of the murders.

"Waverley's beyond our reach, but McCabe and the other man will be charged with felony murder. They'll go to jail for the rest of their sorry lives." He stared at the rain pelting the large window. "We have to find the shooter. He's the key."

"How can we do that? We can't see his face."

A determined gleam lit his eyes. "The tattoo will identify him. A guy like that will be in our data banks. This wasn't the first crime he committed. Nor the last."

He sounded so confident, but how long would the search take? How many people would die in the meantime? And what if the killer wasn't in the police files? Would he get away with his crimes like he had all these years? "What if we stick with our original plan?"

Chase's eyes narrowed, and the furrow between his dark brows deepened. "What are you talking about?"

"I'll take the photographs to Darien, but I'll refuse to give them to him until he tells me the name of the man with the tattoo."

"Are you crazy? I—"

"Darien doesn't know you've seen the pictures. He thinks I'm here on my own. He'll tell me what he knows. Why wouldn't he? He doesn't consider me a threat. He thinks I'm so cowed I'll do whatever he asks."

"No way." He grasped her upper arms, forcing her

to face him. "Do you hear me? No way in hell I'm letting you do this."

She shuddered at the fierce determination on his rugged face, but held strong to her resolve. "You think the man who shot those people in the convenience store is responsible for murdering Waverley and his assistant, and Darien's men. Right?"

"Maybe."

"Come on. You know I'm right. This guy set the bomb in Darien's car, and shot at us at Germanson Point." She freed her arms from his grasp. "He won't stop until he kills Darien and anyone else who gets in his way. We have to find him before he kills again. Darien knows his identity. I can—"

He shook his head before she finished speaking. "It's too dangerous. This bastard's murdered seven people. He'd think nothing of killing you. Hell, he's already tried twice." He shoved his hands in the front pockets of his jeans. "Let the police handle this. We'll have the shooter on file, or we'll find McCabe. You're not risking your life. I won't let you."

"You won't let me?" She pinned him with a fierce look of her own, outraged at his arrogance. He won't let her indeed. "I'll take precautions. We'll make copies of the photos, and you'll be nearby making sure I'm safe."

A look of despair flooded his face. "I can't let you do this. Don't you see? I can't."

Anger hadn't worked, so she changed tactics. "Please, Chase. I want to make amends. I feel responsible for what Darien's done." She blinked back tears. Real tears.

"You aren't responsible for anything that asshole did." His voice was a hoarse croak. "You know that, right?"

She blinked pleading eyes at him. "Let me do this. Please."

"I can't...I can't lose you."

"You won't."

He ripped off his gloves, tossed them in the garbage can and wiped his hand over his eyes, and nodded. "God help me."

"Good. We're agreed." Instead of satisfaction at convincing him to go along with her plan, a surge of trepidation chilled her blood. *God help me, is right*. In order for her plan to work, she'd need all the help she could get.

Chapter 26

Chase turned on the tap full blast and stepped under the shower. Water pounded against his skin in a punishing spray. Why the hell had he agreed to Natasha's crazy plan? He ground his back molars until they ached.

McCabe had shown he'd do anything to stay out of jail. Once she gave him the photos, there was no guarantee he'd tell Natasha anything. Why would he? He'd kept silent all this time even though he knew who killed Waverley and his assistant. And now that he was on the run for his life, the stakes were even higher.

Chase scrubbed his face, rubbing hard, trying to erase the unease prickling his skin. Whoever set this killing spree in motion was one smart bastard. The diamond stud clutched in Henrietta's hand pointed to McCabe. The killer had framed him. He wanted McCabe out of the way badly enough he'd stop at nothing to achieve his goal.

He twisted the tap all the way to cold and stood under the icy spray. McCabe was dangerous. No way in hell was he letting Natasha anywhere near him, with or without the incriminating photos.

Somehow he'd convinced her to return with him to the motel and get a good night's sleep before they carried out her plan. He was surprised she'd agreed. She'd been so determined to find the killer, she was all set to rush out and confront McCabe. But she'd listened to him and now she lay sound asleep on the bed in the motel room.

He'd waited until she was asleep, and then snuck into the bathroom and called Mike and arranged for him to pick up Natasha in the morning and take her into protective custody.

Sticking his face under the spray, he let the icy water numb his brain. He'd gone back on his word, but keeping her alive was his number-one priority. No matter if she hated him forever, she'd be alive to fan her hatred.

Last night hadn't been a piece of cake. Once they returned from Waverley's office, they'd settled in for the night in the small motel room. She'd taken the bed, and holding tight to his principles in spite of every cell in his body vibrating with the need to touch her, he'd slept in the hard-backed chair.

He grimaced. Slept? Hell, he'd hardly closed his eyes all damn night. How could he when he was twisted like a pretzel in that torture rack of a chair?

Instead he'd watched her sleep, her face relaxed, blonde hair spread out on the pillow like a golden cloud, her soft mouth open. Her rhythmic breathing had filled the room, and his traitorous mind conjured images of what she was or wasn't wearing beneath the covers, creating another kind of torture…worse than the damn chair.

His body craved her touch. The bed was queen-size, plenty of room for two. She wouldn't even know he was lying beside her.

But he'd know. Damn straight he'd know. He wouldn't be able to resist touching her, caressing her satiny skin, kissing those sweet lips... So he'd stayed where he was as the hours plodded one after the other until he couldn't handle another second, and he'd crept into the bathroom, called Mike, and stepped under the shower.

He turned off the tap. His skin was red from the pummeling icy water. Rubbing dry with a thick, white terrycloth bath towel, he glimpsed his face in the mirror above the sink. His skin was pale, the whites of his eyes streaked with tiny red lines. He resembled a man preparing to face his execution.

His gut twisted in a Gordian knot. He was about to break his promise to Natasha. She'd kill him, or his self-disgust would make him wish he were dead. Either way he was doomed.

Better to tell her now, than when Mike knocked on the door. He dragged on his rumpled clothes, smoothed a hand over his hair, sucked in a deep breath, and opened the bathroom door.

He froze, his body stiff in disbelief.

The bed was empty, the blankets tossed on the floor.

Cursing, he charged across the room and checked the tiny closet. Her coat and shoes were gone. So was the small daypack she'd had with her and her purse. He swore again, the obscenity reverberating off the walls.

Grabbing his jacket from the back of the chair, he flung open the door and hurried outside. *How could he have been so stupid?* The condemning words followed him like a pack of starving wolves as he raced along the upstairs landing and leaped down the stairs.

He scoured the parking lot. A man stepped out of a motel room on the lower level, closed the door, and strode across the parking lot, pulling a wheeled suitcase, but no Natasha. Where the hell had she gone?

Dumb question.

She'd gone after that scumbag, McCabe. A block of ice lodged deep in his gut.

****

A car's headlights flashed as a man left his room and crossed the motel parking lot, wheeling a suitcase. He used his electronic key to unlock his car. Tossing his suitcase in the trunk, he climbed into the driver's seat and started the engine.

As he backed out of the parking space, Natasha cast a quick glance at the upper landing. Chase had gone back into the motel room. The coast was clear. She rose from behind the black pickup truck where she'd been hiding and scurried over to the car and flagged down the driver.

His face registered surprise, but he stopped and rolled down his window.

She gave him a sob story about having a fight with her boyfriend and needing to get away before he woke up and found her gone. Not a total lie, though Chase wasn't her boyfriend, and he'd been in the shower, not asleep.

He motioned for her to climb in the car and drove off as if picking up strange women in motel parking lots was an everyday occurrence.

His name was George Addison, and he was from Bangor, Maine, in town for a business meeting. He agreed to drop her at the bus depot as it was on his way.

The car purred along on the early morning streets. Either George wasn't a morning person, or he hadn't had his morning coffee, or he just wasn't the talkative type. Either way, the silence was fine with her.

She slumped back on the seat and stared out the window at the passing scenery. Her head still pounded, her anger steaming white hot at Chase's deception. She'd been asleep when a muted buzzing had broken through her dreams and awakened her.

She sat up. Chase wasn't in the room. Her heart raced at the possibility he'd left her, but then she saw the thin line of light seeping from under the closed bathroom door, along with the splash of running water.

He must be having a shower.

The buzzing sounded again.

She switched on the bedside lamp.

More buzzing.

She shoved back the covers and swung her legs over the side of the bed, and clad only in her T-shirt and panties, crossed the room to the chair where Chase had spent the night. His jacket hung over the back of the chair. The buzzing issued from inside his coat pocket.

Shooting a glance at the closed bathroom door, she fumbled in his coat pocket and jerked out a cell phone. The ringer had been set to vibrate. The display indicated the call originated from the Port Hardesty Police Department.

The frantic buzzing stopped, and the phone silenced.

She bent to slip the phone back in his coat pocket when the phone buzzed again. She chewed on her bottom lip. The call must be important or the caller wouldn't keep trying to get hold of Chase. Maybe there'd been a break in the case. Maybe the police had found Darien. She pressed the answer button and lifted the phone to her ear. "Hello?"

A pause. "I think I have the wrong number." A woman's voice filled Natasha's ear. "I'm looking for Detective Brandon."

"This is the right number. Chase...er...Detective Brandon is busy at the moment. May I take a message?"

Another echoing silence. "Who is this?"

Natasha inhaled a deep breath and instilled an air of confidence in her voice as she built her lie. "Janine Stimpson. I'm assisting Detective Brandon." She wiped her damp palm on her leg. "Is this urgent? Would you like me to get him, or do you wish to leave a message?"

The woman hesitated. "I guess I could leave a message. Please inform Detective Brandon that Detective Podborski is on his way. He should be at your location within the hour to retrieve the suspect."

"Suspect?" The hairs on the back of Natasha's neck prickled. "What suspect?"

"McCabe's ex-wife. Detective Podborski's taking her into protective custody." A hint of suspicion flavored the woman's voice. "I thought you said you were working with Detective Brandon. What did you say your name was?"

The breath rushed out of Natasha's lungs, and she struggled to stay on her feet. She muttered a quick goodbye, severed the connection, and stumbled over to the bed. A dozen emotions reeled through her, but anger took the lead. Chase didn't have any intention of allowing her to go through with her plan to exchange the photographs for the killer's name.

He'd stood before her, bold as brass, stared her straight in the eye, and promised. And all along he'd been lying. He'd called his partner while she slept. She glared at the closed bathroom door. Had he snuck in the bathroom and made his furtive call?

She slammed her fist on the bed. If he assumed she'd wait here like a meek little lamb and allow Detective Podborski to take her into protective custody, he had another thought coming.

Her hands shook with outrage as she tugged on her pants and drew her sweater over her head. Careful not to make any undue noise, she tiptoed over to the desk and fished in his coat's inside pocket for the envelope with the photographs. Tugging the envelope free, she stuffed it in her daypack.

The running water stopped.

She froze and held her breath. Her heart beat a rapid tattoo. When the door remained closed, she let out her breath, grabbed her coat and daypack, unlocked the door, and slipped through the opening onto the outside landing.

Chapter 27

George dropped her off in front of the bus depot.

She waved goodbye and crossed the street to a small coffee shop with a neon sign in the front window boasting they served the best java in town.

A bell above the door announced her arrival, and a matronly waitress sporting frizzy gray hair and thick glasses sang a cheery greeting. "Morning. Coffee?"

Natasha nodded.

A mouthwatering aroma of bacon grease, fried eggs, and coffee saturated the air.

The café wasn't crowded. Two bearded men sitting across from each other at a booth in the front of the small café glanced at her with mild interest before returning to their loaded plates.

Another man, engrossed in his newspaper, didn't look up.

Natasha hung her coat on the hook on the end of a booth at the back of the restaurant, and slid onto the cracked plastic bench seat.

The cheerful waitress bustled over with a steaming cup and set it before Natasha. "Want a menu?"

Natasha shook her head, and the woman hurried away. Steam, smoky, with a hint of chocolate, rose from the cup. She sipped the strong, dark brew, exhaling a breath as the coffee slipped over her tongue, sparking tingles of ecstasy on her taste buds. A jolt of caffeine rocketed through her veins and infused her with a burst of energy. She smiled. The sign on the window was right…this place did make a good cup of java.

Picking up her cell phone, she punched in the number Darien had given her. The phone rang a dozen times, and she was ready to hang up when he answered.

"Where the hell are you?"

She winced at the venom in his voice. "What do you mean?"

"You heard me. I've had my men watching your house. You aren't home. You haven't been for days. I thought I told you to go back."

A chill settled over her. "Someone trashed my house looking for your briefcase. I couldn't stay there. The house was a disaster."

"Did you go to Waverley's office like I asked?"

She nodded.

"Answer me, Natasha, damn it."

"Yes, yes, I did. I…I have the envelope."

A long silence ensued. The clatter of dishes and the muted conversations of the other early morning diners were loud as she held her breath and waited for him to respond.

"Are you alone?"

"Of course I'm alone."

"So what's all the noise?"

"I'm in a coffee shop."

"You'd better not be lying to me, Natasha."

Her hand holding the phone trembled. "I'm not lying. I promise."

He harrumphed. "Meet me in an hour at Holden Warehouse on Dickenson Road. Don't be late."

"I...I'll be there." She checked her watch. She'd have to hurry. Dickenson Road was on the other side of town, and rush hour traffic was in full swing.

"And Natasha?"

"What?"

"You'd better be telling the truth. If I see anyone but you in the vicinity, I'll be very unhappy." The call disconnected.

A shiver slid along her spine. Her hands shook as she stuffed her phone back in her pocket and shrugged on her coat. Tossing bills on the table, she hurried out the door of the café and onto the street. She flagged down a cab and instructed the driver to take her to Holden Warehouse.

The taxi swerved off the main highway onto a side road leading through a heavy industrial area of warehouses, automotive repair shops, and shipping companies.

She sat forward on the seat, her heart pounding. The hour was almost up. The road ahead was empty of traffic. "How much longer?"

"Five minutes, give or take." The cab driver steered around a crack in the pavement. "Depends on how rough this road gets. I don't wanna lose a muffler in one of these potholes."

Her breath whooshed out in a puff of air. This nightmare could be over soon. Darien would give her the killer's name, and she'd hand him the envelope. He wouldn't suspect the photographs were copies. He wouldn't know she'd stopped at an office supply store along the way and had the cab driver wait while she made photocopies of the incriminating photographs.

She'd replaced the originals with the copies, and

stuffed the originals in another envelope, addressed that envelope to Detective Chase Brandon at Port Hardesty Police Headquarters, and dropped the envelope in a mailbox.

If something happened to her, the original photographs would be safe. Chase could use them to track down the murderer. She shivered. But nothing would go wrong. Her plan was solid.

She'd convince Darien to tell her the name of the man who had a Celtic cross tattooed on his wrist. And then she'd pass that information onto the police. The killer would be caught, the police would find Darien, and he'd go to jail for a very long time. Best of all—the killings would stop.

Everything would be just peachy.

A sob hitched in her throat. *Yeah. Real peachy.*

She swiped at the tears stinging her eyes and peered out the side window as the cab turned down a rough road and passed by several rundown buildings and warehouses. Most of the buildings looked deserted. Windows were boarded up, and the empty parking lots consisted of garbage, broken asphalt, and straggly weeds. Rust-encrusted machinery, massive, cracked and chipped cement blocks, and broken plastic pipes were strewn amongst the weeds.

The road became rougher, and the cab bounced through one pothole after another. The taxi halted before a metal gate blocking the road and barring access to a vast, deserted parking area. A faded sign hung at an odd angle from a post, warning this was the property of Holden Brothers Shipping Company and trespassers would be prosecuted to the full extent of the law.

She grimaced. As if anyone would bother to trespass on the neglected property.

Except her.

A transport truck, tires flattened, the windows shattered, and the driver's door ripped off, was parked before a large, dilapidated, single-story, red brick building. Four garage bay doors flanked the front of the warehouse. A weathered sign mounted on the roof of the building announced this was Holden Brothers Shipping Company.

"Looks like the place is closed." The cab driver glanced over his shoulder, his bushy gray eyebrows raised. "You want me to take you back?"

She shook her head. "I'll walk from here."

"You sure, lady? This ain't no place to be wanderin' around alone."

"I'm sure." Digging in her pocket, she withdrew money for the fare and a substantial tip and handed the cash to the driver. "Thanks." She climbed out of the cab.

Drawing in a deep breath, she studied the rundown building. Was Darien here, or was this one of his cruel jokes? She had a hard time imagining him hiding out in a place like this. He'd be more likely to choose a luxury resort on a secluded tropical island where the Scotch was old and the women young.

The taxi driver peered through the dusty windshield, his lined face filled with concern.

She waved him off with more confidence than she felt, ducked under the barrier, and hurried down the gravel lane to the distant parking lot before she changed her mind.

The cab's motor grumbled to life.

She glanced back as the car reversed and drove away, leaving a plume of dust in its wake. Ignoring the frisson of unease rippling along her spine, she straightened her shoulders and marched toward the warehouse.

Stepping over torn black plastic bags spilling rotting garbage, scraps of soggy cardboard, and old newspapers, she rounded the hulking wreck of the big eighteen-wheeler.

A shiny black SUV was parked around the side of the building, out of sight of the main road.

The hairs on the back of her neck prickled, and she slowed.

He was here.

Her gut screamed at her to turn and run before Darien saw her, before he had the chance to hurt her. But finding answers was too important. She'd given up everything for this moment…gone back on her word, severed any hope she had of a relationship with Chase, and in the process, shattered her heart. All to confront Darien, a man who terrified her, and get the answers she needed to help Chase find the killer.

A lump thickened in her throat. Chase. This was all about him. Even though his betrayal stung, she was determined to learn the name of the killer so he could solve the case. He'd be a hero, and he wouldn't have to quit the police force.

Inhaling a deep breath, feeling as if she were a soldier marching onto a battlefield where she was hopelessly outnumbered, she walked on leaden feet toward a battered, gray metal door on the end of the building close to Darien's vehicle.

A shiny, heavy-duty lock hung from a thick chain

attached to the door handle. The lock gaped open, and when she grabbed the door handle, the door swung open on silent hinges. She stepped over the threshold into the building's dim interior.

The door closed behind her with a slam, and she jumped, pressing her hand over her chest to slow the furious pounding of her heart. *Ugh, that saltwater stench of decomposing seaweed and rotting fish wasn't helping her roiling stomach.*

Faint light filtered in through several grime-encrusted windows set high in the brick walls. The water-stained ceiling, covered with rusted metal trusses and sheets of steel, soared high above.

A long, narrow corridor stretched before her into the dim interior. Numerous dark doorways opened off the central corridor. A steady dripping of water emanated from somewhere deep within the building. No other sounds broke the ominous silence.

Fishing her penlight out of her pack, she switched on the light. The tiny beam illuminated a few feet in front of her, but the spill of light instilled confidence, and she inched along the corridor. The slap of her shoes on the bare cement floor was eerily loud.

Pausing at the first doorway, she shone her light into the room beyond. Stacks of old wooden crates were piled three high. "Darien?"

No answer. She trudged on.

The next room was similar to the first, except a small window high up on one wall let in enough light to reveal a jumble of rusted metal drums. "Darien?" Her voice echoed off the cracked walls. A clatter from above made her jump, and her heart pounded. She craned her head back and stared at the ceiling.

A bird fluttered in the rafters before settling on a metal beam.

Where was Darien? She hadn't lied to the police, snuck out on Chase, and come all this way to play games.

Stopping at the next doorway, she swung the beam of her flashlight around the room. Crates were stacked against the walls, but no Darien. Was this his idea of a joke? Was he sipping a martini in a fancy hotel and having a good laugh at her expense?

She reached in her pocket for her phone to call him, but yelped, her heart racing, as a shadow detached from behind a huge crate, becoming the shape of a large man. "You!"

Chase scowled and strolled toward her. "Hello, Natasha, or should I call you Janine? That is the name you used when you lied to Officer Daniels, isn't it?"

"But"—she gulped—"I left you at the motel. How…how did you find me?"

His lips curled in a cold smile. "Mike spotted you sneaking out of the motel room. He figured something was up, so he followed you."

"Even if he followed me, there's no way you could have arrived here before me. I didn't know where I was going until I talked to Darien."

He smirked. "What can I say? Good detective work." His phony smile widened. "When you snuck out on me the first time, I had Mike get a subpoena for access to the data on your mobile phone. Once you made the call to McCabe, it was a simple matter for our tech people to follow your digital trail. Lo and behold, the data led us here."

"You had my phone tapped?" She glared. "Is that

even legal?"

His smirk didn't falter. "The subpoena says it is. Besides, I was right not to trust you. The second my back was turned, you took off."

She jammed her hands on her hips. "You didn't trust me?" She was so angry she could spit.

He must have been worried she would, because he backed up a step.

"You agreed that I'd give the photographs to Darien in exchange for him telling me the name of the man with the Celtic cross on his wrist." The words spewed out. "I believed you. I actually thought that for once I'd met a man I could trust, but then"—she swiped at the tears burning her eyes—"but then I answered your phone and learned I was a fool.

"You're no different than Darien. You're a liar." The tears flowed down her face, but she ignored them. "You may not hit women, but you betray them in other, just as hurtful, ways. And to think I actually thought…I thought…" The rest of what she was going to say was lost in her sobs.

"You thought what, Natasha?" His voice was quiet, his body still.

She shook her head and bit hard on her bottom lip. Had she actually been about to tell him she loved him, and he'd broken her heart? Wouldn't he love that? He'd have a good laugh over what a fool she was. The mortifying thought dried her tears and stifled any further confessions. She backed away until she bumped into a wooden crate and couldn't back up anymore.

His face was haggard in the pale light streaming through the high window. He covered the distance between them in two long strides. His eyes sparked fire.

"I'm nothing like McCabe. Nothing."

Guilt riddled through her. She hadn't meant what she said. Not really. He wasn't an abuser like Darien, but his lack of trust stung, and she'd wanted to hurt him as much as he'd hurt her. But she wouldn't apologize, and so she returned his stare and kept silent.

He tunneled his fingers through his hair and drew in a deep breath. "This isn't getting us anywhere. McCabe's car's parked outside, so he's in the building. Mike's scouting the outer perimeter. You and I'll check the interior."

She raised her eyebrows. "You and I? You mean together?"

"I can't leave you, and there's no time to take you back to the safe house." His icy exterior cracked, and his eyes softened. "McCabe's a cornered rat." He stepped closer. "I don't want you to get hurt. Don't you get that?"

The wooden slats dug into her back, but she remained mute beneath the heat sparking in his hazel eyes.

He smoothed a curl behind her ear. "From here on, you'll do exactly as I say. Understood?"

She shivered at the warm brush of the callused pads of his fingers against her skin. Unable to speak over the lump in her throat, she nodded.

"Good." His breath fanned her face. "Don't worry. I'll keep you safe. You're too important to me to let anything happen to you."

And just like that, the lump in her throat dissolved as his words pierced her soul. "You mean you need me for the case."

He shook his head, his gaze fixed on hers. "No,

you're important to me, Natasha." He leaned closer. "To me."

Her heart rate sped up with the certainty he was going to kiss her. She moistened her lips, anticipating, wanting, needing.

His pupils dilated, and he inched a breath closer, but then his eyes shuttered and he jerked back, and the moment vanished. "Let's go." He yanked a gun out of his shoulder holster and motioned for her to follow as he strode out of the room.

She blinked. *What the heck?* Stuffing her penlight in her pants pocket, she hurried along behind him, trying to keep up with his long-legged strides, she struggled to make sense of what had just happened. Why hadn't he kissed her? He'd wanted to. She'd seen that in his eyes. And she'd certainly wanted him to kiss her.

"Let's check in here." He inclined his head toward another dark opening and stepped into the room. The glow from his flashlight revealed this room was larger than the other three rooms she'd checked. Instead of wooden crates or oil drums, large bales of what looked like paper were stacked in haphazard piles about the room.

A snuffling sound echoed from somewhere behind the bales.

The hairs on the back of her neck prickled.

He raised the gun and shot her a warning glance, motioning for her to remain still. Stalking on silent feet across the room, he vanished amongst the stacks.

Heart hammering, she shifted from one foot to the other, clasping and unclasping her hands for a heartbeat before she tiptoed after him. *To hell with his rules.*

The tall stacks blocked the light seeping through the grime-encrusted windows, and deep shadows filled with menace loomed across the floor. She crept around a pile of bales.

The snuffling was louder, sounding like an injured animal suffering terrible agony. A sickly metallic scent hung in the air.

In the pool of bright light cast by his flashlight, Chase crouched before a humped shape on the cracked cement floor.

Her breath hitched in her throat and she stumbled closer.

A man sprawled on his back, his arms spread out at his sides. A pool of dark liquid oozed from beneath him, spreading tendrils of red across the floor.

Chapter 28

Her knees shook, and she staggered.

Chase stood, and holding his gun, wrapped one arm around her. He settled her head against his chest, blocking the grisly scene. "Why don't you ever listen? I told you to wait."

She gave in to the security and comfort of his embrace, but the nightmare image of the bloody, sprawled body was seared into her brain, and she stepped back from his embrace and stared at the man lying on the floor.

The truth struck her like a blow. Even with blood spattered on his face and the poor light, she knew.

Darien's dark-blond hair was mussed, his gaunt face ghostly pale. A snuffling wheeze escaped his open mouth with each shallow breath.

With a sob in her throat, she rushed to his side and crouched on the floor, uncaring she knelt in a puddle of blood.

His eyes were closed, the lids heavy and sunken. The only signs he lived were the slight rise and fall of his chest and the wheezing gasps.

She shot Chase a glance over her shoulder. "Have...have you called for help?"

He didn't answer. A deep furrow ran between his dark brows, and harsh lines bracketed his mouth.

"Chase, did you call for an ambulance?"

He shook his head.

"What? Call them. He needs help."

Chase didn't budge. His eyes were cold and hard.

"Chase?" She fumbled in her pocket for her cell phone. "Damn. My battery's dead." She tossed the useless phone on the floor. "Where's your phone?"

"He's been shot."

"Shot?" Icy dread rushed through her, and she scoured the menacing shadows for a gunman. "Who...who shot him?"

"Hopefully, he'll live long enough to tell us."

Darien moaned, his broken body unmoving and still. He resembled a corpse.

She shuddered. "Please, we have to help him. We can't let him die. Call an ambulance."

Chase studied her for a long moment, his eyes shuttered. "Are you sure you want me to call for help?"

"How can you ask that?"

"He made your life a living hell. I thought you hated him."

Tears filmed her eyes. "I do hate him. I despise him for what he did, but he was my husband." Tears blinded her. "Don't you see? I can't let him die."

"But I can." His gaze was fierce. "The bastard deserves to die."

The steel in his cold voice terrified her. She rose to her feet and placed the palms of her hands on the sides of his face. "Look at me, Chase."

He shook his head, refusing to meet her fervid gaze.

"Look at me." She infused her soul into her plea.

His hazel irises shone with unshed tears.

She released the breath she hadn't been aware she

held. "You can't let him die. That's not who you are. He isn't your father. He's a weak man who made mistakes. Don't let him destroy you."

A tear slipped from his eye and slid down his rugged cheek.

"We have to help Darien. Otherwise, we're no better than he is." She caressed his face, running her fingers over the stubble on his cheeks, wiping away his tears. "You're a good man, Chase. You won't be able to live with yourself if you don't help him."

He blew out a ragged breath. "Okay."

She grazed his lips, the kiss fleeting—a mere brush of air, but the intensity of the contact left her breathless.

He fished in the pocket of his jeans, jerked out his cell phone, punched in the emergency number, and spoke into the phone. When the call finished, he said, "They're on their way."

Relief washed over her, and she returned to Darien's side. She clasped his cold, limp hand. "You'll be okay, Darien. An ambulance is coming."

Chase crouched beside her. He eased Darien onto his side, revealing a blood-soaked hole in his expensive, navy blue, silk suit. Yanking out a pocketknife from the front pocket of his jeans, Chase cut away Darien's suit coat and the bloody shirt beneath, exposing a gaping wound from which a steady stream of blood oozed.

Removing his jacket, Chase slipped out of his gun harness and laid it on the floor. He stuffed his gun into the holster and ripped off his T-shirt, rolled the soft cotton into a ball, and placed the makeshift compress over the gaping wound. Using both hands, he applied pressure, stanching the flow of blood.

Darien's breathing quickened, but he remained

unconscious.

She studied his pale face. The harsh, cruel lines had softened, and she caught a glimpse of the man he used to be, the man she'd married. Her voice softened as memories of the past swamped her. "He wasn't always a monster. I loved him once." She swallowed hard. "I knew he was caught up with some bad people, but I thought I could change him. I thought…"

"Why didn't you walk away?" Chase's voice roughened. "After he started hitting you, why'd you stay?"

"You asked me that before." She shrugged. "I don't know. I guess I blamed myself. I assumed I'd done something wrong to make him angry, and that's why he hit me."

"My mother blamed herself when my father beat her. After all, he loved her, so she must have done something to piss him off." Chase grimaced. "That's what these bastards do. They pass the blame, make the victim guilty. The abuse is never their fault."

Darien groaned and his eyes opened a crack, the sunken lids heavy. He blinked, bleary and confused, and groaned again. "So…much…pain." His voice was a thread of sound.

She tightened her grip on his hand. "Help's on the way."

"Natasha?" He coughed, and a thin stream of blood mixed with saliva trickled from the corner of his mouth.

"Shhh. Don't talk."

His thin, bloodless lips curled in a grimace. "I…I knew you'd come."

Keeping the palms of his hands pressed on Darien's wound, Chase shifted so his face was inches from Darien's. "Who shot you, McCabe? Who did this?" His voice was urgent and commanding.

Darien opened his mouth again. A garbled sound emerged, mixed with another small stream of blood. He inhaled a rattling breath.

Hand trembling, she touched his cheek, shocked at the cold waxiness of his skin.

"I'm...I'm sorry, Natasha...for everything." His reddened eyes bulged as he gasped with the effort to speak.

"I know." And she did know. He was sorry for the way he'd treated her, but sorry wasn't enough. Sorry didn't make up for the years of fear she'd endured at the hands of this man. She couldn't forgive him even though he was dying. A wrenching sob shook her, and she jerked away from his beseeching gaze.

"Ask him who did this," Chase urged.

"Can't you see he's in pain?"

"He doesn't have long. We have to know who shot him."

She shuddered at the blood staining Chase's hands as he pressed on Darien's wound. He was right. They needed to know who'd shot Darien and all those other victims. People's lives were at stake.

Darien's breathing grew shallower, and long gaps settled between each laboured breath.

She swallowed over the thick lump clogging her throat. "Darien, can you hear me?"

His eyelids fluttered, and he groaned, but he opened his eyes and met her gaze.

"Who did this?"

He shook his head, and his complexion lost what little color remained.

She clasped his cold hand between hers. "Tell me, please. Who shot you?"

"He…he wants the diamond. That's why he did this. He won't stop until he gets it."

"Diamond? What diamond?" Chase demanded. "What's he talking about?"

Darien moaned and his eyelids fluttered closed as if they were too heavy to keep open.

Her frustration mounted. Releasing his hand, she withdrew the envelope from her daypack and tugged out the photographs. She held one picture before him and pointed at the man wearing the ball cap and sunglasses. "Darien?" Was she too late? Was he already gone? "Look at the picture. Is this the man who shot you?"

He opened his eyes, but they were bleary and unfocused. "The three of us were best friends." A ghost of a smile flitted about his gray, bloodless lips. "All through grade school we were inseparable." He coughed and winced, his breathing thick and liquid-filled.

"We needed cash. The convenience store was our first hit. It was supposed to be easy. A piece of cake." His voice was so low she had to lean closer to hear. "But then Carter panicked and shot the old lady and the clerk. Jonas and I grabbed the money and ran."

He sucked in a wheezing breath. Blood bubbled from the corner of his mouth. "Later, Jonas needed cash. He…he had the photos from the store security cameras. He wanted money or he'd go to the cops. He made me…made me…" A grimace of pain crossed his face. Sweat beaded his forehead.

"McCabe, where's the diamond?" Chase lifted his

hands from Darien's wound and grabbed him by the shoulders and shook. "Come on, you bastard, tell me."

Darien moaned.

"Stop, Chase." She blinked back tears. "You're hurting him."

"We have to know. Come on, McCabe. Tell us."

"Don't let him hurt you…" Darien gripped her arm, his icy fingers squeezing in a painful vise. "Don't trust…anyone."

She nodded, not understanding his rambling, but sensing his desperate plea for her to agree.

He gurgled deep in his chest. His body sagged, deflating as the last of his life fled.

"Darien, no." Too late. He was beyond hearing. Tears flooded her eyes.

"Damn it." Chase's bare chest heaved. He scrubbed his hands on his pants, leaving red streaks on the faded denim. "We need to know where this treasure Carter's looking for is. He could still be in the building."

She peered into the shadows. "Do you think so?"

"I don't know, but something's not right. Mike should have found us a long time ago."

The distant sound of a door slamming and the heavy tread of running feet echoed in the stillness.

Chase reached for his harness on the floor and drew out his gun. "Stay here." He dashed to the paper pallets and peered into the darkness beyond.

Chapter 29

Chase crouched behind the large paper bale and peered around the edge, gun raised and steady in his hand.

Footsteps approached.

Mike? Maybe, but what if it wasn't? What if it was the murderer? He tightened his two-handed grip on the gun.

A beam of light swept the surrounding darkness, and the footsteps slowed. "Chase?" The voice was filled with tension. "Chase, where are you?"

Chase's breath whooshed out. Easing his grip, he lowered the gun, slipped it into the waistband of his jeans, and stepped away from the concealing crate. "In here, Mike."

The arc of light swept the room and settled on Chase, blinding him.

"For God's sake, turn the damn light away." The light swung to the side, and he blinked in the sudden gloom. "Where the hell have you been?"

"Me?" Mike's brow furrowed. "I've been trying to find you for the past fifteen minutes. This place is a damned maze."

Chase's gut pinged as his body went on cop alert. Sweat gleamed on Mike's lined face, and he gasped for air as if he'd been running. "Everything okay?"

Mike looked away. "Fine. Just took longer than I

expected to check the grounds." He wiped his forehead with the sleeve of his coat. "Where the hell's your shirt?" He stepped closer and shone the flashlight beam on Chase. "Christ, man, is that blood on your hands?" Mike's body vibrated with nervous energy, and his gaze skittered around the room, settling on nothing.

The pinging in Chase's gut ramped up to a thunderclap. *Something was up*. He motioned for Mike to follow and led the way back through the stacks of paper pallets to McCabe's body. This was a crime scene. He'd figure out what was going on with Mike later, after they caught the murderer.

Mike's sharp inhalation of breath filled the room. "What the hell?" He strode toward the body, bent, and placed two fingers on McCabe's carotid artery, checking for a pulse. "He's dead." He stared at Chase and Natasha. "What the hell happened?"

"Someone shot him in the back," Chase said.

Mike rubbed the gleaming slick of sweat off his forehead with the back of his hand. "Did he say anything? Did he tell you who did this? How long's he been dead? Have you called it in yet?"

Chase ignored the blast of questions. "Waverley was blackmailing him." He bent and retrieved the photographs Natasha had dropped. "Take a look at these."

Mike studied the photos and released a long, low whistle. "Are these what I think they are?"

Chase nodded. "Pictures from the security cameras at the convenience store murders."

Mike fixed a hard gaze on Chase. "How'd you get these?"

Chase opened his mouth to explain, but Mike cut

him off. "On second thought, don't tell me. I don't wanna know." He scrubbed a hand over his hair. "This clusterfuck just keeps getting worse." He glanced at Natasha. "I don't suppose you had anything to do with acquiring these?"

Her face flushed, and she turned to Chase. "I—"

"Leave her alone, Mike. She's not involved." Chase strode to her side and placed an arm around her shoulders, drawing her close, protecting her from Mike's scorn.

Her face was devoid of color, her body hunched. Hell, a stiff breeze would knock her over. No wonder. She'd just watched her ex-husband die an excruciating death. And now Mike was giving her the third degree.

Mike scowled at Chase. "What the hell, man? Are you determined to destroy what's left of your career?" He pointed his finger at Natasha. "Why is she here anyway? Is she involved? Or haven't you asked her? Does she have you so pussy-whipped you don't see how badly you've fucked up?"

Natasha gasped and her body sagged.

Chase held her tighter, supporting her. His anger rose to the surface, made all the hotter because of the grain of truth in Mike's harsh words. "None of this is Natasha's fault. She hasn't made me do anything I haven't wanted to do. I knew exactly what was at stake when I allowed her to help in this investigation."

"Help?" Mike snorted. "Is that what they call it these days?" He shook his head. "Oh, man, you're in so deep, you can't see the friggin' light. She isn't worth ruining your life." He jerked his chin at McCabe's body. "She was married to that low-life scum. How can you be so certain she isn't involved?"

Mike's words were like a napalm strike. Chase's outrage skyrocketed into the stratosphere. "That's bullshit, and you know it." The words exploded out of him. He opened his mouth to say more, but Mike was already shaking his head.

"I don't want to hear your excuses. Get her the hell out of here before backup arrives. I don't know how I'll explain this shit to the captain."

As if to punctuate his words, sirens blared in the distance, growing closer with each passing second.

Natasha slipped from under Chase's arm and stepped away. She retrieved her daypack from the floor, and with a last look at McCabe's body, she turned to walk away.

"Where do you think you're going?" Chase's stomach plummeted. She couldn't leave. Not like this. Not with Mike's words hanging in the air like smoke in the aftermath of a missile strike.

She glanced back, anguish reflecting in her blue eyes. "I'm going home."

"No, wait, Natasha, please. It's not safe. The killer could be out there."

Hefting the strap of her pack over her shoulder, she shook her head. Her glance lit on Mike's angry face. "Your partner's right. I shouldn't be here."

Chase blew out a ragged breath. "But—"

She kept walking.

"Natasha." He called again, but she didn't slow her steps. He charged after her.

Mike grabbed his arm, stopping him.

He struggled, fighting to shake him off, but Mike's grip was too strong.

"Let her go, man. It's the right thing to do. You

know it is."

Keeping his gaze fixed on her receding back, he shook his head. "I can't. Not like this."

"You have to. You know what'll happen the second the captain gets here. She'll be taken into custody and interrogated. Could be months before she clears her name. Do you want that for her?"

Chase cast one last look at where Natasha had been, but she was gone. And just like that, his anger evaporated, leaving him exhausted. He stopped fighting Mike. Even though he ached to go after her, to explain that what Mike said wasn't true, to convince her that he cared. Hell, he loved her. Instead, he stood there, his heart breaking, and listened to the sound of her footsteps as they died away.

Mike was right. Once the police team arrived, the processing of the murder scene would begin, along with the hard questions. Natasha would be in the middle of the investigation. With her connection to McCabe, she'd be a prime suspect. She'd be taken to headquarters and mercilessly grilled.

Better to let her go. He'd done a piss-poor job of protecting her, but he could do this for her. This was when he stepped up and became the man he'd always wanted to be, the man who protected the woman he loved at all costs.

He shivered and rubbed the goose bumps on his bare arms, knowing he'd never be warm again.

****

Each step required superhuman strength as she stalked away from Chase into the shadows beyond. Tears stung her eyes and clogged her throat, but she refused to cry. Crying wouldn't help. Nothing would erase Mike's hard-hitting words.

The worst of it was, he was right.

She was responsible for ruining Chase's career. Because she'd convinced him to let her be involved in the case, he'd be drummed out of the police force. He loved being a cop. It made him who he was, and now, because of her, his dream would die.

The piercing wail of sirens ceased, and the distant slam of car doors reached her through the brick walls of the old warehouse. The door at the end of the corridor burst open.

She ducked into the room to her right and hid behind a stack of old metal drums. Her presence in the building would cause Chase more problems. Hicupping over a sob, she crouched behind the drums and waited for the stream of uniformed men to pass.

The uproar died down, and once again the building was silent.

Slipping from behind the drums, she tiptoed to the door and peered into the hall. The corridor was empty, but a rumble of male voices echoed from the room down the hall where she'd left Chase and Detective Podborski.

Breathing in a deep breath, she stepped into the hallway.

The clomping of boots pounded on the cement floor behind her, and she broke into a shambling run, hoping to reach the exit before she was discovered.

A car door slammed in the parking lot outside.

Veering to the right, she sprinted through the next open doorway into the dark. Stumbling over unseen objects, she raced on, desperate to get away before she was discovered.

She sagged against a cold, damp wall, her chest heaving. As her breathing slowed and the pounding of her heart eased, she cocked her head and listened. The steady drip of water sounded from somewhere behind her, and from above, the old building's metal roof creaked as the steel warmed under the morning sun.

She fished in her pocket and withdrew her penlight. The thin bead of light revealed a small, windowless room. The floor was strewn with bits of broken pipe, white plastic pails, cardboard boxes filled with rusty screws, and tangled strands of yellow nylon rope. Wooden shipping boxes were piled against the walls.

Careful to shield her light with her hand, she crossed to a doorway on the far side of the room and hurried down the corridor. This old building had to have another exit.

She lost track of time as she wandered the endless rooms. Each room was the same—damp, cold, and filled with junk. Sagging against a crate, she wiped the dampness from her brow. The sweeping arc of the penlight revealed yet another cavernous room. Her head throbbed. Hadn't she already passed that black bin? She was wandering in circles, going nowhere.

The soft glow from her penlight dimmed. She shook the metal tube. The beam of light brightened for a brief moment and then faded to black.

Chapter 30

Where was she?

The frantic refrain rang through Chase's mind as he searched one endless room after another. He shouldn't have let her run off. He should have stopped her. Instead, he'd stood there like a fool and listened to Mike.

The second she stormed away he knew he'd made a mistake. He'd wasted a few precious minutes arguing with Mike, but then he'd run after her, ignoring his partner's furious shouts. His career was over. He knew that. He didn't have to hear Mike spell it out, but he had to find her.

Sprinting down the long corridor to the exit door, he dodged the paramedics rushing into the warehouse rolling a stretcher between them. He thrust the door open, ignoring the questions thrown at him by the uniformed cops climbing out of their cruisers. He scoured the parking lot, but there wasn't any sign of her blue coat or shiny fall of blonde hair.

He turned back to the warehouse and grabbed one of the cops by his arm. "Did you see her? Did you see a woman with blonde hair?"

The man's mouth gaped, but he shook his head.

She was still in the building. She had to be. But where? The place was a labyrinth. His gut screamed that she was in danger.

Crazy, right? McCabe's killer wouldn't still be around. The place was swarming with cops. So why were alarm bells ringing through his head?

For the first time in years, memories of the prayers he'd learned as a child when he'd attended church service every Sunday returned. Mouthing the long-forgotten words under his breath, he flung open the door and ran back into the warehouse and along the corridor, stopping only long enough to glance in each room he passed.

He didn't dare call out for fear he'd alert the gunman to her presence. Besides, after the way he'd treated her, he wasn't certain she'd answer if he did call. Sweat beaded his brow, and his palm grew slippery on the hilt of the revolver he gripped.

A scraping sound caught his attention, and he froze, trying to pinpoint the location of the noise.

Natasha?

Or the killer?

He tugged out his cell phone and crept forward, ready to call for backup. There was the sound again. He raced down the narrow corridor passing one room after another. He stiffened.

Footsteps, heavy and moving fast in his direction.

He raised his gun.

A body hurtled into him with bruising force.

Chase's head snapped back and cracked into the cement wall. The gun and his phone flew from his hands and vanished into the darkness. A tsunami of pain flooded his body. Blinding fireworks burst before him. The sharp iron taste of blood filled his mouth. He struggled to stand, but his muscles refused to obey; his knees turned to rubber, and he slumped to the floor.

"You don't take a hint, do you, Brandon?" The assailant lashed out with a foot, smashing it into Chase's jaw. "I warned you to stay out of my business."

Chase blinked, fighting to clear the thick fog. Through the blasts of agony peppering him, he recognized the thin, blond-haired man in the black leather jacket towering over him, a cruel sneer on his lips. Natasha's drawing of the man who'd shot at her was bang on. Ignoring the shattering pain, he scrabbled in the dark for his gun.

The man raised his foot, clad in a heavy-soled work boot, and stomped on Chase's chest.

The loud crack of a rib splintering split the air, and white hot agony scorched him. He screamed. The world went dark.

****

Someone was coming. Natasha's mouth dried.

The slap of hard-soled shoes on the cement floor grew louder.

The police? No. The footsteps were too furtive. Feeling her way in the dark, she edged along the side of a large wooden crate and crouched behind it. She strained to hear over the furious pounding of her heart.

The arc of a light flared, lighting the concealing shadows, and the shuffle of boots grew louder.

The footsteps stopped. Heavy breathing and the clunk of metal striking wood filled the room.

She inched further into her hiding place, but jolted at the loud crack of splintering wood.

A curse, uttered in a deep, gravel-filled, male voice echoed in the small room.

What was he was doing? Slipping along the side of the crate, she peered around the edge.

A wide beam of light from a lantern set on top of a nearby crate illuminated the room, creating shifting shadows on the high ceiling. A man wearing a black leather bomber jacket and black jeans bent over an open crate. Pieces of broken slats lay scattered on the floor beside him. He stood and rubbed the small of his back.

She slapped her hand over her mouth to smother the scream. *Him*! The man who'd shot at her in the ravine. She'd never forget his face—the cold eyes, the scraggly blond hair skinned back into a knot at the back of his head, or his cruel mouth.

Her heart beat a frantic tattoo. He'd murdered Darien. He was Carter. He had to be.

He muttered something she couldn't hear and moved on to the next crate. Using a metal crowbar, he ripped at the top of the crate, prying off the wooden slats and rummaging inside.

She inched ahead. Her foot struck something on the floor and metal clattered. She held her breath.

He tilted his head as if listening. Lifting the lantern, he shone the light around the room.

She ducked, her heart pounding as light swept over the crate where she crouched.

After a minute, he set the lantern back on the crate. The crack of splintering wood was loud as he pried off another slat of wood.

She released her breath and once again peered around the corner.

With the lid removed, he searched the crate. He gave a grunt of triumph and withdrew a small bundle wrapped in some sort of white padding. The light from the lantern shone on his face, revealing a feral grin.

He unwrapped the covering from a small wooden

box. Lifting the lid, he peered inside. "Yes!" Grinning, he closed the lid, rewrapped the object in the padding, and stuffed the bundle in his coat pocket. He pulled out a small flashlight from his other pocket, and with a last, furtive glance, he hurried out of the room, leaving the lantern behind. His footsteps faded as he ran along the corridor.

Creeping out of her hiding place, she wiped the grime off the knees of her pants and scurried over to the crate where the blond man had been searching.

The container was filled with the foam peanuts used for packaging fragile items. The diamond Darien had mentioned must have been in this crate. That's why the killer had remained near the scene of the crime even after he'd shot Darien.

She crouched and studied the outside of the crate. A faded label was affixed to the side. She rubbed away the layer of grime. The writing was faint and spattered with watermarks, but she made out the words El-Mataf and Yemen.

Her stomach lurched. The antiquities expert the police had hired to study the dagger from Darien's briefcase said the ivory and jewel-encrusted gold knife had been stolen from El-Mataf, a museum in Yemen.

She tried to think over her rising excitement. The box the man had just taken from this crate had to have come from the museum in Yemen. It was probably another stolen artifact, shipped illegally out of the country. But how had the crate ended up in this deserted warehouse? And what had Darien known about it?

She had to tell Chase. He had to know about the blond-haired man and the object he'd taken from this crate. Picking up her pack, she hefted the lantern in one hand, and raced out of the room.

The hallway was dark after the relative brightness of the room, but the lantern's glow guided her way. The old building creaked and groaned, and she hurried her steps toward where she hoped she'd find the exit.

She rounded a corner, and her steps faltered as she stumbled to a stop. Her heart thumped in her chest. Holding the lantern before her, she inched ahead. The fingers of light revealed a body on the floor.

Chase!

He slumped on his side, his knees drawn to his chest, his arms flung out at an awkward angle. Blood stained his clothing and streaked his face.

She collapsed to the floor, and fighting disabling fear, she felt his neck. His skin was cold and clammy, but a pulse beat beneath her touch. His eyes were swollen almost closed, and his nose was bent at a crooked angle. A deep cut sliced across one cheek, and blood seeped from a gash on his forehead. Dark bruises were already forming along his jaw.

The worst of his injuries seemed to be a deep wound on the back of his head leaking a steady stream of blood. She swallowed back the sour taste of nausea, refusing to give in to panic. Her hand shook with her visceral ache to hold him, but she jerked her hand back, leery of causing him more pain. She had to get help.

She'd tossed her phone after the battery died, but Chase had one. He'd used his cell phone to call for help when they'd found Darien.

Searching his pants pockets, she came up empty. Where was the damn phone? She checked his pockets again. Nothing.

Her heart lurched at the gray cast of Chase's skin. She swallowed over a sob and threaded her fingers through her hair. He needed help. Detective Podborski or one of the other cops must still be in the warehouse. She had to find them.

Leaning over his still body, she brushed her lips against his bloody forehead. "Be strong, my love. I'll be back as soon as I can." She rose but halted, frozen in place.

The blond-haired man loomed before her, blocking the hall. His mouth twisted in a cruel grin. "What a touching scene." His grin widened. "Too bad he's too far gone to appreciate your adoration." He widened his stance, and his leather jacket swung open. Dark stains covered his white T-shirt. Dried blood.

"You! You did this."

He shrugged in mock sheepishness. "Guilty." A smirk tugged at the corner of his thin lips.

"You killed Darien."

"Right again." He raised his arm and smoothed back his hair, and the sleeve of his coat rose above his wrist, revealing a faded tattoo of a Celtic cross.

She gulped, her mouth desert dry. "You're Carter. You killed those people in the convenience store all those years ago. And you murdered Jonas Waverley."

"Among others." He preened as if proud of the heinous acts he'd committed.

Her mind whirled. "Henrietta Kinkaid, Waverley's assistant. You killed her, too."

"I didn't want to. She was a damn good lay." He shrugged. "But she was going to go to the cops. She was upset I killed Waverley." He pouted. "What the hell did she think would happen when she gave me the security codes to Waverley's building and told me about the secret passage?"

She reeled from the cold calculation in his pale-blue eyes. "The police are in the building. They'll find you." She prayed to any listening gods she was telling the truth, and the cops would ride in here like in the movies and save the day. "Why are you still here? What do you want?"

He nodded toward Chase. "Lover boy hasn't figured it out?"

"We know you, Darien, and Jonas Waverley robbed the convenience store. You killed that old woman and the clerk. We also know Waverley was blackmailing you. That's probably why you killed him."

"Don't get me wrong. Jonas had his uses, but he got greedy. We went back a long way. I put up with his foolish blackmailing for sentimental reasons, but I got fed up with paying him every damn month." He made the shape of a gun with his hand and pointed at her, miming the clicking of a trigger. "Bam, bam, bam." His hand jolted with each bam. "No more blackmailer."

Chills rippled along her spine. "Why don't you take what you want and leave us alone?"

He smirked and patted his jacket pocket. "I already have what I want."

"So why are you still here? Why don't you leave? " She slid a glance at Chase's still body. "He needs medical attention. You don't want to kill a cop."

He shrugged. "One less cop in the world. No loss." His gaze swept over her. "You saw me, didn't you?"

"What?"

"Don't lie to me. I'm not in the mood. You saw me

searching the crates."

She opened her mouth to deny his claim, but realized the futility of lying. "I won't say anything. I don't care what you took out of the crate. It's none of my business."

He chuckled, the sound chilling in the dim room. "Now that's a good one."

His icy gaze pierced her to the bone.

"I should have killed you in the ravine after I popped McCabe's meatheads, but I didn't know you were McCabe's bitch. I missed my chance again when you and your boyfriend were making out at the beach. You were sitting targets."

He reached in his coat pocket and yanked out a gun. He twirled it so the dull, black metal gleamed in the light from the lantern. "This place is filled to the rafters with damn cops"—he spun the gun again and aimed the pistol at her—"and this won't be quiet, but…" He shrugged.

Her heart stilled. At this close range, he wouldn't miss. Terror threatened to engulf her. "Kill me if you want, but help Chase, please. He's not part of this. He was just doing his job."

"You're a real Juliet, aren't ya? And he must be your Romeo." He sniggered. "You know how that little romance turned out." He shook his head. "Poor sap. He's better off dead. Never met a woman worth the skin she's wrapped in."

She struggled to think of something, anything to distract him and stop him pulling the trigger. "What was in the crate? Was it really a diamond?"

Lowering the gun, he fumbled in his coat pocket and tugged out the bundle he'd taken from the crate.

"Wanna see?" He unraveled the muslin covering and revealed a square box the size of the palm of his hand. The glossy wooden box gleamed in the lantern light. "Take a look at this." He lifted the lid.

She sucked in a breath. Inside the box, lying on a bed of purple velvet, was the largest diamond she'd ever seen.

"She's sure somethin', ain't she?" His gaze fixed on the glittering jewel. "Two hundred and twenty-two carats, and she's all mine." The diamond's multi-faceted surface drew the light from the lantern and reflected flashes of vibrant colors.

"You stole that from a museum."

"Nope. I stole it from McCabe. He stole it from a museum." He stroked the diamond as if caressing a lover's skin.

"Darien stole the diamond?" She struggled to get her mind around this shocking news. "How is that possible?"

"McCabe, Waverley, and I had a profitable little enterprise going until they fucked up and had to be dealt with. Waverley paid the museum security guards to look the other way, and his people lifted the antiquities from museums in the Middle East. McCabe arranged the shipping and stored the merchandise. I found the buyers."

He traced a finger over the diamond as if he couldn't resist touching the glistening surface. "This little bauble's worth millions. It was supposed to be our last score, but with Waverley dead, McCabe tried to cut me out." He grinned a feral smirk, revealing stained, crooked teeth. "Never a good idea to cross me."

"I don't believe you."

"Who do you think owns this place?" He closed the lid on the box, rewrapped it in the cloth, and stuffed the bundle in his pocket.

"Darien owns this warehouse?" As soon as she asked the question, she knew the answer. Of course this was Darien's warehouse. That's why he'd arranged to meet her here. He'd stolen priceless works of art and worked with this monster who thought nothing of murdering anyone who got in his way. "You killed all those people for money?"

"What else?"

"You're despicable."

"Maybe so." He raised the gun, his eyes icy and flat. "One more loose end to snip, and then I'm outta here." His finger tightened on the trigger.

Horror seized her. This was the end. He'd kill her, and Chase would bleed to death. A sob caught in her throat.

She blinked.

A flicker of movement shifted behind the man with the gun. Detective Podborski stepped out of the shadows. "Carter!"

The killer spun, gun raised, ready to fire. "Oh, it's you." He lowered his gun. "What—?"

The detective's gun barked, and a small black hole appeared in the middle of the blond man's forehead. He staggered, arms flailing.

Detective Podborski fired again, and a hole tore in the other man's coat.

The killer's knees sagged, and with a heavy thump, he landed on his back on the floor. His body convulsed and then stilled.

Blood poured from the hole in his forehead and

pulsed from his chest, staining the white T-shirt a brilliant red.

Chapter 31

Natasha stared in open-mouthed shock at the gunman's bleeding body.

Detective Podborski strode over and kicked the gun away from the limp hand, and crouched before the body and felt for a pulse. He looked up. "You okay?"

"I...I think so." She stumbled to Chase's side. His breathing was stronger, and his face had lost some of the gray pallor, but he was still bleeding. "Chase needs help. That man beat him pretty bad."

"I already called. Another ambulance should be here soon."

"How'd you find us?"

"When I couldn't contact Chase on his phone, I grew concerned and decided to do one more check of the building. I knew he wouldn't leave without telling me." He stood, knees cracking, and replaced his gun in his shoulder holster. "Good thing I did."

A sob hitched in her throat, and she pointed at the dead man. "He told me everything. He murdered Darien and Jonas Waverley, and he strangled Waverley's assistant. He...he killed all those other people too."

The detective nodded, his face grim. "I heard."

An uneasy flutter stirred deep in her gut. "How did you know his name?"

His craggy brow furrowed. "Whose name?"

She pointed to the dead man. "His."

The furrows in his brow deepened. "What are you talking about? I've never seen him before."

She licked her parched lips. "You called him Carter…before you shot him. I heard you."

"You're mistaken. The man had a gun pointed at you. He was going to kill you. You were terrified. You weren't thinking straight."

She shook her head. "I was scared, but I heard you."

Silence stretched between them. The urgent peal of sirens seeped through the warehouse walls.

He blew out a puff of air and smoothed a hand over his buzzed gray hair. "I really wish you hadn't heard that." Tugging a handkerchief from his coat pocket, he darted to the killer's gun. Using the handkerchief to cover his hand, he picked up the gun. "I hoped I wouldn't have to do this." He pointed the gun at her.

Her heart stuttered. "What are you doing?"

A sad look crossed his weathered face. "Come on, Natasha, you're a smart girl." He swiped sweat from his brow with the sleeve of his coat. "I'm sorry this has to end this way, but you don't leave me any choice. You know too much."

He shook his head. "I knew you were trouble the minute Chase laid eyes on you. He's a damn good cop, and now he has to quit the force because he fell for your pretty blue eyes."

"You won't get away with this." Her heart thundered so loud she feared it would burst out of her chest.

His mouth twisted in a semblance of a smile, and he jerked his thumb at the body of the gunman. "That guy shot you." He held up the gun in his handkerchief-covered hand. "His fingerprints are the only ones on the gun. I heard a gunshot and found you dead. The killer was going to shoot me as well, so I shot him." He shrugged. "Self defense. Pure and simple."

The sirens shook the walls. He cast a quick look over his shoulder and then swung back and raised the gun. "Time to end this."

"Not so fast, Mike."

The detective's eyes widened.

She spun at the sound of Chase's voice.

Under the coating of dried blood his face was ghastly pale. His hands trembled and sweat beaded his brow. He looked like he'd collapse at any moment, but he stood, his gaze steady and locked on Mike. "Put the gun down." The steel in his voice revealed no trace of weakness.

Mike shook his head. "I can't. I'm in too deep."

Chase's eyes blazed out of his pale, battered face. "You sure as hell better."

"And you're going to make me? Christ, man, you're half dead, and I have a gun." He shook his head and blew out a breath. "This wasn't supposed to happen. Why couldn't you have stayed unconscious?" His eyes shone with unshed tears. "I don't want to do this. Shit. You were like a son to me."

Her heart chilled. Mike was talking about Chase as if he were already dead. "Let him go, Detective Podborski—Mike. Please."

A tear leaked down his weathered cheek. "I can't."

Chase swayed and grabbed for the wall. Face paling, he drew himself up inch by inch until he stood upright. He wiped a shaking hand over his eyes, smearing blood across his face. "Don't do this, Mike.

You're throwing away your life. All those years on the force—"

"That's right. All those years on the force." Mike sneered. "And what do I get for my hard work? A cop's pension is shit. I'd be eating cat food and lining up at the food bank if that's what I had to live on."

"You won't get away with this. We'll hunt you down until the day you die."

Mike nodded. "Probably, but I'm in too deep to stop now."

"Jesus, man. What happened to you?" Chase's voice was anguished. "I respected you. You were one of the good cops."

"I didn't mean to get so involved." He swiped his eyes. "Really I didn't, but I was broke and—"

"And you sold out," Chase spat.

"Little things at first." He grimaced. "Look the other way when something went down, misplace evidence, make a call... Nothing that hurt anyone. Not really."

"You stole the video tapes from the cameras at the convenience store murders all those years ago, didn't you?"

"I didn't want to, you have to believe me, but Waverley didn't give me a choice. Either do what he wanted, or he'd turn me in. I couldn't lose my job." Mike shook his grizzled head. "I just helped. I didn't kill anyone." His gaze shifted to the dead man. "Well, not anyone important, anyway."

The blaring sirens ceased, and a distant door banged. Loud voices and hurried footsteps echoed from the far reaches of the gloomy warehouse.

Mike shot Chase a hard look. "I don't expect you

to understand." He raised the gun and pointed the lethal weapon at Chase.

She swallowed. This time there'd be no rescue. Help would arrive too late. A sob tore at her throat. "Please, Mike, don't do this. You don't want to kill us. You and Chase have been partners for years."

Mike's tortured gaze swung from her and back to Chase. Sweat gleamed on his brow. He cursed and relaxed his trigger finger. "Stay where you are." Walking backward, the gun held steady and pointed at them, he edged to the body lying in a pool of drying blood. Bending down, he rummaged in the man's leather coat and removed the cloth-covered, wooden box. "This little trinket will make my retirement a lot more pleasant."

"Don't do this, Mike. You know this won't turn out well." Chase's voice was strained. Sweat beaded his upper lip and glistened on his forehead.

"A man's gotta do what a man's gotta do." Mike saluted, and then raced out of the room.

She hurried to Chase and fell into his arms. "Thank God you're okay." She kissed his bloodstained cheeks, his forehead, his chin. She found his mouth and sealed her lips to his.

****

The room was filled with people, all talking at once. The overpowering racket increased the sledgehammer pounding in Chase's head.

The paramedic leaning over him applied a final strip of tape on the gauze bandage covering the wound on his cheek. "That'll stop the bleeding, but you have to go to the hospital, Detective. The wound on the back of your head requires stitches, and you have a broken rib.

You probably have a concussion as well."

Probably? Chase dabbed the back of his head. A lump the size of a baseball had formed, and his hair was stiff with dried blood. If the pounding in his head was any indication, he had a cracked skull. "I'll get checked out later."

He rose to his feet, and the room reeled. Grabbing onto the wall, he closed his eyes and held on until the spinning stopped and the nausea subsided. Blinking to clear his blurry vision, he searched the organized chaos.

Natasha stood stiff and still against the wall as a sea of uniformed cops, detectives, paramedics, and crime scene investigators ebbed and flowed around her. Her face was pale, and she clenched her hands into tight fists in front of her, looking like a lost waif.

Inhaling a shaky breath, fire burning in his chest, he strode over, pleased his steps were steady and he didn't fall. "You okay?"

She nodded, although any fool could see she was anything but okay.

He eased open her clasped fingers and rubbed the palms of her hands where red marks from her nails marred the tender skin. "It's over."

Her blue eyes filled with shadows. "Is it? Is it really over? What about Mike?"

He drew her into his arms, no longer caring who observed them together. "Don't worry. We'll find him." He smoothed her golden hair and tightened his embrace, ignoring the stab of pain in his side. Holding her, knowing she was safe, was worth any discomfort. "We'll find him."

"Detective Brandon?"

Reluctantly, he released her and turned to the

waiting police officer. "What is it, Sergeant?"

"We searched the warehouse like you ordered. We found more antiquities."

Chase nodded. He wasn't surprised. Once Natasha had told him the warehouse belonged to McCabe, he figured more valuable artifacts were hidden in the shipping containers stored throughout the warehouse. The old, deserted building provided the perfect location to hide stolen treasures. No one would think to look here for priceless artifacts.

He still couldn't believe Mike was involved in this mess. The hammering in his head revved to a new level of agony. He and Mike had been partners for seven years. He'd looked up to the older man. Wanted to be like him. And now—

"Detective? You should see this."

Chase blinked and glanced over to where a technician crouched over the floor near the door studying something.

He nodded at the technician. "Give me a minute, Jakowsky." He turned back to Natasha. "I'm sorry. I have to go, but I'll be back."

"You're busy. I should leave." Her voice was small, lost in the hubbub.

He leaned closer. "Don't go." Even with the stench of death filling the room, her clean feminine scent of lilacs and roses surrounded him. For the briefest second, he closed his eyes, inhaled, and forgot the death and mayhem.

"Detective?"

He blew out a breath and opened his eyes.

Her gaze was fixed somewhere in the distance. Once again her hands were clasped, the knuckles white.

She'd been through hell these past few hours—finding her ex-husband lying in a pool of blood dying of a gunshot wound; encountering the gunman who'd attempted to kill her; confronting Mike with his astounding confession of complicity in the vile crimes. And she was still standing.

She'd given a preliminary statement to one of the other detectives in the department, but that was only the initial interview. As a prime witness to the disastrous events, she'd be interrogated countless times in the coming days. The questions wouldn't stop until the department was satisfied she'd told everything she knew.

"Detective!"

"I'll be with you in a second." He frowned at the irritation lacing his voice and gentled his tone. "Sorry, Jakowsky." The technician was just doing his job. The crime scene had to be analyzed and time was of the essence. "I'll be right there." He rubbed his temples. Would the infernal pounding ever end?

He cupped Natasha's shoulders with the palms of his hands and drew her close. Her slim body was so frail he worried he'd break her bones if he squeezed too hard. "Look, I have to leave you for awhile, but I'll be back. I promise."

She nodded, but he wasn't sure she understood what he meant. He couldn't say the words. Not here, not now, not with a dead body on the floor and blood spatter on the walls. He tightened his hands. "Wait for me, okay?"

Again she nodded.

He studied her face, but her expression was unreadable, her eyes cloudy. "Wait for me." When she still didn't respond, he lifted his hands from her shoulders, turned away, and plodded over to the waiting technician. He didn't look back, petrified of what he'd see, what he'd do if she asked him to stay.

The next time he looked for her, the place by the wall where she'd been standing was deserted. He scanned the busy room, but couldn't see her shiny golden head amidst the throng of cops.

She'd left. Run away like she always did, even though he'd practically begged her to stay.

Chapter 32

Natasha plopped down on the couch, picked up the television remote, and switched on the set. Two weeks had passed since the nightmare events at Darien's warehouse. Two long, lonely weeks hiding in her house with the curtains drawn, as the shocking details played out on the television news and in the newspapers. The murders, the thefts, her connection to Darien…all fodder for a ravenous press.

She'd been hauled into the police station, and forced to sit for hours in a windowless room reeking of stale sweat and rancid coffee while grim-faced detectives shot one question at her after another. In spite of their suspicions, she'd maintained her innocence and told them every sordid detail.

Well, almost every detail. She'd omitted any mention of Chase and her making love, and she certainly hadn't told them she loved him. Bad enough her life was in tatters. She refused to ruin his career. As far as the police knew, Chase had been against her getting involved in the case, so she'd gone behind his back.

She wasn't sure if they believed her, but after she confessed to interfering in a police investigation, accepted responsibility for her actions, and agreed to appear in court as a material witness, the endless interrogations ended, and she was free to go.

Free.

She sniffed, fighting the ever-present tears. Free to do what? Free to live a bleak, desolate life? Free to face a shattered heart? She was drained and empty inside.

Darien was dead. He'd ruined her life, but now he was gone. She had a chance to heal, an opportunity to start again. So why wasn't she celebrating? Why was she wearing the same stained clothes she'd worn for days, her hair a greasy, tangled mess, tearstains streaking her face?

The nightly news came on, and her breath hitched in her throat as an image of Darien's warehouse flashed on the screen. She switched the channel, hoping to find a sitcom, reality TV show, even a soap opera…anything but the endless rehashing of the gruesome details of the murders and museum theft ring.

Captain Redding appeared on the screen. He was standing on the steps in front of the Port Hardesty Police Station. A bouquet of microphones bristled in front of him as reporters recorded his statement.

Grateful the volume on her TV was muted, she pressed the button to change the channel, but stopped when the camera swung to Chase, standing at attention beside the captain. His handsome face was swollen and discolored with bruises. A neat line of stitches trailed along the top of one cheek, and one eye was puffy, his eyelid a rainbow of vivid purples and yellows.

Natasha drank him in—his battered face, his tall, strong body, those piercing eyes. The hollow ache in her chest throbbed. She swiped at the tears blurring her vision. Seeing Chase, even on television, felled her like a blow to her stomach, but like a junkie who needed her fix, she couldn't look away.

She hadn't seen him since she'd walked out of the old warehouse. The times she'd been at the police station being interviewed, the chair behind his desk was empty, and she'd been afraid to ask anyone about him.

Every night she dreamed of his hazel eyes, his gentle caresses, his torrid kisses. Every day she awoke to the devastating reality he was gone from her life, that he'd chosen his career as a police detective over his love for her. And once again, her heart shattered.

For the thousandth time she wondered what would have happened if she'd done as he asked that night and waited for him.

But she hadn't waited. She'd run away from the busy crime scene and out of his life.

He loved being a cop. She refused to stand between him and his love of his job. He'd made his choice and she had to live with that.

But could she?

The news conference ended, and the screen now focused on a bombing somewhere in the Middle East. More sad news. She shut off the television and sank back against the cushions. Tears streamed down her face and dripped off her chin.

The sudden peal of her front door chimes startled her, but she sank lower on the couch. She didn't have to wonder who was at her door. The press had hounded her day and night, calling her on the phone and ringing her doorbell, bombarding her with requests for interviews, determined to get a sound bite for their networks.

Reporters milled on the street blocking traffic and tromping over the neighbor's lawns, crushing flowers and shrubs, cameras ready, hoping to catch a glimpse of

Darien McCabe's infamous ex-wife.

Of all her neighbors, Betty Houston alone loved the attention. She was all over the news spouting lurid details about her neighbor's criminal husband and her frequent run-ins with the police.

Taffy was an Internet sensation. The little white dog had thousands of followers on his social media page.

The whole circus would have been funny if Natasha's life wasn't destroyed. She was a prisoner in her own home. It was impossible to even slip out to the grocery store without being pummeled with dozens of shouted questions.

The throng of reporters had thinned over the past two days as other tragedies occurred in the world. She hadn't seen anyone lurking on her front lawn today, and the street was clear of news vans.

The bell chimed again and continued ringing as if the person on her doorstep kept a thumb jammed on the doorbell.

Enough! She stormed over to the door and threw it open. "Look, this is harassment. If you don't leave me alone, I'll—" The words died in her mouth. "Chase? What…what are you doing here?"

He grinned, his teeth flashing white. "Aren't you going to invite me in?"

****

Chase resisted the urge to scrub his damp palms on his pants. His heart pounded so hard in his chest he feared it would burst through muscle and skin. He kept the grin pasted on his face, though his cheek muscles cramped, and no doubt his smile resembled a rictus of pain.

The minutes ticked, each one lasting an eternity. He hadn't expected her to leap into his arms, but when she didn't speak, didn't smile, the painful truth struck him, and he staggered as if reeling from a blow. He blinked back the sting of tears. "This wasn't a good idea. I'm sorry I bothered you." Turning away, he crossed her small porch, his feet leaden, the cloth bag bumping against his thigh.

"Wait."

His steps slowed. Had she spoken, or was her voice a figment of his imagination, his desperate desire for her to want him? He kept walking.

"Chase, wait."

He stopped, and as if moving in slow motion, he turned and squinted against the light shining from the hall behind her.

Her face was in shadows. "Do you want to come in?" The sweet, musical tones of her voice flowed around him like a symphony.

Did he want to come in? His heart soared, and he fought the urge to fist pump the air. He schooled his expression. "I'd like that. I'd like that very much."

She studied him a minute more, then wheeled around and headed down the hall toward her living room.

He blew out a breath and followed, closing the door behind him.

They faced each other in the living room.

He couldn't look away from the luminous depths of her eyes. His mouth dried, and he struggled to swallow. "How have you been?" He could have smacked himself on his already damaged head. Could he be any lamer? How did he think she'd been? He'd heard about the hours of interrogation she'd endured at the precinct and the flood of reporters who'd laid siege to her house.

He'd wanted to come to her sooner, but his presence at her house would only have inflamed the media frenzy. He'd already caused her enough pain. Instead, he'd ignored his desperate craving and stayed away, though it was the hardest thing he'd ever done.

Two weeks of hell. It felt more like a thousand years. And now here he was.

At last.

Was he too late? Would she let him explain?

"I'm fine."

Her voice, a husky whisper as if her throat was raw, broke into his tortured thoughts. "And you? How have you been?"

Any remaining moisture in his mouth evaporated. "Okay."

She stepped closer, narrowing the void between them. "Your face looks better."

He grimaced and traced the healing stitches on his cheek. "I wasn't any too pretty for a while there."

"How's your head?"

He touched the lump on the back of his head. "Healing. I still get headaches, and my rib hurts like a hot damn." He shrugged. "But you know, I'm getting better."

She nodded.

Come on. Sweat broke out under his arms. *Say something. You didn't come here to give her a medical report.*

She broke the strained silence. "Do you want something? Coffee?"

You. I only want you. The words flashed through him, but he shook his head. He couldn't tell her that. Not now. Not after she'd left him. After he let her leave. "We caught Mike."

"You did? Where?"

"We knew he needed to get rid of the diamond, so we staked out the known antiquities fences. The cops in Canada caught him trying to sell the diamond." His mouth twisted as the pain of Mike's betrayal sliced like a knife into his gut. "He didn't have a chance. He knew we'd catch him. It was only a matter of time. A diamond that size, that valuable, has a limited number of buyers." He rubbed the back of his neck. "I think he wanted to be caught."

Another lengthy silence.

"What's going to happen to him?"

Her scent wafted in the still air, and he closed his eyes and breathed deep, inhaling her very essence. He blinked, realizing she'd asked him a question. "What? Oh, he'll be extradited back to the US." He shrugged. "After that, I expect he'll stand trial for homicide, tampering with evidence, collusion, police misconduct..." He shook his head. "A long list. He's looking at prison for the rest of his life." Was it his imagination or had she moved closer? He swallowed.

"I feel sorry for him."

"He made his choices. There's a line. Once you cross that line, you can't go back."

"Prison won't be easy. He isn't a young man."

"Inmates don't take kindly to cops."

"I'm sorry." She touched his arm, the warmth of her hand burning through his jacket, searing his skin. "This must be hard for you."

He stared into her eyes. Had they always been that deep shade of blue? "Mike was a good cop, but he made mistakes, and he has to pay for them. That's the law." He didn't want to talk about Mike, not now. He'd spent too much time these past weeks talking about his partner. The deep pools of her eyes tugged, and he dropped the bag and leaned into her, enfolding her in his arms, ignoring the sharp stab of pain in his chest.

Her body stiffened.

He dropped his arms. His shoulders slumped, and it was all he could do not to collapse in a boneless heap on the floor. She didn't want him. He didn't blame her. How could he? He'd deserted her and left her to face the endless interrogations.

He turned to leave, but halted. Inhaling a deep breath, he asked the question that had burned through his soul for the past two weeks. "Why didn't you wait?"

Her smooth forehead creased. "What?"

"At the warehouse. You didn't wait for me like I asked."

"I...you were busy. I was in the way. You had a job to do. I didn't want to interfere."

"I wanted you to wait." He swallowed hard. "I had something to tell you, something I needed to say."

She nodded. "I know. You wanted to tell me you weren't resigning from the police force, that what happened between us was a mistake." She backed away. "I get it." Her laugh was brittle. "It's okay. I understand. Thank you for telling me. Don't worry. No one will know what happened between us. Your job's safe."

Fear congealed like a casing of ice around his heart. "No, that's not—"

She cut him off. "I appreciate you coming here to tell me about Mike." Her mouth tightened. "Now, I'd like you to leave."

He struggled to think through his numbing fear. "I brought you something." Before she kicked him out, he picked up the bag he'd dropped and handed it to her.

"What's this?"

"Look and see." He held his breath as she opened the bag and tugged out a rectangular object wrapped in white tissue paper.

She slipped off the paper covering and stared at the framed picture.

Time passed, each second an eon.

His shoulders slumped. *Okay, so this was a mistake.* "Sorry to have bothered you." He turned to leave.

"You...you did this?" She held up the framed drawing. Unshed tears glittered in her eyes like diamonds.

He nodded. After he'd cleaned up the mess McCabe had made of her artwork, he'd taken the balled-up drawing to an art restorer and asked him to repair it. The guy had been skeptical, but he'd worked magic and the drawing was as good as new. "I thought you'd like it."

"I do. Very much. Thank you."

Her gratitude gave him the courage to speak up, to try and explain why he'd waited two weeks to see her. "I guess you're wondering where I've been."

"You don't have to explain anything. You're a busy cop. You had a case to finish. I get it." Her eyes glistened with moisture, dampening her long sweep of lashes. Her tears belied her cool tone.

"I was under investigation by Internal Affairs."

"What?"

"The captain didn't like some of the choices I made."

"You told him?" Her throat worked as she swallowed. "About us?"

He nodded.

"What…what happened?"

"They cleared me." He shrugged. "They didn't have much choice. The mayor was thrilled the murderer was caught and a multi-million dollar smuggling ring destroyed. It wouldn't have looked very good if the lead detective in the investigation was charged with improprieties. Things were already bad enough, given Mike's complicity."

"I'm glad, Chase. You must be pleased."

"I quit."

"You quit? But you love being a cop."

"That's true, I do." Sweat prickled under his arms. "But you're what counts. I realized that when I looked for you in the warehouse and you were gone. I put my job before you. I shouldn't have done that."

He scrubbed his head, uncaring about the stab of pain of his injury. "I wanted to tell you that if it came to a choice between you and the job, I'd choose you. Every time. But you left. And then it was too late."

He took her hand in his. His heart surged when she didn't yank her hand free. For the first time in weeks, he dared to hope. "I couldn't come to you before; not until it was over. Once the press heard I resigned, they were all over me wanting to know why. If they put two and two together, you'd pay the price. I wouldn't put you on the front page of a supermarket tabloid."

Her scent filled his senses, and the air between them sizzled. "Look, I'm not saying this right." He chewed on the inside of his cheek. "Hell, I've never done this before, never wanted to, but…" He squeezed her hand. "Okay, look. Here's the deal." Emotion clogged his throat, and his voice was a raspy croak. He coughed. "I love you."

She blanched.

"I love you." He managed to say it louder this time. "I've loved you probably from the first time I saw you in Waverley's office." He coughed again. "I love you more than I ever thought it possible to love someone." He waited, afraid to breathe, afraid to stir a muscle. He'd played his hand. The rest was up to her.

A slow smile curled her full lips, and the corners of her incredible eyes crinkled. "You love me?"

"I do." His chest tightened. He couldn't breathe. But then a miracle happened and she leaned into him, her body soft and welcoming, and kissed him on the lips.

Their bodies fit together like two pieces of a puzzle, and the kiss deepened. Heat devoured him as sensation flooded in, melting the block of ice around his heart. The ferocious pounding in his head eased. She was everything he'd dreamed of these past lonely weeks and more, so much more.

When the kiss ended, his body buzzed as blood coursed through his veins, but he held on to his sanity for a heartbeat more. "Well, what do you say?"

"No."

He frowned and his gut tightened. "No?"

"You love being a cop. It's who you are. I won't let you give that up. You wouldn't be happy doing anything else. Eventually you'd resent me."

He nodded. "Did I forget to mention I've been hired by the FBI to work as part of an art theft investigation unit? I start next month."

"You didn't mention that."

"Now will you answer my question? Do you"—he coughed, winced—"do you love me?"

She clasped her hands at the back of his neck and drew him down so close their breaths mingled. "I love you, Chase Brandon, forever and ever."

He'd read of this kind of love in books, watched romance play out on the big screen, but he hadn't fully believed until now, right this second.

True love did exist. He half expected an orchestra to start playing and doves to appear.

He grinned.

He was a lucky guy.

He kissed her, pouring his heart and soul into the kiss. He swore to God he heard the swell of violins and the flutter of wings.

Yep, he was one hell of a lucky guy.

A word about the author…

C.B. has always loved reading, especially romances, but it wasn't until she lost her voice for a year that she considered writing her own romantic suspense stories.

She grew up in Canada's Northwest Territories and Yukon. Graduating with a degree in Anthropology and Archaeology, she has worked as an archaeologist and an educator.

She enjoys hiking, canoeing, and snowshoeing with her husband and dog near her home in the wilderness of central British Columbia.

Visit her on Facebook:

cbclarkauthor@facebook.com

And follow her on Twitter:

https://twitter.com/cbclarkauthor

And Instagram:

https://www.instagram.com/cbclarkauthor/

Check out her blog:

https://cbclarkauthor.wordpress.com

Goodreads Author Page:

https://www.goodreads.com/author/show/15029617.C_B_Clark